THE LOVE DARE

PRAISE FOR ABIOLA BELLO

THE LOVE DARE

ABIOLA BELLO

SIMON & SCHUSTER

First published in Great Britain in 2024 by Simon & Schuster UK Ltd

1 3 5 7 9 10 8 6 4 2

Simon & Schuster UK Ltd
1st Floor
222 Gray's Inn Road
London WC1X 8HB

Simon & Schuster: Celebrating 100 Years of Publishing in 2024

www.simonandschuster.co.uk
www.simonandschuster.com.au
www.simonandschuster.co.in

Simon & Schuster Australia, Sydney
Simon & Schuster India, New Delhi

A CIP catalogue record for this book
is available from the British Library.

PB ISBN 978-1-3985-1693-9
eBook ISBN 978-1-3985-1694-6
eAudio ISBN 978-1-3985-1695-3

Typeset in Times by M Rules
Printed and Bound in the UK using 100% Renewable
Electricity at CPI Group (UK) Ltd

MIX
Paper | Supporting
responsible forestry
FSC® C171272

*To my amazing brother Gboli and sister
Lola. Thank you for always supporting me.
So happy I get to do life with you both. To my
great-aunty Sadé, who was the inspiration
behind Grandma in the book. Love you! x*

ONE

I come from a line of very dramatic Nigerian women. When Mum and Grandma asked to see my carnival costume I hesitantly showed them the video of my fitting appointment that I had recorded on my phone.

For years Aunty Lola – who is my best friend Sharisha's aunt – had a float at Notting Hill Carnival, and when I was younger I was happy taking part playing the steel pans. I've played the double tenor since primary school and was part of a steel band up until I was fifteen. We performed at festivals and, of course, at Carnival on Aunty Lola's float, and Mum didn't mind me doing that because my costume was always a T-shirt and shorts. But for a while now I've been dying to be on a float as one of the dancers. Unlike my friends, who all have summer jobs, I've struggled to get one so I begged Dad for the money to get the package deal that includes my costume, food and unlimited drinks. Plus, we'd have a VIP toilet! No nasty portaloos or paying someone to use their bathroom like everyone else.

I was very careful not to let Dad see my costume and I booked everything before Mum could interfere. I would have bet money and won knowing how she would react when she saw it. She didn't disappoint. She took a sharp intake of breath before she shouted, 'Make you no vex me, Eva! You want your bum bum out for everybody?' Her accent at that moment was a strong Nigerian one. Mum is a chameleon with her voice and can switch between Yoruba, Pidgin English and the King's English.

I explained that everyone would be dressed like that and Mum looked me up and down and said, 'Does everyone live in this house?'

Grandma cried, 'Ah God-o!' and shook her head so hard that her black wig slipped slightly to the side. She then said something to Mum in Yoruba which I didn't understand because I was never taught it, but she kept gesturing at me. Her tone alone told me that whatever she was saying wasn't good.

Mum warned me not to talk to any man when I was at Carnival dressed in my costume. Better yet, I shouldn't make eye contact. I tried to explain to her that that would be pretty impossible given how many thousands of people would be attending, but she wagged her finger at me and told me to remember that I'd be representing the family. Technically I'd be representing Aunty Lola's carnival float, but I kept quiet. I made sure to delete the video in case they moaned to Dad and he wanted to see.

It will be no surprise that since Mum and Dad have been in

Nigeria from the beginning of August I've felt more relaxed. I love my parents, but they can be a bit much, especially Mum. She scrutinizes what I'm wearing, how long I'm on the phone, who I'm talking to, what my plans are for the future. I'm constantly trying to be the 'good' daughter and it's exhausting. I wish I could be more like my older brother Dami. He's five years older than me and we're pretty close, although we don't hang out as much as we used to since he's been with Amara. Somehow Dami manages to block Mum and Dad out and just do his thing, but I struggle with that. The only time I feel like I'm really me is with my friends.

Finally, after all the preparations, the carnival weekend has arrived and when I get to Aunty Lola's float, even though Mum isn't around, I admit I suddenly feel super self-conscious about how revealing my outfit is, even though everyone on the float is dressed identically to me. It takes me a while to feel comfortable, but once everyone starts feeling the vibe and we all get in formation, the excitement starts to build.

I'm wearing the most stunning golden, crystallized bralet with matching knickers – well, more like a thong – and flesh-coloured fishnet tights so at least my bum cheeks are somewhat covered. On top of my head is a golden headdress that looks like a crown with ocean-blue gems on it. My favourite part though is the huge yellow and orange wings that are attached to straps that go over my shoulders. I'm basically dressed in a crystallized bikini and have had to shave literally everywhere. When I first tried the costume on I almost backed out of being on the float altogether because I thought it was too revealing, but once I stood with my friends to have a group picture taken, I started to love the outfit.

We've all been in charge of our own hair and make-up. Thankfully I got braids put in only a few days ago and my baby hairs are laid in the most intricate swirl designs. Amara, who's been secretly staying with us since our parents went away, is a brilliant make-up artist and helped me this morning with my 'look'. She actually laughed when I told her I would do my usual carnival make-up, which was going to be pretty much my go-to, everyday, simple look only this time with bright eyeshadow to fit the carnival theme. Instead, she picked up her make-up brushes, told me to close my eyes and relax, and proceeded to work her wonders. So, thanks to her, I have long, fluttery eyelashes, gold and blue eyeshadow that's blended beautifully, gold highlight that shimmers, plump red lips, and cheekbones for days.

Notting Hill Carnival is the only place where you will find the most bougie area of London covered in feathers, glitter and sequins. It's vibrant, colourful, joyful – the soundtrack of summer in London. You're never far away from the smell of jerk chicken and everyone is there to enjoy themselves. Despite the boiling August sun, it's pure vibes and a community feel that you just can't buy. People everywhere are waving West Indian flags – from Jamaica, Trinidad, Barbados, Dominica, Haiti. It's a parade of floats, dancers, stunning costumes and music. I cannot believe that I'm up here on a float at Notting Hill Carnival, surrounded by people all dancing like me in the most stunning costumes, with the beautiful hot weather, the soca music . . . I honestly feel like a whole queen!

The advantage of being on the float is that I can whine all day long without having random guys try and dance up on me. There's also my old steel band that take turns playing in tune with the DJ. It's like a soca orchestra, where almost a hundred of us dance to the melody. Aunty Lola has positioned the dancers. I'm in the middle of everyone. Oyin is front and centre and she's a sick dancer, Sansa and Fatima are on opposite sides in front of the crowds, and Sharisha's next to me. I can't believe my friends and I are actually dancers on a float, in costumes, at Carnival! There are masses of people on either side of us, waving flags, filming us on their phones, cheering and clapping along to the beat.

Sharisha's deep dimples appear as she grins excitedly at me. We've known each other since nursery, and out of our group of friends we're the closest. We actually played the steel pans together when we were younger, but she stopped once we got into secondary school. Where I'm tall, lean, with small boobs and curvy hips, Sharisha is short with curves all over and in all the right places, so she looks ridiculously sexy in her outfit. Her thick, black, curly hair is slicked up into a top bun. And she's sprinkled pink and gold glitter all over herself.

The steel band starts to play the intro to the next song. I close my eyes and lose myself in the music, whining my waist to the melody as the glitter on my arms catches the sun so my skin sparkles. I feel like I'm in another world.

'Ow!' Melanie shoots me a dark look over her shoulder when I spin, lose balance and bump into her.

'Sorry, Mel!' I shout over the music, cheeks burning.

5

Sharisha bursts out laughing.

'Oh, shut up!' I say, but I'm smiling.

I'm waving at the crowd, blowing kisses at people filming us. It's like we're famous. I hope our costumes are good enough to make it onto the Notting Hill Carnival Instagram page. Imagine if we're featured on the news! There'd be hell to pay at home if that happened. It would be worth it though.

'I want to look around,' Sharisha moans, interrupting my thoughts. 'We've been doing this for hours.'

'I'm down.' Every year I've seen girls who look absolutely stunning in the most amazing costumes. Today I'm that girl and I want to embrace every second of it.

'Let's get the others.' Sharisha grabs my hand and we dance our way through the dancers until we reach Fatima, Sansa and Oyin. We really do look like a girl band. Fatima is tall and lean like me, with the same brown skin tone but a more angular face, and light brown, almost golden, eyes behind her glasses. Sansa and Oyin are a little shorter in height. Sansa's pale in skin tone with sun-kissed blonde hair, green eyes and a small frame, whilst Oyin has beautiful, dark brown skin, jet-black hair and small eyes which are emphasized with the longest, fluffiest eyelashes. Sharisha and I met the girls in Year 7 and we've been stuck together ever since. Just as Sharisha and I live super close, Sansa and Fatima live up the road from each other, so they see each other more. I wish we had another person in the group to even out the dynamics as sometimes I think Oyin feels left out.

The float moves so slowly that we can come and go as we

please. As we mill about down on the street, people are in awe of our costumes and ask to take pictures of us. I silently cheer as we pose together. This really is the best summer with my girls.

'Can you take one of us?' Oyin asks a random person before we squeeze in tight as they snap the picture.

'Eva, I swear you're a real-life Bratz doll,' Fatima says, zooming in on the pic.

Oyin shields her eyes from the sun to study the picture. Her hair tickles my arm as she brushes against me. 'She is the pretty one,' she says, with an edge to her voice.

I don't even know who started the nicknames at college but I know it was a guy. A dumb one at that. They did this stupid list where they nicknamed all the girls. For what reason? I don't know. But for a while it was the talk of college and something that all the girls obsessed over. So Oyin's the feisty one, Sansa's the sweet one, Fatima's the smart one, Sharisha's the fun one and I got to be the pretty one. It pisses me off that all my friends got nicknames based on their personalities, but mine's based on how I look. Why didn't I get 'the smart one'? Or 'ambitious'? I mean, I'm the one who's going to study law at university! But when I moaned to my friends about how it made me feel, that I was reduced to my physical attributes and not who I am deep down, they didn't get why I was irritated. 'You got "pretty",' they said, like that was the best label to get. They couldn't see how it made me feel like I was just a face and nothing more, like I am only worth something if I look good. So I've tried to drop the whole nickname thing, and yet – and this is the worst part about that list – it's still managed to affect how we girls see ourselves, how different it's made us act, like we each have to live up to our individual labels. Even I started to feel that if I didn't look pretty today I wouldn't be living up to the label – the label that I didn't want in the first place! It's so messed up and still rattles me. I wish I knew who wrote it so I could really cuss them out.

'Okay, shall we start?' Oyin smirks rubbing her hands together. Her dark skin is covered in gold shimmer and as the sun hits her she seems to glisten from head to toe.

'Nah, I'm not doing it,' Fatima says, brushing back her curls.

'How can you back out of a dare that we already agreed to?' Oyin argues.

A few weeks ago, when we realized how little time we had left together because we're all heading off to different unis after the summer, we had an impromptu sleepover at Sharisha's house, where we shared all the things we wished we had done together, like going on a road trip or throwing a house party. I'm actually doing that last one, throwing a house party, for my eighteenth birthday, which will be in a few days. After we'd made our 'I wish we'd . . .' list, we started daring each other to do things on it, so that we could achieve our goals.

Most of the dares involved boys. Even though I'm known in the group as the pretty one and I do get a lot of male attention, I've never had a boyfriend. I haven't even kissed a guy. Not that I haven't wanted to. But I think that a first kiss is special and I want to make sure I experience it with the right person. My friends think I'm over-romanticizing it, especially when I say that kissing is part of seeing if you have a genuine connection with someone. They keep on telling me that it's not that deep and that if I stopped over-thinking it I could have kissed lots of guys by now. I think they think being liked by guys is such a great thing. As for me though, I would rather be liked by that one special person. That's what I'm waiting for. But then, at the sleepover, Oyin asked me if I was worried I'd be bad at kissing because of my lack of experience. It may sound silly, but I hadn't even thought of that. I mean, I want my first kiss to be special, but also one that will make him faint because it's so good, you know? So now I'm not sure. What if I've messed up by waiting for so long?

There's no prize for doing the dares, but if you refuse or don't manage to do one then your punishment is that you *have* to do the next dare. Once the float was confirmed, Oyin thought it would be fun to bring the dares to Carnival. So we agreed to dare each other to dance with as many guys as possible, but the catch is someone else has to pick the person for you.

Something about this costume and being at Carnival makes me bolder than usual. In my everyday life I would never go up to a hot guy and start dancing on him. I'm used to guys approaching me, but today it's time to switch it up. I spotted a group of hotties en route that I want to catch again, but everyone knows that if you see a good-looking person at

Notting Hill Carnival, the chances are you won't see them again because it's just so busy. There are thousands of people here, so if you miss them, you miss them.

'I hope they're not expecting me to throw it back.' Sansa looks back at her small, pert bum and Sharisha smacks it, making Sansa jump.

'Small butts matter!' Sharisha says, making us laugh. 'Oyin, why don't you go first and show us how it's done?'

'Okay, cool. Who should I go for?' Oyin has a dangerous glint in her eyes as she watches guys walking past.

We've already attracted quite a bit of attention just standing here in our costumes. Guys always moan that girls travel in packs, but so do they. I'm scanning the groups of guys trying to find someone for her and then I spot him. Tall, Black, looks around early twenties with a fresh cut and beard. His muscles are popping out of his vest top, a bit of chest hair pops through. He sort of looks like Logan, the guy Oyin's dating, so he's totally Oyin's type.

'What about him?' I point and the girls all turn.

'Damn,' Fatima says, peering at him over her glasses as if she can't see. 'He is fine.'

'And all mine,' Oyin sings. She waves her fingers at us as she struts – yes, struts – over to him.

The bearded guy slowly smiles as she comes closer. She grabs his hands, spins herself round so her feathers are touching him, and starts to whine to the beat of the soca music blasting in the background.

'Yes, sis!' Sharisha yells.

His boys are hyping him up. And because Oyin is such a performer and I wouldn't expect any less from her, she takes his hands and puts them on her waist so he can really feel the pressure of her whine. As the music stops, so does she, pressing her bum one last time against him to let him know what he's losing before she struts back over to us. The guy has a fist in his mouth and his boys are clapping him on the shoulder, even though he didn't do anything.

'Bitch, you better werk!' Sharisha says, and Oyin laughs giving her a high five.

'Yeah, I can't be doing all that,' Fatima says. 'What if an aunty sees me?'

We look her up and down in her sparkly bra and burst out laughing. Fatima is too dramatic.

'All right, Sansa girl, it's your turn,' Oyin says, and Sansa groans.

I don't know why she's stressing. Sansa may be white but she knows how to move her waist. Oyin puts a finger to her full lips and searches the crowd. 'Him.'

We follow her finger and she's pointing to a policeman!

Sansa's eyes widen. 'No way!'

I swear I'm going to piss myself laughing so hard, but Oyin shrugs.

'A dare is a dare,' she says.

Sansa hesitates. She and Oyin are the most competitive girls I've ever met. She adjusts her headdress over her blonde hair. 'I better not get arrested,' she says before she walks over to the policeman.

11

'She's actually doing it?' I gasp. I would have asked for another guy or taken the next dare.

'Oh shit!' Sharisha laughs. 'Nah, I'm going live for this one.'

The policeman looks pretty young and I don't know what Sansa is saying to him but she's smiling a lot and at one point he starts laughing. Sansa looks at us over her shoulder and winks before she starts to move her hips round in a circular motion and the policeman joins her.

Oyin's mouth drops open and Fatima pushes it back up, making me laugh out loud. Sansa rotates her hips fast to the dancehall track and now people are stopping to watch them, cheering them on. The policeman's a bit stiff, bless him, but he's trying his best to keep up with Sansa.

Everyone applauds them when they're done and the policeman's face is bright red. He even starts to fan himself with his hand and I don't know if he's hot from the weather or all the fire that Sansa just brought to the table.

Sansa hurries back over to us and we cheer the loudest.

'That was top tier,' I say.

'My heart is racing!' Sansa says, breathing fast. 'Thank God he was up for it. Okay, my turn to pick and I choose Eva.'

'Me?' I squeak suddenly feeling nervous. Oyin and Sansa have made it look so easy. When I agreed to do these dares, I somewhat forgot that people will of course stop and form a crowd to watch girls dancing in the elaborate costumes.

'Is that Jayden?' Fatima asks.

I follow her gaze and sure enough it's Jayden, with Miles,

Logan and Arhvee from college. There's another guy that I don't know with them.

Okay I'll admit it. The one guy I would love to kiss is Jayden Lawal. I've fancied him since I met him on the first day at college and we have this very flirtatious relationship. We tease each other a lot, find opportunities to sit next to each other, text or chat on the phone every other day, put love heart emojis under every Insta post. Everyone's waiting for us to get together but neither one of us has made the move. I think he can sense that I'm nervous about possibly taking it to the next level.

I've been on dates, but none with Jayden. I dunno what it is with him. It's like when I think he will ask me out he doesn't, even though I've made it clear that I'm very interested in him. Jayden wants to play football as a career and we all think he's good enough to achieve this, but he's still waiting to trial for a professional team. He's invited me to a few games with the rest of his mates, but I've always wondered why he won't invite only me. If he did, I could watch him play and then we could hang out together afterwards. Just us two, alone. Sort of like a date but not a date-date, if you know what I mean. But soon we're all going our separate ways and I want him to do something. Anything! If he tried to kiss me, I know I won't pull back.

And now here he is, looking extra sexy in a tight T-shirt that pops against his dark skin, showing muscles upon muscles. This dare business isn't so bad after all – I will very happily dance all over *him*.

Sansa's looking around and I whisper to myself, 'Jayden, Jayden, Jayden.'

'Him.' Sansa points at the Black boy that's beside Jayden, the one I don't know. He has a lighter skin tone than Jayden, with long, thick curly hair – the texture suggesting that he's mixed-race. He is shorter and slimmer than Jayden and is wearing an anime design T-shirt with jeans. His arms aren't as defined as the rest of the boys' and one of his is decorated with tattoos. The boys are all chatting and laughing loudly, but he's quiet and observing everybody.

'That's cold, Sansa. He's clearly one of Jayden's friends,' Fatima says.

'Oh, I just thought Jayden might expect you to come for him, and maybe he'll wake up if he sees you with someone else,' Sansa says quickly, and I know she means it. She's not fluent in shade yet.

'It's okay,' I say, gently squeezing her arm and she smiles looking relieved.

I take a deep breath. All I've got to do is walk past Jayden and dance on his friend. Sansa's right. Maybe Jayden will finally make a move.

TWO

'You've got this,' Sharisha says, massaging my shoulders like I'm about to enter a boxing ring. 'Do you know what? Don't even talk to Jayden.'

'Don't talk to him?' I say, alarmed, spinning around to look at her. 'Isn't that rude?'

'No! You've gotta be like, *I'm Eva Òjó and if you're not gonna holla, I'm gonna dance on your friend and let you see what you're missing,*' Sharisha says, and the girls agree.

I'm still not sure if this is the right move but I nod anyway and walk over to them. Immediately Logan, who's standing next to Jayden, runs a hand over his fresh trim and is looking at me up and down. Inside I cringe. I always feel funny seeing Logan, ever since he asked me out a few months into starting college, despite being one of Jayden's best friends *and* knowing that Jayden and I liked each other. When I turned him down, he then asked Oyin out and she said yes. I know Logan is Oyin's type. She's attracted to him and they seem to get along, but I would never want my friend's sloppy seconds. The whole situation is messy. Sometimes I catch Logan staring at me. If Oyin notices, she never says anything.

Arhvee, the only Filipino boy in our year who also plays football, spots me and nudges Jayden. Jayden looks at me, making my heart race, and he slowly smiles. He's almost smug, like he thinks I'm coming over just for him. But then I adjust my focus to the boy in the anime T-shirt.

I always get compliments on my eye contact. Apparently, I draw people in. My friends say that's how I get the hottest guys' attention. I've never understood that because I'm legit just staring and not doing anything special, but right now I hope this amazing eye contact I supposedly have works. At first the guy is looking left to right like he's not sure if it's him that I'm staring at. When he realizes that it *is* him, he's focused only on me.

From the corner of my eye Jayden's frown is getting deeper and deeper. I grab the boy's hand and at first he resists, which surprises me. The last thing I need is being rejected by Jayden's friend *in front of Jayden*! I flash the guy a reassuring smile and this time, when I pull his hand, he walks with me. Jayden's mouth opens like he's about to say something but I keep my eyes on the guy, not giving Jayden a second thought. I place the guy's hands on my hips and start to move. I get a whiff of his aftershave – vanilla and something smoky, and, I'll admit, he smells sexy. But it's like he doesn't know what to do with his hands, as he quickly withdraws them before reaching towards me again. His thoughts are etched all over his face – *should he dance with me or not? Is he standing too close? Is it okay for him to touch me?*

'It's okay,' I say gently, as I grab his hands again and put them on my lower back so his fingers graze the top of my bum. To ease him into the rhythm I move my waist slowly, despite the fast bashment music coming from a nearby carnival truck. People have stopped to watch and my girls are cheering me on. At first the guy is really stiff, like is he *even alive* stiff, but after a moment he starts to warm up, catching the whine, and for the first time he smiles and I notice the dimples in his cheeks that remind me of Sharisha. The beat takes over my body and I start to rotate my hips faster in time to the rhythm.

'I'm trying really hard to keep up,' his deep voice says in my ear, and I laugh.

'You're doing great.'

I turn around, trying not to laugh when I hear him say, 'Oh wow.'

The track changes so I stop dancing, a little relieved that my dare is over, and everyone claps for us. I grin suddenly, feeling exhausted. The guy dramatically fans himself, which makes me burst out laughing.

'That was something,' he says, smiling at me. 'Your costume is amazing.'

'Thank you! What's your name?' I ask. He responds, but just then someone blows a horn nearby that drowns him out. I step closer so his lips are near my ear. 'Sorry, what?'

'Saint,' he says.

17

'Nice to meet you, Saint. I'm Eva. Thanks for dancing with me.'

'Oh no, thanks for dancing with *me*!' Saint laughs.

I glance over his shoulder and Jayden is glaring at me. Good! Maybe this will push Jayden into making his move. Saint follows my gaze. 'That's my cousin,' he says.

'Cousin?' My voice is louder than I meant it to be. I glance from one to the other and I can't see any resemblance. Saint shoots me a questioning look. 'Oh,' I say, 'we're friends ... from college. Actually, I know all the guys from college.'

'Damn, Eva!' Miles says. Nice guy, but he's always following Jayden and Logan around like a lost puppy. He's smiling as he walks over. 'Is it my go?'

I scoff. *He wishes.*

'Sexy Eva strikes again,' Logan says, and I ignore him. This guy has no shame.

'I didn't know you could do all that,' Arhvee adds.

I flick my braids. 'There's a lot I can do,' and the boys all go 'Oooh.'

'You look ... wow,' Jayden says, drinking me in.

Inside I'm screaming.

It feels a little awkward, with Arhvee, Miles and Logan gawking at me, Jayden admiring me and Saint recovering from our dance, so I quickly change the subject. 'So, are you guys excited for my party?' I ask.

In two days I officially turn eighteen! Seeing as my parents are still in Nigeria, I'm throwing a birthday house party that's the talk of college. I've had to lie to Grandma, telling her Dami and I will be out that day so she doesn't swing by. She's been cooking us food and checking in on us since Mum and Dad left, which is helpful because neither Dami nor I can cook anything great. Dami doesn't care about the party as long as I don't tell our parents that his girlfriend Amara is staying with us while they're away and that I clean up after the party. Most importantly, if I get caught or if anything breaks, I have to make it clear that he was not involved and he is not paying for any damage.

'No doubt,' Jayden says, completely cool like he's unfazed.

'Eva!' Sharisha and the girls hurry over. 'That was so good! Hey, guys.' Everyone hugs in greeting and Jayden introduces Saint, who waves shyly at us. Sansa, who's a hugger, goes to greet him with one and he turns to the side, giving her a stiff one-armed hug that reminds me of the way some of the boys at church hug me if their girl's watching.

'Can you lot keep these costumes just for me, please?' Miles brings his hands together in a praying position.

'Thirsty much?' Fatima rolls her eyes at him. 'Let's grab some food.'

We actually get free food from the float but as I want to hang around Jayden for a bit longer I don't say anything. We begin to walk through the crowds of people. The feathers help because they're so big that people are forced to move out the way, clearing a path for us.

'You really do look beautiful,' Jayden says walking beside me. 'But you always do.'

I look up at him. Big brown eyes, long lashes, white teeth.

He's been growing out his hair so now it's a small afro, but he has a clean shape up. Jayden's so handsome that his selfies get thousands of likes on Instagram. He doesn't even need to put captions on his social media posts, like it's purely him that gets the love. I definitely see the girls who walk past us check him out. They don't matter today though because he only has eyes for me.

'Thank you! So you liked my dance?' I flutter my lashes and Jayden laughs.

'Would have liked it better if it was with me.'

'It could have been with you, if I knew that you wanted it to be,' I say in a sultry tone.

Jayden laughs and says, 'Oh, for real?'

And as we fall into our usual flirty banter, I play my ace card, my out-of-this-world eye contact, and hold Jayden's gaze as he glances down at me, his eyes switching between looking into mine and looking at my lips.

'I could eat a fucking horse!' Fatima breaks our moment as she clutches her stomach dramatically. 'I'm losing too much weight with all this walking.'

'And all that dancing!' Oyin laughs along with her.

'Just don't lose that ass,' Logan jokes, grabbing Oyin round the waist and pulling her in for a kiss. He does seem to like her, but then I do question his feelings when I catch him looking at me. To be honest, once they head off to uni I doubt they will last. Oyin can do so much better.

Everyone's talking back and forth, and I spot Saint walking a bit behind us, watching our conversations, and I feel bad that he's being left out. So I leave Jayden's side – he still has his boys he can talk to – and I hang back until Saint's next to me.

'Who's that on your shirt?' I ask, pointing at the weird alien creature, and Saint looks down at it, brushing back his thick curly hair.

'Oh, it's Frieza.' He looks at me expectedly but I frown. 'From *Dragon Ball Z*? It's an anime TV show.'

'Oh. I think my brother used to watch that. What's it about?' I'm not really interested in anime, but for the sake of being friendly and welcoming to the new guy in the group I lean into his interests.

'It's about a warrior … well, a Saiyan called Goku …' Saint's face comes alive as he talks to me about the show and I try to keep up with all these weird names he's throwing around – Piccolo, Krillin, Vegeta.

'Sounds good,' I say interrupting him mid-flow. 'Maybe I'll watch it.' I have no idea why I said that when I know I won't, but it makes Saint smile – and there, his dimples are back. His brown eyes, with flecks of green in them, light up.

'Let me know what you think,' he says.

'I will. You must hear this all the time, but your hair is amazing!' It's dark brown tight curls with streaks of light brown running through them, and it's so long that it comes down to his chest. I'm already wondering whether I can get a wig like that and if it would suit me.

Saint laughs. 'Thanks. A bit of a handful. Not sure why I thought leaving it out in this heat was smart.' He shrugs.

21

'What college do you go to?'

'Woodside in West Ham,' Saint replies.

'Oh, no way!' Sansa was talking to a guy that goes there. 'You know Anthony? I think his surname is Watson.'

'Yeah, I know Anthony, he's my boy.'

It gives me an idea. 'You should come to my birthday party. It's in two days. Bring Anthony. Jayden and the boys are coming too.'

'Yeah? I don't want to feel like I'm imposing.'

I shrug. 'Nah, it's fine. You seem like cool people.'

Saint smiles. 'Okay, sure. Thanks.'

There are multiple stalls selling Caribbean food with queues of people that stretch far. The smell is drifting down the line making my stomach rumble – jerk chicken, curry goat, oxtail. I didn't realize how hungry I was until now. The problem is I'm such a messy eater . . . really messy, like crumbs will be in my hair and rice will fall on my chest. I don't want Jayden to think I'm a slob.

We eventually get to the front of the queue and the boys order a large meal each before going to find a bit of pavement to sit down on and eat. While Fatima is asking the servers what they have that's halal we notice Oyin only gets a patty.

'You not hungry, babe?' Sansa asks.

'I want to dance, so I'll eat properly later,' she says.

Sharisha goes back and forth about the jerk chicken. 'I can't eat chicken properly with a fork, but I left my hand sanitizer.'

'You already know I'll be a mess if I eat the chicken,' I say before I turn to the server. 'Can I get dumplings and ackee and

22

saltfish?' That should keep me going until I can pig out later in all my messy glory.

We get our food and head over to the boys. Jayden taps the space next to him and smiles at me. My heart jumps as I sit carefully beside him, trying not to mess up my feathers.

'Saint said you invited him to your party,' Jayden says. 'That was cool of you.'

'Of course he can come. The more the merrier.' I eye his juicy jerk chicken enviously.

'Maybe you can save a dance for me?' Jayden whispers in my ear, his lips gently brushing against me, and I catch my breath. Dancing with Jayden at my party would be the highlight of my year. I can already see us now in the middle of the dance floor, dancing to the music, focusing only on each other, pressed up close together.

'If you're lucky,' I say coolly, and Jayden grins at me with that smile that literally makes me feel weak.

THREE

We don't leave the float until the evening and my feet are begging to get out of these trainers. Because it's a residential area and there are noise restrictions, once it hits a certain time the music cuts off. Originally, we had wanted to go to an after party to keep the vibes going, but I underestimated how exhausted I would be. Dancing and walking in the sun all day is not a joke. Thankfully we were able to eat some jerk chicken from our float later in the afternoon and grab some drinks, and by then, because the carnival was winding down, I didn't care that I had sticky sauce on my hands.

'Best. Day. Ever,' Sharisha says once we've changed back into our normal clothes.

'Them feather wings have mashed up my back.' Fatima rolls back her shoulders.

I carefully place my costume in a bag, wishing to myself that it was perfectly normal to walk around like that every day. We've still got our elaborate make-up on but now with our regular clothes so we do look a bit odd, but I don't care. It was my first time being in costume, I had the best day with my girls and I want to keep as much carnival on me as possible.

'Hello?' I call as I open the front door.

It feels like I've been travelling home for hours. Getting out of a very busy Notting Hill and fighting my way onto a packed tube took my last bit of energy and I'm desperate to sleep. I place my bag containing my costume on the floor and my cat Yum-Yum puts his ginger head right inside it. He raises his paw as he sees the feathers ready to attack, so I have to pick the bag up and put it on the coat stand instead to avoid having my outfit ruined.

'In here!' Dami calls from the living room.

I walk in and the heat in the room hits my face. It's boiling hot despite the two fans that are on. Dami and Amara are lying on the sofa, him in shorts, a white tee and some socks. Who wears socks in summer?

'Hey, Eva,' Amara says, removing her legs from my brother's lap. 'Oh good, your make-up held up. I forgot to take a pic this morning. Okay to take one now?'

Amara jumps up not even waiting for me to reply, pulling down her short skirt in the process. Amara kind of reminds me of a fairy. Petite with cute features and she's usually wearing something short and floral. Her long hair hangs down her back and her gold bangles tinkle as she holds up her phone.

Dami is stockier and towers over her. He could probably pick her up with one arm. They've been dating for two years now and I can't lie, Amara has been a positive influence on him. Dami used to hang out with a bad crowd and seemed to be doing nothing with his life, especially when he dropped out of uni. Since Amara, he's got his act together. He's still figuring out his career but at least he has a steady job doing admin for a tech company.

'How was it?' Dami asks.

'Yeah, it was—'

'Don't move!' Amara says, and I instantly fall silent. She gently brushes a stray braid out of my face. After a few moments she says, 'Got it. Oh, you look so beautiful. Do you have pictures of your costume?'

I hand her my phone.

'I had the best day,' I tell Dami, who pulls a face at whatever Amara shows him.

'Shut up! Like you don't go Carnival to look at the girls in the costumes,' I say.

'Used to,' Dami replies quickly as Amara glares at him. Once she turns away, he mouths, 'What the hell?'

I always forget how sensitive Amara is. Me and my brother, we can go back and forth teasing each other, but she's a little bit . . . tense and can be petty. Like when Dami grew his beard because an ex-girlfriend suggested it. When they broke up and he got with Amara, she seemed to like the beard at first. But when she found out he'd grown it because of his ex, she wanted him to shave it off. I'm not being funny, but the beard completes him. He'd look about fourteen without one. Thank God he didn't listen to her and kept it.

Amara sighs. 'I wish I went on a float.'

'Not dressed like that,' Dami says, handing me back my phone.

I would hate it if a guy tried to tell me how I could dress, but Amara loves it. She cuddles into him, smiling like he just said the most romantic thing.

'So, your party. How many people are coming again?' Dami asks.

'Err . . .' I try to think about how many I initially said but I can't remember. What I do know is there are now way too many people coming. At the beginning, it was a select group, a limited number of friends that I invited, but somehow that became a 'tell a friend to tell a friend' situation. Every day I've had someone message me asking if they can bring someone else too. I don't know why I kept saying yes. A part of me was worried that the party would be dead if I was too fussy, but now I've lost track of the names and numbers of who is coming.

'Not many,' I eventually say.

Dami nods in response. 'We're gonna be out. We'll be home around midnight. Make sure you wrap it up by then. I don't need the neighbours complaining.'

'Midnight?' I groan. 'I was thinking more three a.m.'

Dami gives me a look and I know not to push it. He's a real one for even letting me have this house party for my birthday. I force a smile on my face. 'Midnight it is.'

Our family WhatsApp group pings and Dami and I both look at our phones. The group is always going off. Mum and Grandma are forever sharing bible scriptures or some unsolved mystery, but right now it's Grandma saying she's dropping food off tomorrow morning. Thank God! We're down to our last pot of jollof rice. For someone so tiny, Amara can eat! Dami and I are both pretty rubbish in the kitchen, and I have no clue whether Amara can cook. She just seems to snack a lot throughout the day.

I head up the stairs to wipe off this make-up. Yum-Yum follows me and jumps on my bed, stretching himself out, trying to paw me as I sit beside him and look through my pictures. It really was the best day. I select my favourite ones and post them on Instagram. Straight away the post racks up likes and comments, and it doesn't take long for the one comment I'm looking for to appear. Jayden's.

One word, *Eva*, followed by a series of heart eyes. I squeal making Yum-Yum jump.

I cannot wait for this party.

FOUR

I hear Grandma before I see her. Only she would come over at eight a.m. blasting a church sermon on loudspeaker on her phone, the pastor praying in tongues as the smell of fried egg wafts into my room. Yum-Yum has left my bed and I hope Grandma let him out into the garden to pee. Sometimes she's a bit off with him. Apparently, when she grew up in Suparé, a village in Nigeria, she thought cats were souls of witches, or something weird like that. Then Dad asked her if she used to eat them and she threw back her head and laughed . . . but she didn't deny it. It took her months to stop praying whenever Yum-Yum entered a room.

I pass Dami's closed bedroom door and head downstairs in my shorts and T-shirt. The back door is wide open and through it I can see Yum-Yum out in the garden eating a piece of grass. Our neighbour's white-and-brown kitten is sitting near him. Golden, buttery omelettes and freshly boiled yams are on the counter. Grandma, wearing a long floral dress, sandals and a printed headscarf over her grey hair, is wiping her hand on a tea towel.

'Grandma,' I say, kneeling to her in a traditional Nigerian greeting before wrapping my arms round her. She kisses my cheek before grinning at me, showing off the large gap between her front two teeth.

'Good morning, sugar,' she says in her thick Nigerian accent. 'Are you hungry? Do you want breakfast?'

'Yes please.' I watch greedily as she piles my plate with way too many yams and a massive omelette. 'Do you want coffee, Grandma?'

'Please,' she says. Grandma only drinks two things – coffee and Coke. 'Where is your brother?' She doesn't wait for me to answer as she walks to the banister and shouts, 'Dami! Oluwadamilola! Get up o!'

I can hear my brother's heavy footsteps and a muffled 'Coming!' followed by Amara's high-pitched voice, but Grandma has already walked back to the kitchen and misses it. She would lose it if she knew Amara had stayed over. Grandma is very traditional and a devout Christian, plus she claims to know a lovely girl from Abeokuta who attends her church that she thinks would be perfect for Dami. She won't listen, no matter how many times we tell her that he's in a relationship.

Grandma sighs as she sits at the kitchen table. One of her legs plays up on her sometimes. She says it's old age, but I think it's because she always walks everywhere. I've tried to tell her to ask Dad for a lift or to stay home and rest, but as usual she doesn't listen. That's Grandma though – hard-headed, but loves hard.

I quickly make her her coffee and myself a tea. I hand her the cup and she spoons heaps of sugar into it.

'Are you missing your parents?' she asks loudly over the sermon which is still playing, and I reach over for her phone and turn the volume down.

'Err . . . a bit.' The truth is, I've loved the freedom. It's felt like a breath of fresh air, but Grandma would be offended if I said all that.

'You must keep this house clean and keep on top of your brother. He is acting lazy being in bed at this time.'

I reach for my tea and take a long sip. There's no point mentioning that it's still only eight fifteen and he doesn't work Tuesdays.

'Why don't you join the prayer line?' She wags her finger at me. 'I send you the link every morning at seven. The prophet said some wise words yesterday. He said to look closely at our households and to banish any deceitful behaviour.'

What? How did he know that? Oh shit, does Grandma know about my birthday party tomorrow? Is she trying to suss me out? I lose focus, thinking of all the worst-case scenarios, and the tea that should be going in my mouth tips onto my chest and the kitchen table.

'Damn it!' I shout, jumping up, as the hot liquid seeps through my top. I wipe it with my hand.

'Pele,' Grandma says, wetting a cloth and handing it to me.

'Thank you. I may as well get ready for the day.'

I hurry quickly out of the kitchen. If Grandma does know about the house party, I don't want her to start questioning me. I'll crack under the pressure. Maybe I should have just asked my parents if I could have a party? But deep down I know they would have said no. As long as they never find out it should all be okay.

Dami comes out of his bedroom as I reach the landing.

'Do you think she's staying long?' he asks, clearly not bothered that I'm holding a cloth on my chest.

'She's listening to her prayers,' I say walking past.

'Babe, you're going to have to stay up here for a while,' I hear him say to Amara.

Grandma doesn't leave until midday and then it's only because she wants to go to the market. Poor Amara's been stuck upstairs for hours and we couldn't even sneak food to her because we're not allowed to take food upstairs. The kitchen is now full of meat stew, jollof rice and meat pies. This should last us for a few days, which means Grandma won't pop by tomorrow and I can start decorating the house for my party.

Sharisha and Oyin have come over to help. The theme is Coachella ... but a budget version. I've envisioned having this festival theme for years, with photo booths and food stands ... but then I remembered I don't have a summer job, my garden is tiny and my parents wouldn't pay for a party. So instead, we're going to decorate the living room with balloons, streamers and dreamcatchers, and everyone has to wear their best festival attire.

I've got this fitted dress, white crochet and fringed, and I'll wear it with boots. A DJ is not in my budget so I've spent weeks putting together the best curated summer party playlist. Sharisha's pretty good with drinks so she's going to mix up some cocktails for us, and I ordered little cocktail umbrellas to give the drinks a summer vibe. Fatima is picking up the birthday cake for me. My friends got together and paid for it and I already know it's from an amazing bakery close to where I live, so it's going to taste *so* good. Sansa's mum has a membership to Costco so Sansa is going to buy the snacks and drinks. It's all coming together.

After we've been decorating for what seems like hours we finally step back to admire our handiwork. It's looking good. The only thing is the weather's so hot and even with all the fans on and windows open it still feels too warm. I pile my braids on top of my head, which makes me feel a little cooler.

'Thanks, girls,' I say, collapsing onto the sofa. My T-shirt is stuck to my skin with sweat. 'Couldn't have done it without you.' Sharisha and Oyin sink onto the sofa beside me.

'You're welcome. The baby of the group is finally turning eighteen!' Sharisha grabs my cheeks and squeezes them, and I laugh and swat her hand away.

'What's the one thing you would love to happen for your birthday, Eva?' Oyin asks.

It would be impossible for me to pick one thing. I want to learn to drive, go on a girls' holiday, secure a job as easily as my friends have managed to do . . . but there is one other thing that I've wanted for so long.

'Maybe for Jayden to finally ask me out on a date,' I say.

Oyin leans forward, resting her elbows on her knees. 'What

do you like about Jayden? Like, he's cute and everything, but what is it specifically about him?'

'I guess it's more about how he makes me feel. Like when he's close by, everything in me is alert, or when he compliments me it makes my entire day better. Plus, we have good chat and laugh a lot. We just seem to work well together – and I haven't met a guy before that's made me feel like that.'

Oyin pretends to wipe tears from her eyes, and I laugh and grab a pillow and chuck it at her. She catches it.

'You just like the challenge. He's the only guy not to have tried it with you,' Sharisha says matter-of-factly. 'I swear all of his boys have moved to you or asked for your number at one point during college.'

I shoot Sharisha a look, willing her to shut up.

'Hey, watch it!' Oyin says, clearly thinking of Logan. I know Oyin can get super insecure about the whole me and Logan situation, even though I've told her that there isn't a situation and reassured her loads that I do not like Logan in that way. Like, at all. Oyin taps her lips before she smiles. 'I dare you to get Jayden to give you a kiss at your birthday party.'

I swallow, my throat tight. A kiss! We haven't even gone on a date yet. Not even to Nandos or the cinema. Would Jayden be happy if I tried? When I'm on a date, if the guy makes a move, I very politely turn my cheek so their lips land there. I used to worry it would put guys off, but, if anything, it made them more determined to chase me. Some call it playing hard to get, but that's not what it is. That's not who I am. To me, kissing is really intimate and I don't want to do that with just anyone. But Jayden isn't *anyone*, so maybe kissing him would mean something?

I glance at Oyin. She has that look on her face like she knows I'm freaking out and on the verge of pulling out of the dare, but I'm not going to give her the satisfaction. Anyway, if I pulled out, then I'd have to do another dare instead, which could be worse. At least this one is something that I want.

'Okay, cool,' I say, and Oyin grins. 'I'm gonna get Jayden to come and meet me upstairs in my room, and not only am I going to get a kiss, I'm gonna get my man too,' I say confidently.

Oyin cheers but Sharisha gives me a nervous look. I smile at her to show her it's okay. I can do this.

FIVE

I wake up to my phone ringing and I reach over, half asleep. 'Hello?'

'Eva?' Mum calls in her loud voice. 'Happy eighteenth birthday, my darling.'

'Thanks, Mum.' I sit up and yawn. 'How's the holiday going?'

'It's okay. Too hot and my cousins are asking me for money. They think I'm rich because I live in England. I said, "Me?" Ah, they do not know my struggles.' Today her African accent is stronger than ever. 'Any special plans today?'

'Oh, just hanging with my friends.' Technically not a lie.

'That's fun. Have you done your university shopping yet?'

'Mum!' I moan. Any chance she gets she brings up uni and it's the last thing I want to think about. 'Not today.'

'Okay, okay.' She huffs. 'We left your present in our closet.'

'You did?' I jump out of bed, tiredness forgotten, praying my present is the Air Dunks I've been drooling over and not so subtly told my parents about. I practically run to their room

36

and pull on the closet door. I already know it's trainers from the size of the gift.

'I'm opening it now,' I cry.

'Open it gently so I can reuse the wrapping paper.'

I roll my eyes as I peel back the sellotape. It feels like it takes forever before I'm able to lift the lid of the box and, yes! The black, white and red trainers are there inside, almost gleaming like treasure.

'Thank you, Mum!' I squeal. Even though I've been hinting for weeks, I can't lie, the trainers are mad expensive. My parents would usually make me wait till they are on sale, so the fact that they paid for these lusted-over trainers is kind of amazing.

'You're welcome, darling. Oh, your dad wants to speak to you.'

'Happy birthday, Eva.' Dad's rich booming voice comes through the phone.

'Hi, Daddy. Thank you for the trainers.'

'It's okay. But one hundred pounds for trainers? Ah ah! It should be no more than forty pounds. I get my trainers from the market. Fifteen pounds max.'

I can't help but laugh. Dad loves a bargain just as much as his non-branded market trainers, so I know this was Mum making him spend this amount.

'My Lyca is running out. Tell Dami I will call him later. Make sure to listen to him, don't have people staying over, no being outside late and no driving my car.'

I groan. Honestly, I'm not ten years old. 'Yes, Daddy. Bye – speak to you later.'

'Bye-bye. Enjoy your birthday,' Dad says.

I can hear him talking to someone in Yoruba and I wait in case he wants to say something else to me. But clearly he's forgotten that he hasn't hung up and I don't want him moaning at me that he's out of money on his phone, so I end the call.

Eagerly, I try on the trainers and they look so good on. My friends are going to be so jealous! Everyone wants these Dunks.

My phone is blowing up with happy birthday messages and I'm being tagged in lots of stories on Instagram. Jayden has posted a picture of us all at Carnival and has wished me a happy birthday. That's a good sign, right? This public display of affection. Everyone is tagged in the picture, including his cousin Saint, and because I'm curious I click on Saint's profile.

Saint Rowe-Falade's Instagram is full of old comic book covers and the comments are people geeking out over them. There isn't even one selfie of him. A notification flashes on my phone and Saint has re-shared Jayden's picture to also wish me a happy birthday and he's followed me. I'm not really into seeing comics on my feed but I follow him back anyway.

But I need to get a move on. The party doesn't start till seven. Thankfully my braids are still fresh, but Dami said he would pay for me to get my nails done as a present. Nothing makes me happier than fresh acrylics.

I get home a few hours before the party. My birthday nails are so beautiful. I went for my usual long almond shape, but with a fancier design this time. Each nail is painted white and there's a small gem on all of them apart from my fourth nail, which has white flowers to add to the festival theme. Dami gave me enough money to get a pedicure too, so my feet have been scrubbed and massaged and my toes are white and glossy. Being pampered has almost made me forget that tonight I'm going to get a kiss from Jayden!

'There you are,' Amara says looking stressed. 'I thought I was doing your make-up?'

'We've got time. No one will come at seven on the dot.'

'I don't like rushing,' Amara argues as I sit down. She has everything spread out on the dining room table, from foundations and blushers to highlighters, lashes and lip gloss. I see so many brands, like Fenty, Mac, Nars, Huda Beauty, Tower 28.

She begins with my foundation. 'I'm thinking a bronze, golden look,' she muses, 'with thick but natural lashes, a bold eye, and glittery highlighter for that festival look. Maybe a nude lip – or should we go red?'

'Red,' I say, already envisioning my whole look. 'Thanks, Amara. And please don't cover—'

'Your beauty spot, I know.'

I have a beauty spot under my left eye and I hate when it's covered up. It's unique to me and I feel like it gives my face more character. I love it.

'Eighteen. How do you feel?' She squirts foundation onto the back of her hand.

I shrug. 'The same really.'

I always thought once I turned eighteen I would feel this immediate maturity, like I'm grown now and no one can tell me anything. Kind of hard to think like that, I suppose, when I have no job and my parents are still telling me what to do from over four thousand miles away.

'You're doing law at uni, right?' Amara asks.

That familiar clammy feeling engulfs me when people ask about my future. Yes, I'm going to uni to do law, but it's only because my parents have pushed me into it. I blame Dami. He was meant to be the lawyer but then he changed his mind, dropped out of uni and is now working full time at the tech company. The pay isn't the best, which is why he can't afford to move out. My parents channelled their disappointment in him into pushing me to have a career in law. The trouble is I know deep down, just like Dami, that I don't want to do law either, but I don't know how to tell them. I even picked a uni in another city, Nottingham. At the time I thought it would be cool, getting my independence and just having space from my overbearing parents, but now I'm not so sure about moving away, and the closer it gets to the start of term, the more I'm regretting it. None of my friends are going to the same uni as me. I've only been to Nottingham once, so I don't really know it. And what if I don't make any friends? Although I hate to admit it, I'm quite reliant on my parents and I have no idea how I'll look after myself.

'Yep, I'll be off to Nottingham soon,' I tell Amara, forcing a chipper tone.

'That's cool. I kind of wish I'd gone to uni and had the experience everyone talks about.'

'You think you missed out?' I ask.

Amara shrugs. 'Kinda. But I guess I can live it through you.'

I know Amara didn't say it to add pressure, but now it feels like she's another person relying on me to go to university.

Despite her complaining that she doesn't like to rush, Amara works quickly, humming under her breath. She pauses for a second and stares at me. 'Ugh! Your face is perfectly symmetrical. I'm so jealous.'

'Err, thanks,' I say uncertainly.

'You could always do modelling. If you were taller you could have done runway. Maybe you can be an influencer and Insta model?'

'Ha! Modelling? Have you met my parents?' I laugh, even though I did want to be a model when I was younger, especially when other people said I should do it. But then, when that list came out, I realized I didn't want to be known just for what I look like. And anyway, Dad barely understands what Instagram is. He would not be impressed if he saw me posing on there and sharing my life. He would probably say something like, *What life will you have with no degree?*

Amara opens up the mascara. 'Sit still please.' She gently opens my eye and starts to apply the mascara. My phone starts vibrating back to back and I instinctively turn to look, causing the mascara brush to poke the edge of my eye.

'Amara!' I yell squeezing my eye shut. Fuck, that hurts.

'You moved!' she shouts defensively. 'Let me see if your eye is red.'

I can barely open it for her to check. 'I'll get you some ice,' she says.

41

I pick up my phone as she leaves, looking with one eye, ignoring our Bad Bitches WhatsApp group chat, and see that the girls have each messaged me separately. I click on Fatima's message first and work my way through the others.

Fatima
They spelt Eve instead of Eva on your birthday cake – have you got icing?

Sharisha
Girl, these shorts are not fitting these thighs. Can I raid your wardrobe?

Sansa
Got the snacks but I left my ID! So I couldn't get the alcohol. I'm sorry, hun. Can Dami help?

Fuck's sake, I do not need this stress right now! I quickly fire back responses to each of them.

Deep breaths. Don't panic, Eva, I tell myself.

SIX

It's ten p.m. and the party is in full swing. My house is rammed with teenagers dancing to my playlist. Pretty much everyone stuck to the festival theme and there's lots of denim, floral and bright colours. Most of the guys have their shirts open, which I'm loving – very Coachella! There's a few that made zero effort, like Robbie, who I've known since primary school, who's in a full tracksuit despite it being insanely hot in here.

Dami wasn't happy that he had to go out to buy alcohol for my party and he left the receipt on my bed. Not sure how he thinks I'm going to pay for it, but I'll deal with that later. Right now, he and Amara are out and aren't due back till later tonight and everyone thinks I'm amazing because I've thrown a party with zero adult supervision.

'Have you texted him?' Sharisha shouts over Beyoncé's 'Alien Superstar', handing me a red cup that's full of something alcoholic. She looks amazing in my short skirt with fringe at the bottom and a brown halterneck top that just about holds in her large chest.

I shake my head. Jayden is yet to make an appearance. I don't want to text him. He'll know that I've noticed he's not here. But I can't lie – his absence is stopping me from really enjoying myself. I've got to wrap my party up by midnight. *Where is he?*

Fatima and Sansa are talking to some guys at the other end of the room. Oyin's been stuck to Logan all night. His hands haven't left her butt, which is spilling out of the bottom of her short shorts. Oyin has barely spent any time with me at my own party. I down the drink in one go and Sharisha raises her eyebrows at me.

'I'm thirsty,' I say defensively. 'I'm getting another drink.'

I head to the kitchen and am surprised to see that most of the drinks have already gone. The only refreshment that's left is half a bottle each of rum and Coke. I mix a small amount together, not wanting to get drunk in case anything goes wrong, and when I head back towards the living room I see Jayden walking in through the front door, followed by Saint and a few other guys. I recognize one of them, a slim, white guy with dark hair, as Anthony Watson. Sansa will be pleased!

Jayden's saying hi to everybody as he passes so he doesn't see me straight away. He's wearing a blue Hawaiian shirt, shorts, and fresh white Air Forces. On anyone else the combo would look ridiculous, but Jayden pulls it off with an effortless swag. Saint sees me first and raises his hand in a hello. His long hair has been cornrowed straight back and he's wearing a white T-shirt with a dragon on it, denim shorts and white trainers – maybe not the most festival-looking outfit.

'Hey!' I walk over to them and because Jayden isn't looking in my direction I hug Saint first, surprised to feel his muscles through his top. I see Oyin watching us over Saint's shoulder, and she raises her eyebrows as if to say, *Ooh, you're hugging Saint?* I roll my eyes in response, which translates as *Relax.* 'Thanks for coming,' I say aloud.

'Thanks for the invite. Happy birthday.' Saint hands me a card.

I don't know if it's weird, but my friends and I never buy each other birthday cards. A shout-out on Instagram and a WhatsApp message is what we do best. Only family tend to spend money on cards. I do secretly love a birthday card though; it's another way of someone showing they care about you.

'Thanks, Saint.' I smile at him.

At this point Jayden finally looks at me and his mouth makes an 'O' shape as he sees me. This crochet dress is so tight and the lacy pattern has big holes in so you can see my white bikini underneath. I think it's meant to be a beach cover up, but tonight it's my party dress.

'You look hot.' Jayden wraps his arm round me and for a moment I let myself lean into him, breathing in that citrus woody smell of his that I love. 'Happy birthday, Eva.'

'Glad you could make it! Drinks and snacks are in the kitchen,' I say.

'You still gonna save me a dance?' Jayden asks, his eyes

shining, and I nod. What I want to do is pull him to the middle of the dance floor right now, but I can't be out here looking too eager.

My friends are dancing in a group together in the living room and they cheer when they see me come back in.

'He's here!' I say with the biggest grin on my face, and they cheer even louder.

Coi Leray's 'Players' is blasting from the speakers, Jayden's here and I'm dancing with my friends in what has so far been a successful party. Nothing is broken, no crazy spills, the vibe is just right and I'm eighteen! This is the happiest I've felt all night. I can see a few boys watching us and someone grins and waves at me. In the dim light it takes me a second to realize it's Logan. I don't want to risk upsetting Oyin, so I don't wave back. But when I turn back to my friends, Oyin is already watching me.

'What's that?' she asks, pointing at the envelope in my hand.

'Oh, a birthday card. Saint gave it to me.'

'We never do birthday cards . . . Is that weird?' Sharisha asks.

'I never really thought about it,' I say.

Sansa gasps. 'We haven't done the birthday cake yet!' She snatches the envelope from my hand. 'I'll put the card with the gifts. Fatima, help me light the candles.'

'I'll get the music,' Oyin says and wanders off.

'So, are you still going through with the dare with Jayden?' Sharisha asks.

'If I can get him alone,' I say. I look around the living room but can't see him anywhere. He must be stuck out in the hall.

That's the problem with being popular. Everyone wants your attention.

The main light comes on and the music abruptly stops, making everyone groan.

'Oi, listen, yeah?' Oyin shouts. 'It's time to sing happy birthday to Eva, so none of that moaning,' which makes me laugh.

Sansa walks carefully through the parted crowd, carefully carrying in the cake on its sparkly pink board and leading the happy birthday song. The big '18' topper twinkles at me and Sharisha gently pushes me forward towards the cake. Everyone takes out their phone and starts to film.

The cake is gorgeous. It's all white but it looks like it's been torn in the middle to reveal a pattern of sunflowers, my favourite flower. Then, on top, there are real sunflowers, pink gerberas and gypsophila.

'Make a wish, babe,' Sansa says, and I close my eyes.

I was going to wish for a kiss from Jayden, but I've already made plans for that so there's no point wasting a wish on something I've already got in hand. So, what *do* I want? Then it hits me.

I wish that I can be brave enough to follow my desires.

I keep my eyes closed and blow. A cheer goes round the room as the candles go out and everyone starts clapping. I'm smiling and waving, loving the applause, loving the attention, when all of a sudden Fatima puts two fingers in her mouth and whistles loudly and we all fall silent.

'There's one more surprise,' Fatima says. 'Pull the topper up, Eva.'

I frown. Why would I need to do that? I hold the number '18' and start to pull it up and gasp. A chain of five-pound notes are coming up out of the middle of the cake! They're stuck together in a long streamer and are covered in some sort of plastic.

'This is . . .' I'm lost for words. My friends know that, unlike them, I've struggled to get a summer job. I'm so low on money it's ridiculous, so this is one of the most thoughtful things they could have done. There's at least fifty quid here. 'Thank you! I can keep this, right?' I ask and everyone laughs.

'Of course you can!' Sansa kisses my cheek.

'I love you girls!' I hug Sansa, Fatima, Oyin and Sharisha one by one. I really am so lucky to have the best girlfriends.

Sansa heads back to the kitchen to cut up the cake and I follow her to wash my sticky hands. Everyone is hugging me on the way and wanting to take pictures. My cheeks start to ache from smiling so much. I finally spot Jayden surrounded by a group of girls and he doesn't even look up when I walk by. Great.

'First slice is yours.' Sansa hands me a plastic plate and I take a bite. Mmm. This cake is banging! My stomach rumbles and I realize that this is the first food I've eaten since breakfast this morning— *Oh shit, Yum-Yum!* I haven't even checked on him.

'I gotta feed my cat,' I say putting my half-eaten cake down.

'Don't forget your money,' Sansa says, wrapping it up in a few sheets of kitchen towel so my hands don't get sticky all over again.

Grabbing Yum-Yum's food, I squeeze past the people in the hallway. The music is back on as I walk to the beat up the stairs. Despite the noise, Yum-Yum is on my bed, fast asleep. His long ginger body is stretched out on the cover and he looks so adorable I can't help but gently stroke his head. He briefly opens his green eyes before happily closing them again. He has enough water and food in his bowl but I add a bit more anyway.

I place the kitchen towel with the money on my desk before looking at my reflection. My make-up has held up, but I grab my Fenty lip gloss so my lips can look extra juicy. There's a gentle knock on my door and, in the reflection, Jayden's head pops round.

'Jayden!' I quickly put the lip gloss down and flick my braids back. 'What are you doing up here?'

He's so tall that he makes my room look tiny.

'Feel like I haven't had a chance to speak to you and I saw you come up. Is it okay?'

'Of course.' I glance round my room, which tonight looks like a bomb site. Clothes and shoes are everywhere and Yum-Yum's litter tray is in the corner (clean, thankfully, so at least my room doesn't smell funky).

Jayden looks around, smiling at the pictures of my family and friends on the wall. He glances at Yum-Yum and his smile gets even bigger. 'Cute.'

'He is,' I respond. My heart races as I walk towards him. Damn, this boy is so fine. My shoe catches on something and I stumble but Jayden catches me. My cheeks burn hot and I look back to see one of Yum-Yum's toys on the floor.

'Thanks,' I say.

'No problem. I see I'm not on your picture wall.' He's still holding onto me.

'You're there somewhere – maybe in the background,' I tease.

He clutches his heart like I've broken it. His other arm is round my waist. 'Okay, okay. Can we get a picture now, then?'

'Yeah, sure.' He takes out his phone and he has to bend down so he can fit in the picture with me. I'm counting slowly in my head to control my breathing, which is trying to match my racing heart. We take lots of photos, switching it up from smiling to serious faces and then pulling silly faces.

'These are cute.' I look through them. I always knew we would look good together and we really do.

When I look up at him, Jayden's smiling down at me. He very gently traces the side of my face with his thumb. 'Why are you so perfect?' he asks softly, before glancing at my lips.

My brain goes into overdrive. *Does he want to kiss? Is he going to kiss? Should I go for it? Oh fuck, is this really happening? Brain: shut up!*

Before I can even make a move, I hear loud shouting from outside my window.

'Err ... sorry ... one sec—'

What idiots are ruining my moment?! I open my window and stick my head out and can see a crowd of people from my party outside. Two boys are nose to nose, squaring up beside my dad's car, and people are shouting, encouraging them to fight. What do they think they're doing? My neighbours are going to freak out!

'Sorry, Jayden, I just need to—'

The sound of glass smashing makes me freeze.

SEVEN

'Shit!' I race down the stairs with Jayden on my heels. 'Excuse me!' I use my elbows to get through the crowd and my mouth drops open when I see the two guys, neither of whom I know, standing on either side of my dad's car. They're both looking nervously at me. My stomach bubbles like I'm about to throw up. The corner of the car window on the driver's side is smashed in. Glass is on the ground under the driver's door and – shit – on the leather seats inside too. When I tell you Dad loves his silver Mercedes probably more than he loves me and Dami put together, I'm not exaggerating.

Everyone is still, staring at me. This must be a bad dream.

'W-w—' I can't even get the words out.

'This is bad,' Jayden says unhelpfully.

In the distance a police siren wails, getting closer. Fuck! Did a neighbour call them? There's a moment where everyone is looking at each other before they all run in different directions.

'Wait!' I manage to yell, but it falls on deaf ears.

'I ain't dealing with the feds,' someone shouts.

'The car!' I say, but no one cares. The boys that caused this are long gone and I didn't get their names. I don't even know who they are. How could they leave me with this mess?

'What's going on?' Sharisha asks from behind me.

I turn and see her, Oyin and Saint by the front door. Their eyes widen when they see the smashed car window.

'Damn,' Saint says. 'Who done that?'

'Cuz, we gotta bounce,' Jayden says. He smiles apologetically at me.

'You're leaving?' I ask in disbelief.

'Sorry, Eva.' He gives me a kiss on the cheek before he nods at Saint and begins to jog off up the street. Saint hesitates for a second before he gently squeezes my arm and follows Jayden.

'What the fuck?' I put my hands on either side of my face. This isn't happening, this cannot be happening.

'Shit, girl.' Sharisha puts her arm round my shoulder. 'Who done it?'

'Some random guys were fighting. Now my dad is going to kill me. Dami *can't* see this!'

Oyin looks at her phone. 'We've got an hour. Let's sweep up this glass . . . and we need some type of sheet to cover the car. Does your dad have anything for when it snows?'

'I think so,' I say.

Jayden just left! A stupid kiss on the cheek and he bounces without even asking if I'm okay. And how am I going to pay for a new car window? It must cost hundreds of pounds. Money I don't have. I am so fucked. It takes me a moment to realize

53

that the police sirens have gone. They clearly weren't coming for us.

'Eva!' Sharisha snaps, grabbing me out of my thoughts. 'We gotta move. Grab the car keys as well.'

'Yes ... sorry. I'll find the car cover.'

I hurry into the house, where the music is still loud and there are still some people partying, clearly unaware of anything wrong outside. Sansa is grinning and chatting to Anthony in the corner. Fatima is dancing in the middle of the room with Ruby, a girl from college. I turn off the music and everyone looks at me.

'Sorry, guys, but the party is done.'

'Oh, I thought it was finishing at midnight?' Fatima asks looking at her phone.

'There was a fight—'

'A fight!' Everyone starts talking at once and goes to the window, where they gasp when they see the damaged car.

'Oh, Eva.' Sansa grabs my hand and my eyes start to water. 'Who done that?'

'Some stupid dickhead boys.'

'Really? Ugh, what arseholes! Don't worry, I'll start tidying in here, okay?' Sansa turns to everyone else and shouts, 'Unless you're going to help clear up, please make your way out!'

Most people leave, which doesn't surprise me. Why did I throw this stupid party?

'Hey, Eva, what do you need help with?'

It's Anthony asking me, and two of his friends stand beside

him. How can people I don't even know help me out but my so-called college friends just leave?

'Err . . .' I look around the room.

With everyone gone I can now see that the living room is a mess. There are crumbs all over the floor, drinks have been spilled on the table and there are sticky marks on every surface from where people have put down their paper cups and bottles. Pictures have been moved and there's a dark stain on one of the sofa cushions. How are we going to clear up all this before Dami comes back?

'Let's start sweeping, people!' Fatima claps her hand on every word. 'I want this place spotless.' She turns to me. 'I'll clean up the kitchen.'

'Thanks – shit, I need to get the car cover. I'll be back.'

There's a room in our house that's meant to be a guest room but it's basically a general dumping ground. Everything is in here, from boxes and suitcases to clothes that Mum says she's keeping to 'send back home to Nigeria' although she still hasn't. It's an organized mess and I'm able to locate the grey car cover quickly. I know Dami's going to ask me why the car is covered in summer, and he might even believe me if I say I did it to protect it while we partied, but how will I explain why it is still covered now that the party is over? I groan. I wish we had a garage, then nothing would have happened to the stupid car.

Anthony stops me as I grab the car keys from the side drawer in the living room. He's holding the stained cushion.

'Sorry, I've tried, but I don't think the stain is coming out,' he says regretfully.

'I'll wash it,' I say. 'Just leave it on the hallway floor.'

Outside, Sharisha is staring at the broken window. The glass that was on the ground has been swept up

'Oyin went to help in the kitchen. Keys?'

'Yeah.' I unlock the car and grimace at the shards of glass on the leather seats. 'Are we dumb for doing this with no gloves on?'

'Very,' Sharisha says. 'We've got to be gentle with the seats so it doesn't pierce them.'

Picking up tiny pieces of glass and wrapping them in newspaper then plastic bags feels like it takes forever. It doesn't help that all we have for light is the torches on our phones. Every time we think we've got every last shard of glass, there's another piece hidden somewhere. Thankfully the seats are fine, but I'll still need to get the car cleaned inside in case we missed any stray pieces. How am I going to pay for that?

Once we've picked up all the glass, we put the cover over the car and I feel better not having to see the smashed window glaring at me. I glance at my clock. Twenty minutes to midnight.

'Thanks, Sharisha. Couldn't have done it without you,' I say.

'You're welcome, babe. Hopefully everything inside looks good?'

We go into the house and, yes, it looks pretty spotless. Sansa's in the middle of the living room and she wipes her brow with the back of her hand. Her other hand is holding the hoover.

'This okay?' she asks me.

To be honest the house hasn't looked this tidy since Mum and Dad left.

'It looks great. You guys are awesome – thank you,' I say gratefully.

'There's loads of full bin bags in the kitchen so we'll put them outside,' Anthony says, and his friends nod in agreement.

'Isn't he amazing?' Sansa gushes once he leaves the room. 'Such a gentleman.'

'He is,' I reply. Unlike Jayden, who ran off as soon as he could.

I do one last check around the house to make sure everything is okay. It all looks good. Miraculously, we still have five minutes left to spare!

'Thank you!' I call to the boys, and they wave as they leave. I don't miss the wink Anthony throws back at Sansa, who now can't stop grinning.

We all collapse on the couch, sweating and exhausted. My muscles are aching so bad. I kick off my boots and curl my feet underneath my bottom.

'I literally can't thank you girls enough,' I say looking at Sharisha, Oyin, Fatima and Sansa. 'What would I actually have done without you lot?'

'I can't believe those losers mashed up your dad's car. Wish I knew who they were,' Sharisha says.

'This is what I get for letting any hood rat come to my house.' I rub my face, not caring about the make-up. 'Seriously, guys, how am I going to pay for this mess? I can't claim on my dad's insurance because then he'll know.'

'Can't Dami help?' Fatima asks.

I scoff. 'He left me a drinks receipt for what he got for the party today. No way is he helping me. Actually, that was our agreement for the party – he is not involved.'

'Let me check how much it will roughly cost,' Fatima says. She types into her phone and a moment later she whistles. 'Damn. For a Mercedes it's about four hundred quid.'

'Four hundred!' I shout. 'For a window? What the hell?'

'We'll think of something,' Sansa says optimistically.

'Like what?' I question.

We all fall silent. That's it. Dad's going to murder me. Better start planning my funeral now.

'I saw you and Jayden go upstairs.' Oyin raises her eyebrows. 'Did you kiss?'

Me and Jayden. Feels like that happened days ago not a few hours. I shake my head.

'So, you didn't do the dare?'

We all stare at Oyin. Is this girl serious right now?

'What?' She shrugs. 'A dare is a dare and you know what happens if you don't do it.'

'Oyin, please, man – nobody cares,' Fatima sighs.

'We agreed on the rules,' Oyin argues. 'If you don't do a dare, you have to do the next one.'

'Oyin, this isn't the time,' Sharisha snaps at the same time as Sansa says, 'You're being stupid.'

'That's what we all agreed!' Oyin says loudly and now everyone is yelling over each other.

I knead my forehead with my fingers. I can't deal with this shit right now.

'Fine!' I shout. 'Whatever! I'll do another dare! Fucking hell.'

Sharisha, Sansa and Fatima glare at Oyin, but Oyin crosses her arms over her chest with a satisfied smirk on her face.

'I have some extra money from my uni fund that I was going to spend during freshers' week, but I can give it to you to pay for your dad's car and you won't even have to pay me back,' Oyin says, and my mouth drops open in surprise. 'If you complete the dare.'

We all look at each other. Is she being for real? A part of me wonders why Oyin can't just lend me the money if she has it. That's what a good friend would do, wouldn't they? At least, I know the other girls would. But if I win then I won't owe her anything, which is perfect.

'How much money are we talking?' I ask her.

'Four hundred pounds' she replies, with a slight smirk. 'And if you get it cheaper than the four hundred Fatima saw online, then you'll have some spare money.'

'What is it? What's the dare?' I ask.

'Well, you know how we always say that all the boys move to Eva and she doesn't even try,' Oyin says.

'Yeah,' the girls say slowly.

Is this another Jayden bet? I think.

'So I noticed that there's one boy that didn't seem to fall for your charms,' Oyin continues.

'My charms?' I scoff. She's acting like I go round putting

some sort of spell on guys that makes them like me. I don't. I'm just being myself.

'All you need to do is get this guy to ask you out on a date.'

Oyin shrugs. 'Easy.'

Sharisha frowns. 'What guy?'

Oyin's fully grinning now. 'Saint.'

EIGHT

For a second my mind goes blank. *Saint who?* But then I see him standing there in his dragon T-shirt, initially resisting when I tried to dance on him at Carnival. There's no way Oyin is suggesting that.

'Saint? As in Jayden's cousin?' Sharisha asks. She taps her finger at her temple. 'Oyin! Are you mad?'

'It's a good dare!' Oyin says defensively.

'I can't lie, that is pretty good,' Fatima says. 'Savage though.'

Sansa huffs. 'She can't move to Saint! Jayden won't have anything to do with her if she does.'

'Eva can say no if she wants,' Oyin says. 'I'm not forcing her.'

Isn't she? If I say no, I'm back to having no money to fix the car. And I'll just have to do another dare, no doubt a worse one. What if she dares me to kiss Saint? But if I say yes, Jayden will lose it. Maybe. Would he? What if this thing that I think is there between Jayden and me isn't really anything deep? I mean, he couldn't wait to leave the party, whereas Anthony, who doesn't know me, and who Sansa has only spoken to a few times via DM before they saw each other tonight, stayed behind to help me. One date with Saint could fix Dad's car. He's not my type but he seems nice. Kind of quiet though. I definitely didn't get any vibes that he was into me, so I'm not sure how I would get a date out of him. This could be difficult.

'Define "date",' I say slowly, and Sharisha and Sansa's mouths drop open.

'*E-va*,' Sharisha says pointedly. 'Seriously?'

'Well, what's a date? Is going for a walk a date? Cinema?' I ask.

'A date would be he has to ask you out,' Oyin explains, 'take you somewhere romantic *and* he has to pay. No splitting the bill business.'

'*Romantic!* How the hell am I going to get *that* to happen?'

'You can do that,' Fatima says encouragingly.

What is this bad-bitch, city-girl vibe they think I've got going on? I can't make someone who's not into me be into me, especially not on a 'romantic' level, and, on top of that, spend money on me too? What if I try it with Saint and he's like, no thanks, and then Jayden actually does have something deep for me but now he knows I tried to get with his cousin and so it's a wrap for us?

My head starts pounding.

'I think you should think about this,' Sharisha says, holding my arm gently.

Before I have a chance to respond, the front door opens and Dami's deep voice calls, 'Hello?'

I jump to my feet.

'Let me just double check the kitchen.' Sansa quickly runs out of the room.

I hurry out into the hall, with Sharisha behind me, and spy the stained cushion on the floor. I'd forgotten I told Anthony to leave it there. I quickly kick it behind me and Sharisha whispers, 'Got it.'

'Hey, guys!' I say loudly. 'How was your night?'

'So fun!' Amara says. 'Party good?'

'Yeah,' I say leaning on the banister, trying to look causal.

'Hey, Sharisha,' Dami says.

'Hi!' Sharisha grins at him with the cushion behind her back.

Dami jerks his thumb to the front door. 'What's up with Dad's car being covered?'

'Oh, it was just to keep it safe once the party started,' I say. 'Everything was good. You can check the house yourself.'

'Hmmm,' Dami says, but he makes no move to explore. 'Good turnout?'

I nod. 'My girls are still here, but they're going home soon. There's some cake in the kitchen.'

'Yum!' Amara pats her flat stomach. 'They ran out of the dessert I wanted at the restaurant. Come on, baby.' She grabs Dami's hand and leads him to kitchen. I hear them say hi to Sansa.

I sigh heavily, praying that Dami doesn't feel the need to remove the car cover.

'Eva, our taxi's outside,' Fatima says, coming out of the living room and opening up her arms.

I hug her tight. 'Thanks again, Message me when you get home.'

'Is it cool for me to stay over?' Sharisha asks.

I nod gratefully. I need to talk to someone about this Saint dare. If not, my brain will just go round and round in circles.

Sansa and Oyin come through to the hall and I quickly hug them as Fatima tells them to hurry up. Their heels *click clack* on the wooden floor and then the three of them are out the door.

Dami and Amara are still in the kitchen, so I grab the stained cushion from Sharisha and run upstairs with it, Sharisha following behind. I'm going to have to wash it tomorrow when Dami and Amara are both at work. For now, I dump it in my laundry basket. I open the window wide, hoping for some breeze to cool the room.

Sharisha sighs as she collapses on my bed, careful not to disturb Yum-Yum, who carries on sleeping. 'What a night,' she murmurs. She turns on her side, propping herself up on her elbow, her thick hair falling over her arms. 'Did you enjoy your birthday though? Obviously minus ... you know.'

'I did, actually.' I grab the make-up wipes off my desk and take a handful out before throwing the pack to Sharisha.

'This dare – I really don't think you should do it. Oyin suggesting it makes me really uncomfortable. And I don't think it's cool for her, as one of your best friends, to put you in a situation which could mess up things for you with Jayden.'

'I hear that,' I say, wiping my glittery eyelid. 'But what are my options? I can't tell my dad about the car, I have no money to fix it myself, and my parents are back from Nigeria in two weeks. Trust me when I say they will send me to live in Nigeria if they see the car like that.'

'But don't you think your parents will go easier on you, seeing as you never normally mess up? This is really a Dami-type situation,' Sharisha says.

She's right about Dami. He once threw a house party when I'd gone with my parents to stay in Kent for my cousin's wedding. Dami said he was sick so didn't come with us. Then when we got back to a trashed house, Dami passed out in the bathroom, a bottle at his feet and his head literally on the toilet.

'No,' I tell her, 'I think it will be worse. Because I'm the child that *doesn't* get into trouble and would *never* do something like this behind my parents' back. They will be so disappointed in me. If I can avoid them ever knowing then I should do that, right?'

'By going on a date with Saint?' Sharisha shakes her head. Half of her face is now void of make-up.

'At least I can ask him his hair care routine,' I joke.

Sharisha doesn't laugh. 'Seriously, how are you going to pull this off?'

I groan. 'I don't know! I know nothing about him. And his Instagram is just full of comic book stuff.'

'Really?' Sharisha sits up properly. 'Let me see.'

I find Saint's Instagram account and hand the phone to

Sharisha. She scrolls through his page as I remove the many layers of foundation from my face.

'Wait, did you go to the bottom? There's some stuff here.'

'Is it?' I hurry over and sit beside her. There are a few pictures of Saint – one where he's surrounded by people who are in cosplay and he's laughing at something, his dimples showing to full effect. In another he's standing next to shelves of graphic novels and in a third he's in front of a superhero mural that looks familiar.

I tap the last picture. 'Where have I seen that before?'

'Oh! It's ... err ... damn, what's the name?' Sharisha taps her leg as she tries to think then her eyes widen. 'Wonderland, the bookshop on Stoke Newington High Street. Remember when we went there to see that hottie Trey Anderson?'

I laugh. 'Yeah, I remember.'

Two years ago, it seemed like everyone was talking about Wonderland, the Black-owned independent bookshop that was going to close down at Christmas, but then the campaign went viral and all the donations kept it open. My friends and I, we all watched Trey Anderson's appeal over and over again because that boy is so hot! We were all a bit obsessed with him and his artist girlfriend, Ariel. They're like this teenage Black power couple. Trey has a singing voice that will literally make you want to do anything for him, and Ariel had a whole exhibition at the National Gallery. How can so much talent exist between them? The day we went to take pictures in the bookshop, we didn't see either of them, but we did see the murals. One Ariel had designed; the other was the superhero one.

'Do you think Saint drew that?' I ask.

'Nah, I think it was Trey's little brother. Apparently, he's also good at art. Maybe Saint knows them or goes to the bookshop a lot. Look at the caption – *Favourite day at Wonderland*. There's a pretty big graphic novel section. Let's see what his stories are saying.'

'Not on my account!' I say, but it's too late. Sharisha has already clicked on his profile picture and Saint's face appears. It's from earlier today, sometime in the afternoon, and he's walking down a busy road, filming himself talking to his phone screen.

'Just finished my talk at Wonderland bookshop, now heading over to work. If you're planning on coming to the Speak Your Truth event on Friday night, make sure to register.'

I frown. 'Talk at Wonderland? About what?'

Sharisha shrugs. 'Maybe we should go there tomorrow and see what we can figure out?'

I grin. 'So you're helping me now with this dare?'

'I still think you should say no,' Sharisha says, rolling her eyes. 'But I don't want my bestie being sent to Lagos or whatever.'

'Thank you, thank you!' I squeal, hugging her tight.

NINE

My head feels like someone is punching me in the skull. I tossed and turned all night dreaming of the different ways my parents will punish me and now I'm awake and exhausted. The other side of the bed is empty, but Sharisha's bag is still on the floor. Yum-Yum is nowhere to be seen. I drag myself out of bed.

The first thing I notice downstairs is the living room table covered in cards and presents for me. A race of excitement shoots through me as I hurry to open them. Sharisha is sitting on the sofa holding a plate with a stack of American-style pancakes covered in strawberries and blueberries. On the side are sausages, bacon and maple syrup. An identical plate of food is on the table waiting for me.

'Just made them,' she says. 'How did you sleep?'

'Breakfast looks great – thanks, girl. And I slept terribly. What is this?' I hold up a piece of neon material that was in the present I've just unwrapped, not sure if it's meant to be a bandeau top or a skirt.

Sharisha tilts her head to the side. 'Is it a headband?'

'God knows.' I put the material back down, pick up my plate of food and sit beside her. 'Did you sleep okay?'

'Like a baby.' She grins showing off her dimples. Without make-up she looks years younger than eighteen. 'Did you see the Bad Bitches chat?'

The group chat is always going off with anything happening in our lives, from college gossip, local drama, uni prep, birthdays and, more recently, our dares.

I shake my head. 'Phone's upstairs. What's it saying?'

Sharisha taps away on her phone with her long acrylics as I open a birthday card. The card has a light blue background with yellow and orange feathers floating in the air and in the middle a girl drawn in an anime style is holding a bunch of pink balloons. The girl has rich brown skin, long black braids, brown upturned eyes with a beauty spot under one of them, and she's wearing a golden, crystallized bralet with a golden headdress covered in ocean-blue gems. It looks exactly like my carnival costume. Is this girl me?

The birthday card reads *Happy 18th Birthday, Eva. From Saint*.

Sharisha turns her phone to me. 'Read this,' she says.

Oyin

Morning! Hope everyone hasn't got a banging hangover from last night. The party was sick! Just realized @Eva we didn't confirm if you're going through with the dare. Let me know if it's on with Saint x

There are lots of money emojis as well.

Sharisha raises her eyebrows at me. 'So, you're gonna do it?'

'At this point, I don't have a choice.' I show her the card. 'Look at this. Saint's birthday card to me.'

'Wow!' Sharisha gasps. 'Did he draw this?'

I shrug. 'I guess.'

'Maybe he does like you. Come on, what guy goes to all that effort?'

'Yeah, he does not *like me* like that. Read what he wrote.' I hand the card to Sharisha, who chuckles at the message.

I take a bite of my sausage to give myself time to think. Okay, if I can get to know Saint and figure out a way to hang out with him, then maybe he might start feeling something for me and I could pull this off.

'Shit! Do you know what we haven't thought of?' Sharisha says suddenly. 'What if Saint has a girl?'

I groan. 'Do you think he does?' And how would we possibly know, when he shares nothing useful on his social media? Wait, this could work. If Saint has a girlfriend, Oyin would have to change the dare and it can't be anything that includes Saint. Sharisha already knows what I'm thinking because she has her phone to ear. I'm guessing she's calling Oyin to but then she says, 'Hey, Jayden!'

'The fuck?' I hiss and she shushes me.

'Yeah, the party was good! I know, the car ... She's okay ...' Sharisha glances at me and I roll my eyes. If he wanted to know how I am he would call me. 'Quick one. You know your cousin Saint. Is he single? Someone was asking

70

about him . . . Really? You sure? Okay, thanks, J. Speak later.' Sharisha hangs up. 'Dare is still on, babe.'

'Damn it.'

'I mean, we could just tell Oyin that Saint does have a girl . . .' she offers.

I shake my head. 'She'll ask around to make sure. You know what Oyin's like.'

We fall silent. I wish Oyin had picked someone else. It's like she's trying to ruin any chance I have with Jayden before it's even started.

'On the plus side we might see Trey Anderson at Wonderland today,' Sharisha chirps, and that makes me laugh. 'Maybe we can persuade him to sing happy birthday to you.'

'We better dress cute, then!' I say, and Sharisha winks at me. 'And tell Oyin that the dare is on.'

Wonderland bookshop is in the middle of Stoke Newington High Street. We take an overground train and a bus to get there from where we live in Stratford.

It's boiling hot today and I'm wearing a cropped red top with a matching short skirt and my new birthday trainers. My eyes feel even more tired because of the weather, so I've got sunglasses on and my braids in a top bun. Sharisha didn't have any spare clothes for her impromptu sleepover so she's wearing my denim shorts and black vest top.

We head inside the shop, sighing as the cold air from the aircon hits us. It's packed in here. We head over to the comic book mural. There are shelves filled with graphic novels, as

71

well as beanbags scattered around. Teenagers are dominating the space.

'There must be some type of . . . found it!' Sharisha points out the A4 poster that's stuck on one of the walls and Saint's name and face is on it.

Seems like he did a sold-out talk here called 'The Power of Comic Books' yesterday afternoon. I'm pretty impressed. I don't know anyone my age who is giving talks and, even more impressive, giving talks that are sell-out events.

'Okay, we knew two things already,' Sharisha says. 'He likes comic books, and he wore that T-shirt to Carnival so he's a fan of anime,' she says, counting the points off on her fingers. 'So we're right in thinking he designed your birthday card.' Now she's holding up three fingers. 'That's a good start.'

'It is, but how did Wonderland know about Saint to even invite him to talk here?'

I look around the packed store. I can't see Trey. There's an older Black woman with glasses helping a customer. If I remember right, I think she's Trey's mum, who owns Wonderland. A light-skinned boy with light brown eyes and a pretty-boy face walks behind the till. He has this effortless swag in the way that he moves. I've seen him somewhere, but I can't recall where.

'Who is that?' I say.

Sharisha follows my gaze and she quickly pulls out her lip gloss from her bag. 'I dunno but we're gonna find out!' She grabs my hand and practically drags me over, mumbling 'Excuse me' as we push past customers.

The boy sees us and flashes us a slow, sexy smile, making me feel hot all over. He's even more gorgeous up close.

'Hi!' Sharisha says, purposely leaning forward on the counter so her chest is resting on it. He's pretty tall so if he looked down he could catch a view, which is what she wants. 'I'm Sharisha.'

He shakes his head and he's smiling like he knows what she's trying to do but he isn't falling for it. Damn, that makes him even more sexy. 'I'm Boogs.'

Boogs! I remember him now from Instagram. He's Trey's best friend.

'I haven't seen you here before,' Sharisha continues, even though we've only been here once before.

'I'm just helping out for a few weeks. So, what's up, ladies? How can I help?'

Sharisha's too busy fluttering her fake lashes to answer, so I say, 'We saw a poster about a talk yesterday and wanted to know more. Saint gave it, didn't he?'

'Oh, Saint! The one with all the hair. Yeah, the place was packed out.' He points at me. 'You into comics and that?'

'Err . . . yeah,' I say. 'Love all the comics.'

Boogs nods his head. 'You got a favourite?'

'A favourite?' I say, but my voice comes out all high-pitched and nervous. Shit. Why did I say I love comics? I could have just said I'm interested. I glance at Sharisha for help, but she's still too busy checking out Boogs. Who did Saint say that alien character on the T-shirt he wore at Carnival was called again? Wasn't that from a comic book?

73

'Frenzy,' I say, and Boogs frowns. 'The Frenzy one,' I repeat, trying my best to sound like I know what I'm talking about.

Boogs' frown goes even deeper. He thinks I'm a complete idiot. I've obviously got the name completely wrong.

'Oh! You mean Frieza, from *Dragon Ball Z*?' he says, realization suddenly on his face, and I nod. 'Yo that's a classic. We haven't got that here. Saint works at Harley's World of Comics. It's not far from Westfield over in Stratford. Massive collection!' and he opens his arms out wide to emphasize his point. 'They have other anime-related items too, like clothing, collectible figurines, even a gaming section. Here, let me right down the info. You should be able to find *Dragon Ball Z* there for sure.' Boogs presses the till and a strip of blank receipt paper comes out. He writes down a series of instructions on how to find the comic book store and hands it to me.

How have I never heard of this store before when it's only a short bus ride from my house?

Guess this means I'm going to my first ever comic book store.

TEN

Sharisha spent the entire bus ride analysing Boogs' Instagram account, despite him telling her he has a girlfriend when she asked if he was single. So far we've learned that he does in fact have a girlfriend called Santi – she's beautiful – and there are videos of him dancing, pictures of him with Trey, and a countless number of selfie pictures that Sharisha shamelessly likes. I give her a look and she laughs.

'What?' she says innocently.

'You know what.' I play nervously with the receipt paper in my hand. Now that we're almost at Stratford I'm questioning what I'm going to say to Saint. Won't it be weird, just turning up at his workplace? I glance at my phone. It's only midday and, according to Google, Harley's World of Comics closes at seven this evening. I need more time to think.

'You hungry?' I ask Sharisha, who has now moved onto Boogs' TikTok. 'I've got some birthday money with me.'

'Ugh! There's two of them,' Sharisha moans.

I do a double take when I see two versions of his girlfriend in a video and realize that Santi has an identical twin.

'I'll pay,' Sharisha says without looking up. 'It's still your birthday. Wait. Is that Saint?'

'Where?' I look at her phone and she replays the video.

The space looks quite dark and there are candles on the table giving it an intimate feel. Boogs is filming himself and then he moves the phone round so the video scans a table, and Trey, Ariel and Boogs' girlfriend Santi wave at the camera. At a nearby table I can see Saint – he's hard to miss with his long curly hair. Before the video ends there's someone on stage with a microphone.

'I thought it was a concert, but everyone's sitting down and it looks cosy.' Sharisha puts her phone away. 'Maybe it's some neo-soul artist?'

'We'll have to find out,' I reply.

We get off the bus and walk up the steps that lead to Westfield. Me and my friends, we're here pretty much every weekend. I think this shopping centre is one of the best things to happen to Stratford. It has everything you need and there are seats scattered everywhere so you can just chill too. Usually with a bubble tea in our case. Plus, it's air-conditioned, which is perfect in this summer heat. It's the only place round here where teenagers aren't kicked out for just existing.

The food court is busy as usual so we bypass it and head upstairs to the pretzel stand and I breathe in the sweet smell. Sharisha buys a parmesan cheese pretzel for her and pretzel sticks for me as well as two bottles of water. We find an empty table nearby and sit.

'Right, what are you going to say to Saint?' she asks.

I place my sunglasses on top of my head. 'Err . . . "Hi"?'

Sharisha gives me a deadpan look. 'You can't go in clueless. Your parents are home in, what . . . two weeks? Every day counts.' She takes a bite of her pretzel and groans. 'How do they make this so good?'

'What would you do?' I ask intrigued. Honestly, I've got no clue how to go about this and Sharisha is the only person I feel comfortable admitting that to.

Sharisha's quiet for a moment, thinking. 'Okay, I would say I'm interested in comic books for my brother or something, and then when he shows me some, I'll casually mention that I saw he did a talk at Wonderland.'

'Okay, I'll try that. Maybe I can ask if he's doing any more talks? Didn't he say something about an event?' I ask warming to the idea.

Sharisha grins. 'Now you're thinking. You've got this. What guy wouldn't like a gorgeous girl being interested in all of his shit?' Sharisha's phone beeps and she glances down at it, then pulls a face. 'My mum needs me home now to look after Toya.'

'Ah, man!' I need Sharisha way more than her sister does right now. How am I meant to do this without her? I know if she'd been given this dare she would absolutely kill it.

'Sorry, girl, but you've got this. Just go in, ask loads of questions, but also really listen to what he's saying and try and find something – *anything* – that you have in common.'

77

'I'll try,' I say, but deep down I'm nervous that the whole encounter will be awkward and he'll just know I have some ulterior motive. In hindsight, I should have maybe picked up a graphic novel at Wonderland to get some understanding about what the hell I'm going to be talking about. Are graphic novels completely different to comic books? God knows.

We finish up our pretzels and leave the shopping centre together. The sun is even hotter now and I'm already desperate to get back to the air con.

Sharisha hugs me tight. 'Good luck! Let me know how it goes. And I'll wash your stuff and bring it over.'

'No problem,' I say releasing her.

We wave goodbye and I place my sunglasses back down, which helps me see my phone screen better. I have a ridiculous number of notifications from social media. Must be posts from the party and hopefully none about the car. I thought I would have had a message from Jayden by now, but he's sent me nothing. I'm disappointed he's not wanted to check in on how I am. Anyway, according to Google Maps I'm only a ten-minute walk away from Harley's World of Comics so I set off.

I find the store on a side street that I don't recall ever walking down before. It's a white building with lettering in red and black. On top of the H is a black-and-red jester's hat and in the corner is a huge black mallet with red diamonds sprayed on it. The shop window shows a range of comics on display and I can also see a set of stairs to the right. The door is wide open, so here goes . . .

Inside, it's quite busy. There are shelves upon shelves

of comic books, a few racks of anime T-shirts, a gaming station ... There's a massive glass display with figurines. Some I recognize from the Marvel and DC movies – the obvious ones like Iron Man, Superman – but most of them I have no clue about.

It's not hard to spot Saint in front of a section that says STAFF PICKS. He's wearing blue jeans and a white T-shirt with the jester hat from the shop sign and HARLEY'S WORLD OF COMICS underneath. This time I really look at him. I would say he's about five foot ten. Attractive in a kind of hipster way but he doesn't have that swag that I love. Behind the till is a white man with long brown shoulder-length hair. His T-shirt is the same as Saint's but in black. He kind of reminds me of Comic Book Guy from *The Simpsons*.

Taking a deep breath I walk over to the shelf near Saint and stand close enough to him to smell the vanilla scent of his aftershave. It takes him a while to notice me and when he does his eyes widen and he says, 'Eva?'

'Oh, hey, Saint!' I say taking off my sunglasses with the air of someone who hadn't even noticed him.

Saint looks past me as if he's trying to see who I'm here with. 'What are you doing here?' In reality, his tone of voice is giving, *Are you lost?*

'I'm getting a gift ... for my brother. So, yeah ...' I trail off miserably.

'Cool.' He smiles, and dimples appear on either side of his face. 'What is he into?'

'Oh ... err ...' I glance around the store. There are just

too many options. What do I pick? 'He's open to, you know, whatever. What would you suggest?'

'Well, I kinda need to know what he likes so I can suggest something.' Saint laughs.

'Of course,' I say.

We fall into an awkward silence. This is so not working! I should have come more prepared.

'Thanks for coming last night,' I say, quickly changing the subject. 'And the card was lovely. The carnival costume was spot on.'

'Oh, no worries. Glad you liked it. We actually have this new software to design characters. Great if we want to do custom cards, bags or whatever. So I was just trying it out,' he says casually. 'I'm so sorry about your dad's car. I wanted to stay and help, but Jayden . . . Anyway, I'm sorry. It was a great party though. Did you manage to sort the window?'

'No, not yet. I'm kinda low on cash but I've got a few weeks to sort it.'

Saint smiles sympathetically at me. 'Let me know if I can help.'

You can help by asking me out on a romantic date so I can win this dare, I think. Out loud I say, 'Thanks, that's kind of you.'

The white guy from behind the till walks over to us holding a stack of flyers in his hand. 'Your turn, mate,' he says.

Saint groans. 'Come on! I did it yesterday.'

'And I did it this morning,' the man counters. 'It's only fair.' He spots me and he smiles. 'Hello!'

'He owns the store,' Saint explains.

'Oh, so you're Harley?'

Saint and the guy look at each other before they laugh.

'It's named after Harley Quinn, you know – the Joker's girlfriend?' Saint says.

'Oh, of course.' That would explain the jester hat and mallet. 'I'm Eva,' I say politely, very aware that I'm the only customer in the store not dressed in some type of graphic T-shirt. I must stand out like a sore thumb.

'Eva? Do you know Eva Bell?' the man asks.

I frown. 'No, who's that?'

'She's a mutant from *All-New X-Men – Volume 1*.' He looks at me expectantly.

What does that even *mean*?

'Sorry,' I say, even though I don't even know what I'm apologizing for.

'Benji, leave her alone,' Saint says wearily before turning to me and saying, 'He throws random comic book trivia at everyone.'

Benji's eyes widen. 'Oh, is she—'

'No,' Saint says sharply and I look at him, surprised by his tone.

Benji's face reddens. 'My mistake. So, Eva, who do you think would win in a fight? Kitty Pryde or Jubilee?'

'Sorry, what?' I ask, confused. Who the hell are *they*?

'Ignore him,' Saint says quickly. 'They're X-Men. He's always asking customers about who would win what battle and, for the record, my money is still on Jubilee.'

Benji gasps loudly and I look from him to Saint. I have no idea what is happening.

'For that you've got to get rid of all of these.' Benji hands Saint the flyers.

'What? Because I said Jubilee?' Saint asks outraged.

'You should know Kitty is the only answer I'd accept.' And with that Benji dramatically walks off.

Saint laughs and shakes his head. 'Unbelievable. Sorry, Eva. Benji can help you with the gift for your brother.'

'Oh, yeah. Of course,' I say, even though I'd completely forgotten about that. There must be at least forty flyers in Saint's hands and from the way his shoulders have dropped I can tell how much he hates doing it. 'Do you need help with them?'

'No, no, no. Don't worry. I couldn't ask you to do that.'

'You're not asking, I'm offering.' I take half the stack from him.

Saint looks at me quizzically like he's not sure if I'm taking the piss or not. I don't know why I'm offering to hand out flyers when I don't even work here, but our conversation can't be cut short because he picked the wrong mutant to win a fight. And I need to spend more time with him to get this dare in motion.

After a moment's hesitation Saint smiles. (Those dimples again!) He glances behind him and Benji is serving a customer. 'Let's just make sure he doesn't catch us.'

ELEVEN

The footfall outside the shop isn't great so we walk up towards the main road in the direction of Westfield. I'm praying that I don't see anyone that I know. Saint has a slow, lazy walk like he's not in a rush to get anywhere so I slow down to match his strides.

'I saw that you gave a talk at Wonderland,' I say.

'Yeah, I did. It was really good. Was you there?'

I shake my head. 'I passed through today and saw a flyer. Have you got any more talks coming up?'

Saint's forehead creases as he thinks. 'No, nothing that I can think of.'

I wait, thinking he'll remember that he did a whole story on his Instagram about an event tomorrow, but Saint doesn't say anything else. Should I just say I saw it? What would Sharisha do? I glance down at the flyers in my hand and they have a mash-up of pictures from different computer games, from *Super Mario*, *Donkey Kong* to *The Legend of Zelda* and *Tekken*.

'"Retro Gaming Day",' I read out and glance at Saint. '"The Arcade Archive in Bournemouth".'

'We host it every year by the beach,' Saint explains. 'But for those that can't come down, they can log in from their homes or come to the store. You a gamer?'

I used to play computer games with Dami as a kid and I remember loving it, but my girlfriends weren't really into it and my guy friends never took me seriously when I told them I could play, so I stopped.

'Used to,' I say. 'And I love the nineties games the best. My favourite was *Street Fighter*. It took me ages to get Chun Li's spinning bird kick.'

'Oh, *Street Fighter* is one of the best,' Saint says. He looks at me intrigued. 'You any good?'

I scoff. 'Of course I am.' Well, I used to be, doubt I'm any good now but I'm not going to tell him that.

'Then you should come! It will be loads of fun and you can show me how good you are.' He grins at me.

Okay, a date? Not really. Romantic? Definitely not.

'Maybe I will,' I say smiling back.

We're now in front of Westfield and it's even busier than it was earlier and there are lots of teens about. Thankfully none that I recognize, but I'm sure some of them will be down to come to a gamer night.

'We just hand them out, one each?' I ask, but Saint is suddenly looking uncomfortable. 'What's up?'

'I hate talking to people. Especially strangers. It's so awkward. The other day I noticed loads of flyers ended up on

84

the floor or in the bin. Maybe people just aren't interested.' He looks so defeated and I instantly feel bad for him.

'But you just did a talk at a bookshop,' I say. 'So obviously there's something about you that people are interested in.'

Saint shakes his head. 'That's different. The people that came to the talk wanted to be there, whereas this, going up to randoms, is having to *make* them care – and it's shit when they don't.'

Weird. I would find talking in front of a crowd, with everyone just staring at me, more uncomfortable than handing out flyers to strangers. All that pressure not to mess up, the scrutiny if I did ... It's one of the reasons why I don't think law as a career is for me.

'Then we have to make them interested.' I step forward as a group of boys around my age walks towards us. One of them looks me up and down, taking in my short skirt and crop top. He stops dramatically then clutches his heart and stumbles back into his friends, who start laughing. Usually, I'd roll my eyes, but I fix a smile on my face instead and hold out a flyer.

'You guys like playing games?' I ask.

'I'll play any game with you, beautiful,' the boy who stumbled back says.

'I don't think you can keep up with me,' I say in a flirty voice and his friends go 'Ooh!' 'Seriously though, this is a gamer event happening next week in Bournemouth but you can join in online. It's gonna be so sick and it's all the best retro games from the nineties and noughties.'

The boys take the flyer from me and study it intently.

'This actually looks good, you know,' one of them says. The others murmur in agreement.

'Thanks!' the first one says. 'We'll check this out for sure. Are you going to be there?'

'Of course,' I lie. 'See you there?'

He nods, grinning and showing all his teeth. A gold one flashes back at me and his friends elbow him, laughing. I wave them goodbye and head over to Saint, who's standing watching by the Westfield steps.

'You see – easy!' I say.

'You're good at this,' he says. 'So confident when you approached them.'

'It was nothing,' I say breezily. 'Why don't we do it together? You'll be able to give them way more info than I can about the event.'

'Okay, sure,' and from then on, while I lure them in with my enthusiasm, with Saint's knowledge we're a winning combo and it seems like everyone we talk to genuinely is interested to come to the gamer event.

By the time we leave Westfield it's almost four and all the flyers are gone. The time seemed to just disappear, but I've been out the house since this morning and I'm ready to call it a day.

'Thanks again, Eva. We've never gotten rid of all the flyers before. And it actually wasn't terrible, doing it today,' Saint says.

'I had fun. Maybe I'll help you out again.'

'Yeah, that would be great. Anyway, I won't keep you. See you around.'

For a second I think about hugging him goodbye, but Saint nods at me, turns and heads off the way we came towards Harley's World of Comics. I watch him walk away but he doesn't turn back.

TWELVE

The next day finds me standing around the corner from Harley's World of Comics, questioning whether it's a good idea to go inside. I called Sharisha on my way home yesterday to update her on what happened. It's not like I was expecting a parade, but yes, some recognition of the progress I made would have been nice. Instead, when I had finished telling her what happened, she said, 'And?'

'And what?' I frowned.

'And when are you going to see him again? What happens now? Did you find out about the event tonight?' she asked.

'Well . . . no.'

I thought I had done well hanging out with Saint for a few hours, like it was a good start, but what did I really learn about him?

He doesn't like giving out flyers.

Hardly groundbreaking.

'Go back to the comic store and ask him outright about

tonight,' Sharisha ordered. 'And then we'll all come. That will show Oyin that you're already making moves.'

I groaned out loud. 'Fine! I'll go tomorrow.'

Which is why I'm here now, trying to hype myself up to go in and talk to Saint. It's not that I'm nervous, it's more that I don't know what to say. The conversation doesn't exactly flow unless we're talking about anime or superheroes and my knowledge of that stuff is pretty limited.

My phone buzzes and there's a message in the Bad Bitches group chat.

> **Sharisha**
> Girls, keep tonight free! We're going to an event. Eva will send the deets 😊

For fuck's sake.

I take a deep breath and walk around the corner to the comic store. The door is open and inside the strong air con creates goose pimples on my skin. It's busier than it was yesterday and today Saint is behind the till. I stare at his arm wondering if all his tattoos have a deep meaning. If I came home with a tattoo, I would be sent to live in Nigeria with relatives I haven't seen in person since I was little.

Saint looks up and smiles when he sees me. 'Eva! How weird. I was just about to message you.'

'You was?' Maybe I did leave a good impression yesterday and now he wants to hang out one-on-one.

He leans on the counter. 'Yeah. I was telling Benji how good you were with handing out the flyers. Trust me when I say we barely give out a quarter of what we did yesterday. I know you have to fix your dad's car, and you mentioned that you didn't have the money . . . so it gave me an idea. We wanted to know if you were available to help us promote the Retro Gaming Day in Bournemouth?'

'Are you offering me a job?' I ask, surprised.

'Yeah . . . well, it's not permanent. Just until the event is done.'

'But I don't know much about all this,' I confess.

'Oh, don't worry. I can teach you. But we mainly need you for your personable skills,' Saint says. He holds up his hands. 'No pressure though. Only if you're free. We can pay you for three hours a week at ten quid an hour. It's not a lot but it's something – if you want it.'

I'm quiet for a moment as I add it up in my head. Mum and Dad will be home in two weeks so I can make sixty quid, on top of the four hundred pounds Oyin will give me if I win the dare. That gives me a little margin in case fixing the window is more than the amount we saw online. And I also need to get the car professionally cleaned inside . . .

Saint is watching me expectantly and I feel a rush of gratitude towards him. He really didn't have to do that for me.

'Thank you, Saint,' I say earnestly. 'That's really sweet and I would love the job.'

'Great! I'll let Benji know and then we can work out the days and hours.'

Just then, a customer comes over to ask Saint a question

so I move to the side as he handles it. I look around the shop. Not gonna lie: never thought I would be working for a comic book store, but money is money and a girl can't afford to be picky right now.

'So, any plans for tonight?' Saint asks as the customer walks away.

'Err . . . I think I'm hanging out with my girls.' I wait a beat. 'You?'

'I'm doing this spoken word event. Should be fun.'

I raise my eyebrows, acting surprised. 'You do spoken word?'

'For a few years now. My ex got me into it.' For a second he looks pained, but when I blink the expression is gone. Maybe I imagined it.

'That sounds cool. Maybe I can come with my friends? If you don't mind,' I add quickly.

'Oh, you're into spoken word? Who's your favourite poet?'

I'm not into spoken word at all. To be honest, I find it all too serious, too deep, and I can never really understand what they're talking about, like the wordplay just goes over my head. I do like the way they deliver their poetry though. The way their voices rise and fall like a rap.

'Oh, I love it,' I say. 'There's a girl on TikTok that I really like. Are you on TikTok?' I ask innocently, knowing already that he's not because I checked. Saint shakes his head like I knew he would. 'Well,' I add, 'she's good, so yes, I would like to come. What's the info?'

'You know where River Run is?' he asks, and I nod. 'It's

happening there. The event is called Speak Your Truth and starts at seven. It's free but just make sure you get there early because it can get rammed. I was there not long ago to watch an event and only just about managed to get a seat.'

'Sounds cool. Thanks! Are any of your family and friends coming to watch you?' And because I can't help myself I add, 'Like Jayden?'

'Jayden?' Saint barks out a laugh. 'Unless it's football or girls, Jayden's not interested.'

'Girls?' I ask, trying not to sound too anxious. 'Is he seeing someone?' But now another customer is there, wanting Saint to help find something.

'He's never mentioned anyone special to me,' he replies, going over to help the customer. 'One sec, I'll be back.'

My heart is hammering in my chest and I feel weird, like I want to cry, but also I'm mad. I know Jayden and me aren't official, but we do have something. Everyone in college knows it. Does Jayden just think of me as a college thing but nothing more than that? And now that I think about it, when I first met Saint at Carnival and introduced myself, Saint had zero recognition of my name. Clearly Jayden hadn't told him about me, so I can't be that special. It's never even crossed my mind that Jayden could be chatting to other girls. When does he have time to do that, when *we* usually chat every day?

'Sorry,' Saint says, appearing next to me again and making me jump. 'You okay?'

'I was thinking about something.' I want to bring it back to Jayden, but I force myself to hold my tongue. Obsessing over

Jayden in front of Saint is not going to win me any points. 'So, you got any videos of you doing spoken word? I didn't see anything on your Instagram.'

Damn it. I squeeze my eyes shut. Why did I say that?

Saint laughs, which makes me open my eyes. 'You checking out my Instagram?'

'No! Of course not.' I brush my braids back into a bun just to give myself something to do.

Saint's still looking at me with an amused smile. 'I'll see if I have something.' He stands a bit closer as he opens his phone, that vanilla smell of his tickling my nostrils. As he scrolls through his photos, I spot a few pictures of him with his arm round a Black girl with short hair. Who is that? Maybe it's his sister or friend . . . or his ex?

I clear my throat. 'Who is—'

'I think this is one.' Saint cuts me off and clicks the video.

It's been filmed lopsided. Saint is saying something about identity but the audio isn't clear, and whoever is filming is whispering to someone out of shot, but in the video it sounds really loud.

Saint winces. 'Sorry, that's not great.' He shuts it off and his phone screen goes black. 'I never ask anyone to come and watch so I'm just grabbing videos of myself that I find online. Clearly it's not working.'

'Oh . . . well . . . I can film you tonight if you want?' I offer.

'Yeah? Thanks, Eva. That would be cool.'

93

THIRTEEN

River Run is a dark bar on a side street in Mile End. It's small and unassuming with peeled paint on the exterior. The kind of place that I wouldn't go into alone. Behind me, Oyin sighs.

'Where are we?' she moans. 'This looks like a crime scene.'

'It's where the spoken word event is,' I say, keeping my voice cheerful.

She was more than happy to come along when I mentioned it in the chat and I never said we would be going to a palace. I mean, it doesn't look great but maybe inside is nice.

'I think it's a good sign that Saint invited you,' Sansa says, sweeping her blonde hair back. 'Clearly you've already made a good impression on him.'

I nod, not trusting myself to talk. The only one who knows that I invited myself is Sharisha. It's not like I don't trust my friends to know the whole truth, but I feel weird letting them know how much I'm having to try with Saint. Especially when they know I usually don't need to try with guys. They think that I've got him hooked and he's going to ask me on a romantic date any day now. How do I tell them that we're so far from that? There's a small part of me that isn't convinced that anything is going to happen at all, but there's no way I'm saying that out loud.

'They just better have air con,' Fatima says, fanning herself with her hands. 'Let's go in.'

I don't have Saint's number so I shoot him a DM letting him know that I'm here. He reads it straight away and tells me he saved us a table near the front. We go down the stairs to the underground bar.

It's much more cosy down here and I instantly recognize it as the bar we saw in Boogs' video. There are some cool globe-shaped lights hanging from the ceiling and a few round tables with candles in the centre of them. At the front of the room are two giant speakers and a standalone microphone. The bar is to the right and there are people already waiting to order drinks. It's clear we're the youngest people in the room. Saint is hovering by one of the tables, looking down at his phone. He's wearing all black and the light from the phone is highlighting the sharp angles of his face. When he looks up and sees me, he breaks out into a smile.

'Ooh, someone's happy to see you,' Fatima says nudging me.

Do we hug? Would it be weird to? Would my friends think it's odd if we don't? Thankfully, the decision is made for me as Saint wraps an arm round my shoulder and pats my back. The way Dami would hug me if I was upset about something. Very brotherly.

'Hey, thanks for coming,' Saint says as we pull apart.

'Of course! You remember my friends – Sharisha, Sansa, Oyin and Fatima.'

Saint waves at them. 'Nice to see you all again. Here's your table.'

'Is Jayden coming?' Oyin asks, and I try not to react.

I've been trying not to think about Jayden since Saint said he'd never mentioned anyone special. I know I'm being irrational. Me and Jayden, we aren't anything, we never have been, but we've been in this weird will-they-won't-they space for two years so I can't help but feel territorial about him.

Saint shakes his head. 'It's not really his scene.'

Oyin reaches over and gently runs a finger over Saint's tattoo sleeve and Sharisha and I share a look. *What the hell is she doing?*

'These are nice,' she says, looking up at him through her thick, fake lashes.

Whether Saint's clocked her flirting and ignores her or he genuinely didn't catch it, I'll never know, but he moves his arm out of reach and says, 'Thanks. Right, I'm on in a few acts so will catch you later.' He locks eyes with me and gives me a smile before he wanders off into the crowd.

Oyin sits opposite me avoiding my gaze as she adjusts her one-shoulder top and I'm trying really hard not to cuss her out. Why is she trying to make a move on Saint? Sharisha, Sansa and Fatima are sitting in silence looking back and forth at us. I wait patiently as there's only so much time Oyin can spend looking at her top. Eventually she looks up.

'"These are nice."' I mimic her tone. 'What's *wrong* with you?'

'What? I never noticed them before!' she argues.

'I mean, it's a bit . . .' Fatima scrunches her face as she tries to find the right word.

'Giving sabotage vibes?' Sharisha adds. 'And why were you bringing up Jayden?'

Oyin laughs. 'Damn, I was just commenting on his tattoos. And, what? Now it's weird to assume his cousin was coming? I'll just shut up then.' Oyin crosses her arms over her chest and looks away from us.

I don't know why she's getting so defensive when she was blatantly flirting with Saint. And it doesn't make sense why, when she was the one who set me this dare to begin with. The only reason the five of us are here is because of her.

'I'm getting a drink,' I announce, not because I want one but just to get away from Oyin and the tension that's hovering over our table.

'Me too,' Sansa says.

Most people have taken their seats or are standing on the sides so there's only a short line for the bar.

'I'm not going crazy, right?' I say to Sansa once we're out of earshot. 'She was trying it on.'

'She was,' Sansa confirms. 'But you know Oyin. She can be extra. I don't think she meant anything by it.'

I don't agree, but there's no point going on about it to Sansa as she'll only be diplomatic. She always stays neutral when there's any friction in the group.

'Can I help?' the girl with the purple hair behind the bar asks.

'A rum and Coke,' I say.

'Make that two,' Sansa chips in.

'ID?'

I whip out my passport excitedly, glad to show her that I'm officially eighteen and legal. Mum would kill me if she knew I've taken the passport out of the house. She's so scared that they'll get lost, so she keeps all of them together.

'It was her birthday a few days ago,' Sansa jumps in.

'Oh yeah?' The purple-haired girl grabs a bottle of Bacardi and pours some into a shot glass. 'On the house. Happy birthday.'

'Thanks.' I look at the glass warily. On second thoughts, I don't want to get drunk, especially when I need to film the video for Saint. 'Sorry, can I get just a Coke with ice?' I hand the shot glass to Sansa. 'For you. I don't want it.'

Sansa shrugs and downs it in one. She pulls a face. 'That's strong! Look, just ignore Oyin. It's obvious that Saint likes you – saving us a table and all of that.' We pick up our drinks and Sansa takes a sip. 'You'll get the money to fix your dad's car in no time.' I grab a straw so I don't mess up my lipstick and we head back to our table.

The MC is on the stage, with a clipboard in his hand. Oyin doesn't look at me when we sit down, just keeps her gaze fixed to the front of the stage.

'And remember, if you like something, we don't clap here at Speak Your Truth. Instead, click your fingers. Let's give it a try.'

The clicks fill the room. Sansa's giggling as she does it and I'm sure the alcohol has gone straight to her head.

The first poet comes on stage. She's rushing through her piece and looking straight ahead, not making eye contact with the audience. She barely gets any clicks, although Sansa keeps enthusiastically clicking until Sharisha puts a firm hand on her arm and tells her to chill.

The next performer is an older man. He's better and tells a piece about London train journeys. It's actually quite funny and I find myself clicking along with everyone else.

The MC comes back on stage with a wide smile on his face, clearly happy to announce the next poet.

'Now we have Saint Rowe-Falade, who's no stranger to River Run. Give it up for Saint!'

I whoop as I hold my phone out ready to record him. Saint comes onto the stage and is standing up against the red background. He gives a half wave to everyone as I press record.

'Hey, everyone. I'm Saint and this is a piece that I've been working on called "Sounds".' He takes a deep breath and begins:

'*Love. Love fills me up like the sound of a church bell that rings at a time of prayer and God's hand is upon my head, as I kneel thanking him. For you.*'

Everyone clicks. But on my table, it's like there's a stillness in the air as we watch in a trance as Saint performs. He seems to hold eye contact with every person in the room, making everyone think he's reciting these words about love just to them. The room is transfixed and is hanging onto his every word.

'Damn,' Sharisha says under her breath.

I'm watching Saint over my phone, at the effortless way he is performing, the pace, the rhythm, the way he's captured everyone, especially me. The piece is so beautiful that for a moment I wish he was talking about me. Talking *to* me and only me. I wasn't expecting him to be so good. Better than good. Brilliant.

'*It's the sounds of you. The sounds of me. The sounds of us. One.*'

Saint grins. 'Thank you.'

It takes me a moment to realize that he's finished. That was the most incredible thing I've ever heard. I get to my feet and clap my hands and everyone looks at me. Saint laughs and gestures at me to click.

'Oh, sorry!' I try to hold the phone against my arm and torso to click my fingers but my phone buzzes and I glance down at it, at the picture that shows up. Dad's smashed car window. I gasp and the phone slips out and lands heavily on the table with a loud *bang*. It knocks over my drink, which lands on Oyin's lap.

FOURTEEN

'Eva!' Oyin screams as she stands up, drawing everyone's attention to us. The light may be dim but I can see the wet patch on her jeans like she's pissed herself.

The MC is back up on stage and starts talking, so everyone slowly looks away from us.

'I'm so sorry!' I say quickly, digging in my purse to see if I have a tissue, but my hands are trembling. My phone rings. *Dami.* I don't answer and a second later it rings again. Shit! What am I going to do? I pick my phone up warily like it's a bomb about to go off and this time I get a text in all caps.

> YOU SMASHED DAD'S CAR? WTF??? GET HOME
> RIGHT NOW!!!!

'No, no, no.' I squeeze my eyes shut, wishing this wasn't my life right now.

'Everything okay?' Saint touches my lower back and I jump.

'Yeah, sorry. I accidentally spilled my drink. Here, Oyin.'

I hand her some tissues and she starts wiping down her arms. Then she begins to dab at her jeans.

'Ugh! I can't see shit in this light,' she says. 'I might be making it worse.'

'Let's go to the toilet,' Sansa says.

My friends all scrape back their chairs and get up from the table.

'I'm sorry, Saint,' I say. 'I'm gonna help Oyin clear up and I've got to run home after.'

'Oh, okay,' he says sounding disappointed, which surprises me, especially as he didn't even invite me. 'Thanks for coming,' he adds.

'I'll send you the video. You were great, by the way!'

I wave goodbye at him as I weave my way through the packed room towards the toilets.

The girls are by the sink and Oyin is standing under the dryer with a massive wet patch on her jeans.

'Oyin, I'm so sorry,' I say again, clasping my hands.

'I think it will dry.' She nods towards my phone. 'You looked like you'd seen a ghost. Everything okay?'

'I wish.' I show Oyin the picture on my phone and she gasps.

'What is it?' Sharisha peers at my phone round Oyin, then covers her mouth with her hand. 'No!'

At that, Sansa and Fatima hurry over to see too.

'Shit, girl,' Fatima says.

'What are you going to do?' Sansa asks.

'I don't know but I have to go home and sort this. Dami

will definitely kill me. Thanks for coming tonight though, girls.'

'I really got into that,' Fatima says. 'And Saint is amazing, isn't he?'

'He is,' I say, and my friends share a look. 'What? I was just pointing out the obvious. I didn't say I was in love with him.'

'Not yet,' Fatima sings, and I roll my eyes.

'Love you all.' I blow air kisses at them. 'If you hear from me tomorrow it will be a miracle.'

I'm a nervous wreck on the journey home. My knees are shaking and I'm tapping my fingers against my thighs, dreading seeing Dami. When I get to the house, the car is still in its parking spot, but whereas I had covered it so that every inch of it was under the sheet, Dami has lazily chucked the sheet back on so you can now see the rims and the bottom of the body.

Taking a deep breath, I unlock the front door and Dami is standing in the hall wearing a T-shirt and shorts, his arms crossed over his broad chest.

'Hi,' I say nervously and his nostrils flare in response. 'Where's Amara?'

'She's gone home. You want to explain how you smashed the car?' he says pointedly.

'I didn't,' I protest.

'So who did?'

'I don't know,' I mumble, looking at the floor. 'Some stupid boys had a fight.'

I hear Dami take a sharp intake of breath. 'At your party?' he questions, and I nod. 'Didn't I ask you how it went? Why didn't you tell me? Where were you when this fight happened?'

I swallow. My throat is dry and tight. 'I was upstairs in my room and then I heard the glass smash—'

'Hold up,' Dami says and I look up. 'You left all those people alone downstairs?'

'I had to feed Yum-Yum,' I explain, and I don't dare mention that Jayden was also upstairs. 'I was only gone a few minutes. Honestly, I don't know who done it, but I have a plan for how to pay for it.'

Dami scoffs. 'You? How? You don't have a job.'

'No, I do! I mean ... sort of. I'm giving out flyers for the comic book shop by Westfield.'

'And how much is it to fix the window?' Dami asks.

'About four hundred pounds.' And Dami's eyes widen. 'Depends on how premium the car is,' I add.

'I think a Mercedes is premium.' Dami rolls his eyes. 'They're going to pay you enough to cover all of that?'

I lie and nod.

'Have you called any mechanics?'

'No,' I say in a small voice.

'Eva. You're not a dumb girl so why are you moving so stupid? You don't tell me what's happened, you haven't called a mechanic to even get an accurate quote, and Mum and Dad are back in under two weeks.'

I rub my temples in a poor attempt to ease the throbbing

pain that's just appeared in my head. 'I know, I know.' Even though my brain is telling me not to, I ask, 'Can you help me?'

'Me?' Dami says pointing to himself before laughing. 'You want me to pay for a car that I didn't break? You better sort this, Eva, or I'll have to claim it on Dad's insurance before he gets back home – and then he'll know everything.'

'Don't tell him!' I plead. 'I can fix this, I promise. I'll have the money.'

'You better.' Dami shakes his head. 'I'm going to my room. Lock up, please.' And with that he climbs the stairs leaving me alone in the hall.

I lock the door and head upstairs too. Yum-Yum is already sprawled out asleep on the floor against my mirror, which he only does when it's hot in my room, and in a few seconds of being up here I'm sweating. I put on my desk fan and stand by it for a while, letting it cool my body.

My phone buzzes with an Instagram DM from Saint. I open it quickly.

Thanks for coming tonight. Hope everything is okay?

The time stamp shows he sent it only a few minutes after I left. I can't help but smile at how sweet he is to check in on me. None of my friends have been in touch with me yet. I look at his message, thinking what to say back. How do I move this forward? A small part of me feels guilty that I'm even thinking this, but I quickly swallow down that feeling. The car needs to be sorted.

I had lots of fun. Like I said, you were really good! Thanks for checking in. That's really nice of you. Send me your number so I can send over the video xx

I'm surprised that Saint reads it straight away and he's already typing. Maybe he is starting to like me? A moment later I get his phone number.

106

FIFTEEN

I wake up extra early, ignoring the messages in the group chat asking what happened with Dami. I'm determined to cook breakfast for my brother as a way of apologizing for messing up. Last night, before I sent Saint the video, I re-watched his spoken word piece and was again drawn into it like I was when I saw him perform in person. I can't believe this is the same guy that can't give out a flyer without looking uncomfortable but can speak these beautiful words in front of fellow poets and a packed-out crowd. There are lots of moments where he's looking directly at me and I'm not sure if it's only because I'm videoing him. Whoever inspired that piece must be someone very special.

'Morning,' Dami says stiffly as he comes into the kitchen, already dressed.

'Morning,' I sing cheerfully. I hand him a full English breakfast – sausages, beans, eggs, bacon, buttered toast – along with a cup of tea.

Dami raises his eyebrows at me as he holds the plate.

'What's this for?' he asks suspiciously, and I don't blame him. I barely put on the kettle without moaning about it.

'Just to apologize about the car and not telling you about it. Are we friends again?'

Dami grunts in response, which I take as a yes. He sits down, eyeing the food greedily. I take my breakfast plate, the same as his, and sit opposite him.

'You home today?' he asks. 'Grandma is dropping off food around elevenish and I'm heading out to meet my boys.'

'I can wait around before I go to work,' I say. 'I've got to confirm my hours. Quick question – what's a good manga?'

Dami pauses, the piece of bacon on his fork hovering halfway between his plate and his mouth. 'Why?'

'Just wondering. Are you still into that?'

'Not really, but I used to like *Attack on Titan*.'

'*Attack on Titan*,' I repeat. 'What's it about?'

'Damn, I ain't thought about that in ages. Okay, so it's about this boy called Eren who loses his family to Titans—'

The doorbell rings, cutting him off, and we look at each other. It's only eight a.m. so I know it's not Grandma. Who else could be at the door this early on a Saturday?

'I'll answer it,' I volunteer.

We have one of those frosted glass doors so I can see an outline of someone tall standing on the other side. I open it as I wipe my mouth with the back of my hand to get rid of any crumbs.

'Jayden?'

Jayden waves sheepishly at me. He works part-time at

Sainsbury's on weekends when he's not training or has a football match. He looks very cute in his burgundy uniform top and black bottoms. I wish I wasn't in my should-have-been-washed-some-days-ago pyjama set with the teddy bear pattern. God, please don't let me have eye gunk.

'Hey, Eva,' he says. 'I was just passing through.'

'Isn't where you work closer to your house than mine?'

The corners of Jayden's mouth turn up and he rubs the back of his neck. 'Yeah, you're right. I ... err ... I just wanted to say sorry for not helping at your party. I don't mess with the feds like that. Did you sort your dad's car?'

He may be hot, but it's not cool that he's only now just talking to me about what happened at my party. I thought Jayden and I had something, but would someone who actually liked me take days to check in? Someone who liked me would damn sure have mentioned me to his closest cousin. Although ... he is here now and my house is a good twenty minutes away from his. He wouldn't have come unless he cared, would he? My brain is battling with itself. *Should I be mad at him? Should I be nice?* In the meantime, I don't say anything – and the smile on Jayden's face wavers.

He clears his throat. 'I spoke to Saint last night and he said you went to his performance. I didn't know you were into spoken word.'

'I'm no—' I quickly shut my mouth. I almost said *I'm not*, like a complete idiot. 'I'm ... nostalgic.' What the hell am I saying?

Jayden frowns. 'Nostalgic? For what?'

'For ... you know ... the good old days.' I laugh even though it's not funny. 'I used to go to spoken word events all the time when I was ... a kid.' *Smooth, Eva.*

But Jayden seems to take what I'm saying as normal and nods like he understands.

'So, I was thinking –' he takes a step closer to me and my heart starts to race, the way it normally does when I'm around him – 'if maybe you and I—'

'Who are you?' Dami demands, making Jayden and me both jump. Jayden quickly takes several steps back. Dami stands next to me. I roll my eyes.

'Hi, I'm Jayden.' Jayden holds his hand out and Dami looks at him up and down like he's a bad smell. Jayden withdraws his outstretched hand and runs it over his head.

'Why you at my yard at this time, bro?' Dami asks.

'Dami!' I snap. Why is he embarrassing me like this?

Jayden takes more steps back and points towards the right. 'I was just saying hi to Eva on my way to work, but I better go or I'll be late. See you, Eva.' He walks off, trying to look super cool, but stumbles on the pavement.

Dami scoffs. I hit his arm as he shuts the door. 'That was so rude!'

'Who is that little boy?'

'His name's Jayden and he goes to my college.'

Dami glowers at me. 'He better not be your boyfriend.'

'Well, there's no chance of that happening with an idiot like you around.' What an annoying person! I'm nice to Amara even though she's in my house, in my space, all the damn

110

time, and the one time – the ONE time – Jayden comes over unannounced, Dami wants to show me up. I stomp up the stairs away from him and his cackling.

Grandma rings the bell just as I've glued on my eyelashes. I'm wearing this tie-dyed halterneck dress that I've had in my wardrobe for ages. I bought it during last year's summer sale even though I knew my parents would never let me wear it. It's got a slit at the side and shows a bit of side boob but I'm small enough that I can go braless. I'm probably a little overdressed for the comic book shop but I've got to get Saint to make a move.

'What is this?' Grandma asks, looking me over. She's pointing at the skin on show.

'It's just the style,' I say, kissing her on the cheek. I quickly take the heavy shopping trolley from her and haul it into the kitchen. 'Grandma, if you need help carrying stuff, I can just come to you.'

'Okay.' Grandma sighs heavily as she sits on the kitchen chair, forgetting about my outfit. 'Dami should come and pick me up in the car. Where is Dami? Oluwadamilola?' Grandma yells.

'He's out. And he's not insured to drive the car.'

Grandma shrugs. 'Who will know? Why is the car covered with that sheet?'

'Oh.' I busy myself putting the containers of jollof rice, fried rice and stewed meat in the fridge to give myself time to think. 'I read that sunlight can harm a car's exterior. You know – UV light and all that? You know how much Dad loves his car.'

111

Grandma kisses her teeth. 'Man should not love material things like that. Ah, I have a scripture to send him.'

I hold up the spinach that's in one of the bags.

'It's for the egusi soup that Dami asked for so you can have it with àmàlà.'

'Grandma! Don't buy things on Dami's request. We appreciate everything and anything that you make us.' Grandma shouldn't be running around the market in this heat because Dami, with his lazy self, has a craving.

'It's okay, it's okay.' Grandma laughs.

'I've got to make a move,' I say, slipping on my sandals.

'Wait, take some puff puff.' Grandma digs into her shopping trolley. The amount of stuff she manages to cram in there amazes me. She hands me the container. 'You can share with your friends.'

'Thanks, Grandma. I've actually got a job so I'm going to work. I'll leave you here, okay?'

Grandma frowns. 'That is your work uniform?' She looks me up and down again. 'This is not professional.'

'My uniform is at work,' I lie, because I know she will make me go and change into something 'suitable', which I know will be something ridiculous and covered-up like a full tracksuit. I kiss her cheek. 'Bye!' And I hurry out the door before she can say anything else.

SIXTEEN

It's a busy Saturday at Harley's World of Comics and I instantly spot Saint and Benji occupied with customers, so I look at the shelves trying to find *Attack on Titan*. Maybe I can have a quick glance to understand more about it, then I can wow Saint with my knowledge. Ah, there it is! I skim through a bit but it's only adding to my confusion. Which one is Eren? Is a Titan like a giant?

'Eva?'

'Hey, Saint!' I turn, putting the comic back in its place.

Today his long, thick curly hair is out. 'I wasn't sure what time you were coming in.' He pauses and looks me over and my face grows warm. 'You look nice.'

'Oh, this old thing,' I say brushing down my dress. 'It's nice and cold in here.'

Saint glances at my chest for a second and diverts his gaze so fast that if I had blinked I would have missed it. He shakes his head. 'What did you say?'

I smile. This dress has got his attention. 'Nothing. So, should we chat about my hours?'

'Yeah, just give me five minutes. I'll finish helping Benji with the rush.'

'No problem!'

As soon as he's gone I search the internet for a summary of *Attack on Titan*. Okay, I think I've got enough that I can mention it and have an opinion. I wonder if Saint is into *Heartstopper* because I can talk about Nick and Charlie all day. Although I've only watched it on Netflix. I'm sure *Heartstopper* is a graphic novel though, so it must be different to a comic, right? I really must look up the difference if I want to woo Saint with our apparently naturally shared interests. Just as I type 'comic books vs graphic novels' into my phone Sharisha rings me.

'Hey, girl,' I say.

'Hey, you didn't answer in the group chat. How was it with Dami?'

'I mean it was okay I guess.' I search around for Saint and Benji and they're over at the tills. Nevertheless, I lower my voice. 'But he deffo won't help me with the car. Do you know any mechanics?'

'Hmmm, I can ask my dad,' Sharisha says. 'We're going to Westfield later. You down?'

Someone is waving at me and it takes me a second to realize that Saint is beckoning me over. 'I'm at the comic book place trying to work on Saint, so will let you know.'

'Bring him!' Sharisha insists. Saint around all my friends again? Last night Oyin was batting her eyelashes at him. *No thanks.*

114

'I'll let you know,' I say. 'I gotta go.'

'Okay, bye.'

Only when I hang up do I realize that I didn't mention that Jayden came over. That's funny. Since I started getting ready this morning, all I could think about was Saint and if he would like what I'm wearing. Jayden had gone out of my mind pretty quick.

I wave at Benji, who is on the till, and follow Saint down the steep steps to the basement and into the staff room, where there are boxes upon boxes of video games, consoles and posters. There's so much stuff that it almost blocks the table with the chairs on either side.

'Sorry about the mess.' Saint pulls up a chair and gestures for me to sit. 'We're just getting stock ready for the Retro Gaming Day. Can you come to it?'

'At Bournemouth beach?' I double check, and Saint nods. 'Let me know the details, but I don't see why not.'

'Okay, cool. It's just a day trip so we'll leave really early and be back in the evening. Benji will drive us down. There's a bunch of local volunteers there to help and, if you're okay with it, maybe you can help to manage them.'

'Me?' I laugh. 'I'm not sure I'm the best one to lead people.'

'Of course you are. You're confident and charming and nice.' Saint shrugs. 'You're perfect.'

Perfect. Wow … Is that what Saint thinks of me? His compliments have caused a warm, fuzzy feeling to travel through my body. But then it feels like my stomach is in knots as I remember why I'm even here. I shouldn't be feeling any type of warm feeling. A day trip to Bournemouth might be the best place to get a date out of him. A dinner with the sun setting on the beach – what's more romantic for a date than that? I would have completed the dare and Oyin would have to give me the money to fix Dad's car.

'Between now and then we just need to keep pushing the gamer event. Benji was wondering what your TikTok skills were like.'

'I love TikTok.'

Saint chuckles. 'We have an account but it's pretty shit, so maybe as well as handing out flyers you can film some content for it?'

Now this is more like it. 'Yes, I'd love that. I can do social media content at Bournemouth as well. I'd feel more comfortable doing that than leading the volunteers.'

'Okay, sure. I'll let Benji know.'

My mind is already thinking about the best places to film in the store. 'Oh, and we can do features on some of the best manga series . . . like *Attack on Titan*.'

Saint's eyes widen. 'Wait, you're a fan of *Attack on Titan*?'

'Obsessed.'

Saint grins. Those dimples appearing again. 'What's your favourite scene? Mine is Commander Erwin's final speech. Best anime speech ever.' Saint's whole face is alive and I wish I knew what the hell he was talking about.

'Same. It literally blew my mind.'

Saint leans back in his chair and crosses his arms staring at me with a look of amusement and surprise. 'I wasn't expecting you to say that.'

'Why? Because I'm a girl?' I tease.

'No. Just, when I met you at Carnival, I thought you knew nothing about anime, and yet here you are loving one of my favourite shows. It's cool, that's all.'

'He thinks I'm "cool",' I say, fanning myself, and Saint laughs. 'Oh, I just remembered ... My grandma gave me some puff puff. Do you want to try some? It's kind of like a doughnut.'

Saint jerks his head back. 'You think I don't know about puff puff? I'm half Nigerian.'

'Falade. Right.' I take out the container from my bag and open it up, offering it to Saint, who takes one, bites into it and closes his eyes. 'And you're half white?'

'Yeah, on my dad's side. This is really good.'

I take a bite of the doughnut-like texture. No one makes puff puff as good as my grandma. 'Have you posted your spoken word video yet?'

'Yep, and it's blowing up. Thanks again.'

I wave my hand as if to say *It's okay*. 'Was it based on anyone?'

Saint shifts in his seat. 'Err ... yeah. There was someone, but not any more.' Immediately the atmosphere changes and it's like a barrier has separated Saint from me. He glances at his phone. 'We've been down here for a minute. You good to give out more flyers today? I can't leave the shop so I won't be able to help.'

'Oh, okay,' I say. 'I can do it by myself and I'll film some stuff as well.'

'There's one more thing.' Saint opens up a drawer and pulls something out. He holds up an oversized white T-shirt with the Harley's World of Comics logo on it. 'You're going to have to wear this.'

'B-but—' My outfit is so cute. I don't want to have to cover it up wearing this ill-fitting top.

'I know it's pretty big but it's all we got. Is that okay?'

I bite my tongue. *Think of the money, think of the money—*

'Sure! No problem.'

SEVENTEEN

Handing out flyers in the boiling sun by myself is actually really shit. Maybe because it's a Saturday and it's so busy everyone seems less interested in talking to me today. One woman actually sidesteps me twice to avoid getting a flyer. I can see what Saint means. Seeing flyers on the floor and in the bin is upsetting.

'You could just say no!' I snap at a man who took a flyer willingly and then tossed it on the floor once my back was turned.

I stretch my neck. I've been at this for a few hours and I'm sweating in this oversized T-shirt, and I'm thirsty. Based on his reaction earlier when I asked him about the spoken word, it seems that Saint doesn't currently have a girlfriend, but I don't know if he's still hung up on his ex. I stuff the rest of the flyers in my bag and head back to the store.

The air con hits my skin as I enter Harley's World of Comics and instantly cools me.

'Eva! How did it go?' Benji asks, looking up from the open comic book that he's reading.

'Great!' I adjust my bag, that's slightly heavy with all the flyers. 'I was wondering if there are other places round here you think would be good to hand out flyers.'

Benji taps on the counter as he thinks. 'There's a funfair not far away. Lots of gamers will be in the arcade.'

'Okay, cool, I'll head over there.'

'Saint mentioned something about going too ... Saint?' Benji calls, looking over at one of the shelves. I didn't notice Saint there tidying up the comic books on display. He walks towards us. 'Are you still heading to the funfair tonight?' Benji asks him.

'Yeah, I wanted to check out the arcade and see what games are popular to make sure we have them for Bournemouth. Why?'

Benji points at me. 'Eva's going to hand out flyers there.'

'Oh, cool. Wanna go together?' Saint gazes at me and that barrier that was hovering around earlier seems to have come down.

Okay, this is my chance. We'll be out, just us two, and maybe us spending one-on-one time together will make him more interested in me. I wish we were going somewhere romantic though. Maybe if I can create the vibe, it might give him ideas.

'Sure,' I say brightly. 'I'm just going to fill up my water bottle.'

I head down the stairs as I google *romantic things to do at funfair*. The first thing that comes up is *share candyfloss* and there's an image of two very attractive people feeding each other clumps of pink candyfloss.

What else is there? *Ride the Ferris wheel.* That makes me pause. We'll be pinned into a seat together, sitting very close, high up away from everyone else for a while, and with the stars shining above us maybe Saint will open up in a way he hasn't before. Maybe this amazing eye contact that I supposedly have but hasn't worked on him yet might actually kick in. Yep. Ferris wheel it is.

We leave Benji to lock up and Saint and I begin the walk to the funfair. The weather is cooler now and the breeze feels so good against my skin. I couldn't wait to ditch the work top. Saint's whistling as he walks, in that slow, relaxed stroll he has. He has a fitted T-shirt on and I find myself staring at his tattooed arm. I see praying hands, a dove, something written in another language, I think it's Chinese, and lots of roses that cover every inch of skin.

'You have one?' Saint catches me staring and I turn away quickly.

'No way! My parents would literally disown me.'

'Oh, you have the strict Nigerian parents?' Saint laughs. 'My mum's a chill one. After my brothers I think she gave up.'

'How old are your brothers?' I ask.

'Twenty-eight. Twins. Apparently, my mum had them, was content – and then ten years later wanted to try for a girl and got me instead.' Saint grins.

I laugh. 'Are you close to your brothers? I always thought being a twin would be so cool.'

'Me too. It kinda feels like them and me. Christian is more

121

laid back and Israel is the party one, but they're both grown now. One is having a baby, the little girl my mum prayed for, so I'll be Uncle Saint soon.'

'That's cute. I like the names Saint, Christian and Israel. It's giving biblical vibes.'

Saint laughs. 'Right? Mum was on one.'

I glance at his tattoos. 'Do they mean anything?'

Saint rubs a hand over his arm and pulls up his elbow to stare at them. 'Praying hands – I'm a Christian and prayer is important to me. A dove is peace. The writing says "Saint" in Japanese. And the roses – they just look cool.' Saint grins.

I chuckle. 'What about that one?' There's a dragon on the side of his wrist. Smaller than the rest so at first I missed it. It doesn't really fit in with the rest of the tattoos, almost like it's too special and has to be set apart.

Saint rubs his thumb across it and for a second his shoulders slump. 'This one is part of a set.' He stares at the dragon and I can tell that his mind is somewhere else, far away from me.

'Where's the other?' I ask gently, bringing him back.

'New York,' Saint says quietly.

Who was she? I want to ask, because it's clear that this is a guy who has lost someone that he cared about a lot, maybe even loved. Suddenly I feel weird and uncomfortable. Saint was the wrong choice to do this dare on. All I want to do now is go home and tell Oyin to pick somebody else.

'There it is.' Saint points ahead of us and the colourful lights of the funfair twinkle through the evening air. 'Isn't a funfair just the best? I swear I spent all my childhood at one.'

'Me too,' I say. 'My brother Dami would take me on the scariest rides, just because he thought it was funny to hear me scream my head off.' Saint laughs and I'm glad the dimples are back. 'Is it lonely without your brothers around?'

Saint shakes his head. 'Not really. I mean Jayden and I are pretty close.'

Shit! Jayden! I totally forgot to apologize to him about Dami's behaviour. I reach into my bag, searching for my phone to text him, but all the flyers I didn't give out are in the way and I can't find it.

We head into the fair and I manage to touch the top of my phone as Saint pays for two tickets and some tokens.

'It's on Benji,' he says, when I go to protest. 'Technically, this is a work trip. Doesn't mean we can't go on some rides though.' He grins cheekily and hands me my ticket and some tokens, so I abandon my phone in my bag. I'll message Jayden later.

The funfair is packed with teenagers, couples and parents with their kids. Every other second, the sound of screaming whizzes past me as a ride dips or does a loop. The air smells of fried onions and candyfloss. All the typical rides you'd expect are here – bumper cars, carousel, chair-o-plane, ghost train, twister, some free-fall rides that I'm definitely not going on. The Ferris wheel sits in the middle of the fair, huge and lit up. To the left of it is the arcade, and a scattering of stalls where you play to win teddies.

'I'm heading to the arcade,' Saint says. 'Do you want me to help you hand out some flyers?'

'Yes please,' I say, grateful that I don't have to do it all by myself. 'But I thought you hated it.'

Saint shrugs. 'Not so bad doing it with you.'

If anyone else had said that I would have thought they were flirting, but Saint's tone is so matter-of-fact I know he isn't.

We walk over to the arcade and there's now a cool breeze in the air. The music from all the different rides overlaps with each other and I'm so busy trying to catch the lyrics to one of the songs that I buckle on the uneven flooring, something that somehow I do more often than I would like. Saint grabs my arm before I go flying and holds me steady.

'Thanks,' I say, my cheeks burning, expecting him to laugh.

'The ground is really bumpy,' he says kindly, and I notice he doesn't let go of my arm until we're inside the arcade.

It's dim but all the lights on the games machines are flashing different colours. And there's so much noise everywhere, from the games, from people yelling and cheering at the screens . . . A man is shouting and banging on one of the machines as the claw inside drops his Pikachu. I thought it would be a good idea to hand out flyers here, but everyone looks so engrossed in their game I'm not sure how we will get anyone's attention.

'Where do you think we should stand?' I ask Saint, but he's busy looking around the arcade.

Suddenly he grabs my hand. 'I have an idea.'

His hand is soft and warm. Saint leads me through the crowds and to anyone noticing us I bet it looks like we're on a date. We pass *PacMan* and *Whack-A-Mole*. For a second I think he's taking me to the dance machine, which I would be terrible at – my co-ordination is so off – but he passes that and stops in front of a game and smiles proudly.

I recognize the artwork, with the good guys on one side and the baddies on the other. Then the iconic orange, yellow and red logo flashes on the screen and I freeze.

'You want to play *Street Fighter*?' I ask.

I haven't played this game in forever and I'm trying to work out why Saint would pick it. Then I remember. I told him it was my favourite game; I told him how good I am at it. Why? Why did I say *that*?

'What draws a gamer's attention is competition, so me versus you, playing the game that you're an *expert* at, is perfect publicity,' he says brightly. 'And, no offence, but you don't look like the type that's into video games. But that's a good thing,' he quickly adds. 'We'll definitely draw a crowd.' Saint smiles, clearly pleased with himself for coming up with this strategy, and I wish the ground would open up and bury me deep.

EIGHTEEN

I smooth my sweaty hands on my dress as I study the buttons. It's different from a handheld console. For one, there are levers with a sticker on the base that have arrows pointing in different directions like the rays of the sun and names like BACKFLIP, CROUCH, JUMP as well as colourful buttons that read PUNCH, KICK, JAM, FORWARD, BACKWARDS. Okay, this might not be too bad. At least I'll be able to do something. When I played on my cousin's old Super Nintendo I had to remember how to do the moves by remembering the sequence.

'Should we start off with something easier?' I say lightly. 'I don't wanna make you look silly.'

Saint laughs. 'Wow! Confident, yeah?' He takes out one of his tokens. 'We'll see who looks silly.' He puts the token in the slot.

The game comes to life and starts playing this really annoying, loud music, with these fighters facing off against each other, bouncing along to the beat, and a crowd is behind them, cheering. It's *Street Fighter II* and I forgot how dated the graphics are.

'Ladies first,' Saint says.

The street fighters pop up with a map that shows where they come from, but I already know who I want. It's the character I always pick and she's never let me down, so I'm hoping she'll come through for me today. I select Chun-Li from China with the iconic blue outfit.

'Okay, okay,' Saint says. 'Who should I go for?'

I think to myself that he'll go for the main guy, Ryu, but instead he clicks Blanka, the green mutant with orange hair from Brazil. I look at him in surprise.

'Bet you thought I was going to pick Ryu,' Saint says.

I scoff. 'Please. I wasn't thinking about what you were doing.'

Saint chuckles.

'*Round One. Fight,*' the computer says.

The background has a massive tree in the centre with an orange patterned snake wrapped round it and there's a straw hut with people watching the fight from inside.

Come on! You can do this, Eva.

Obviously, I haven't played this game in years so I'm not super confident about what I'm doing, but I immediately start pressing multiple buttons and moving the lever up, down, side to side. Chun-Li is jumping, kicking, punching at a rapid speed and Blanka is already losing his lifeline.

'Hey, stop it!' Saint says, who is way more controlled than me with the buttons.

'Ha! I'm kicking your arse.'

I somehow make Chun-Li crouch low and kick and Saint's

127

Blanka has already lost a quarter of his life. I'm going to win!

Suddenly Blanka grabs Chun-Li by the side of the head and starts to bite her!

'What the hell?' I shout and Saint laughs manically.

Blanka won't let go! There's a trail of blood in his mouth. Yuck! I glance up and now I've lost a quarter of my life too.

'How do I get out of this?' I yell at the screen, as I jam the buttons. Somehow, I manage to flip back and when our characters meet in the air I punch and kick and Blanka falls to the floor.

'In your face!' I shout, and Saint kisses his teeth.

We have a fifty-second countdown till it's knockout and I'm back in the lead. *I can do this!*

'Yes!' Saint yells. I gasp. Blanka has electrocuted Chun-Li! Damn! I forgot he could do that. She flashes so I can see her skeleton.

Now our lifelines are neck and neck and Saint is coming at me so aggressively that all I can do is block. *Thirty seconds.* I just need one power move and I can end this, but I can't remember how to do it! I'm pressing whatever buttons I can reach and my heart leaps when Chun-Li goes upside down, bounces on her head and starts spinning with her legs out like a helicopter.

'No!' Saint yells as I completely destroy Blanka, who dramatically falls backwards to the floor in slow motion as the game says, '*KO.*'

'Yes!' I shout. 'Did you see that?'

'You ain't won yet. We've still got another round,' Saint says.

But I win round two and then round three commences, and once again I completely destroy Saint, who huffs when Blanka falls yet again.

'Nah, we gotta go again,' Saint says, already digging in his pocket for a token.

'You were so good!' a girl says behind us and I turn round.

There's a group of teenage girls and a few boys who must have been watching us battle.

'Thanks!' I say. 'Maybe you guys can come to the Retro Gaming event we're hosting.' I dig in my bag and take out a bunch of flyers and hand them out round the group. They all read them, eager with interest. 'If you can't come down to Bournemouth you can join in the battles online.'

'Wow, this looks great,' the first girl says and she grins at me. 'Thanks! I'll definitely register.' A ripple of 'Me too' goes round the group.

'Cool! See you soon.' I wave at them before I nudge Saint. 'How good was that? People just came to us.'

'Another battle?' Saint says, ignoring my comment, a determined look etched on his face. Bloody hell. I forgot how competitive guys are when it comes to video games.

'You sure?' I take off my earrings and place them in my bag.

Saint laughs. 'Not you taking off your earrings!'

'This is my serious, I'm-gonna-whoop-your-butt attire,' and Saint just rolls his eyes in response.

The next game, while I stick with Chun-Li, Saint tries a different fighter. He wins. But I win the next battle and, by the time we're done, we have an impressive crowd surrounding us, just like he predicted. People are asking to have a go against me, but I hold up my hands and announce, 'I'm retiring on a high!'

'So full of it,' Saint says, but he's laughing.

I take the rest of the flyers out of my bag and by the time we've handed them out to the crowd there's only a small pile of them left.

'Just leave those on the side,' Saint says. 'Anyone coming to play will be looking for an event like this.' He smirks at me. 'You were annoyingly good.'

'I know, right.' I flick my hair and Saint shakes his head. 'What shall we do now?'

'We've still got a few tokens so we could get a bite to eat and then you can pick the next thing?'

'Sure,' I say. 'Winning makes me starving.'

'Ha, ha,' Saint says deadpan. 'Come on, Rocky.' He holds out his arm and it feels like the most natural thing to link my arm through his as we head out of the arcade.

The funfair looks even busier now and we have to wait a short while for food. My mum has always told me to never order any meat from the stands because she doesn't trust how it's been cooked, so I get chips. But as we turn away from the stand I can't help looking enviously at Saint's hotdog topped with fried onions.

He catches me looking. 'Want a bite?' He holds it out to me. 'It's really good.'

My mum's voice is sharp in my head telling me I'll get food

poisoning, but the smell of the hotdog is making my mouth water.

'Let's share,' I suggest.

We find a spot of grass on the edge of the fair and sit down, and it reminds me of Carnival when we stopped to eat food. Saint and I are so close together that our knees are touching as we're sharing our food, and it feels comfortable. He definitely isn't being guarded now like he was earlier. This would be a good chance to get to know him better.

'Are you going to university?' I ask him.

'I'm actually taking a gap year.'

I gasp. 'Really?' I don't know anyone who is doing that. All of my friends are off to their chosen uni straight after the summer and that familiar hurt runs through me as I remember that we're going to be separated in a couple of weeks. 'What are your plans?' I ask.

'I want to do some travelling and I've got an idea for a graphic novel.' He shrugs. 'Maybe I can get a publishing deal. My parents are really supportive.'

'Wow! That sounds amazing.' His life sounds so exciting, unlike mine. I'm shortly going to a uni in another city to study something I don't want to do just to keep the peace. 'Wish I was doing something like that.'

'Why don't you?' Saint asks. 'Life's too short not to do what you want.'

'I get that in hindsight, but . . . you don't know my parents.' Imagine me telling Mum and Dad I'm missing uni to go travelling for a year and to write. They would faint, combust, die. And disown me before any of that. 'It's just not worth the hassle,' I say. 'I don't want to disappoint them.'

My friends are the only ones who know how I truly feel about studying law at uni and they get it, but they also don't, because their parents, like Saint's, are supportive of their choices. Sansa is studying philosophy, for goodness' sake! What the hell can she do with that?

'I'm sorry, Eva,' Saint says. 'Have you told your parents how you feel?'

'No. It's hard because Dami, my brother, didn't follow through with his uni plans so it kinda falls on me now. That's why my parents want me to study law. Dad's always on at me about how I, as a Black girl, have to work harder than anyone else and find a secure job. He's always reminding me how he came over here so we can have opportunities.'

Saint nods along as I speak. 'And what is it you would like to do if you had the chance?'

'I don't really know. I was into the idea of being a model when I was younger, but I don't think I really wanted to do it. I just entertained the idea because everyone said I would be good at it. Then this thing happened at college and the idea of making money because of how I look made me feel weird. There was this list where all the girls were labelled and I got "the pretty one". Like my personality is so non-existent and all I am is a face.'

'Oh, the list Jayden started?' Saint says, and I freeze. 'It was so stupid. I still don't know why he did it.' Saint jumps to his feet and brushes his hands on his shorts. It takes him a moment to realize I haven't moved. 'Eva?'

Jayden? Jayden?! Jayden who I've had a crush on for ages wrote that list? The same Jayden I've spoken to for how many hours and yet he still hasn't thought of one single thing about my personality to compliment. The idea of liking someone who thinks it's okay to comment on girls for his own amusement, the way he did with that list, makes me want to take a shower and wash all thoughts of him off me.

'Eva?' Saint says again. 'Are you okay?'

'Yep. I'm fine,' I say with fake enthusiasm as I get to my feet and smooth out my dress, feeling this new sense of loss settle over me. Jayden not helping at my party showed me a side to him I didn't like. Finding out he's never mentioned me to his family should have been a red flag. But when he came to my house today I thought he'd sort of made amends. I was ready to forgive him. Now, discovering that it was him behind the list that has bothered me for most of college, the list that has affected so many other girls too, makes me feel disappointed more than angry. A part of me always thought Jayden and I would get together but now I'm questioning if I even know him.

The Ferris wheel's lights are blinking, calling me to them.

'I know which ride we can go on next,' I say.

NINETEEN

We walk in silence towards the Ferris wheel and I can feel Saint glancing at me. I'm trying not to let it show that this news has bothered me but I'm failing miserably. What I really want to do is call Jayden about it and ask him why he thought that was even okay.

'Tokens, miss?' the guy running the Ferris wheel demands, his hand stretched out.

Saint has to give most of them to him as the Ferris wheel is one of the most expensive rides at the fair. The guy holds the seat steady as I sit down and Saint climbs in next to me. It immediately starts to rock and I grab onto Saint's arm, already feeling nervous. The guy lowers the barrier and it locks in place, but I still check it, like always, just to make sure it's secure. I've seen too many TikToks of young people falling from rides that weren't buckled properly; the danger is etched in my brain.

'It's fine, Eva,' Saint says looking amused. He puts a hand on top of mine and it instantly calms me down.

'Sorry,' I say, taking a deep breath.

The wheel starts to move and it's a little bit faster than I anticipated. I'm not someone that ever thought of herself as being scared of heights but the higher we rise, the more my heart starts to race and this awful sense of dread comes over me as we reach the peak. My body feels strangely light and I make the mistake of looking down. Everyone looks tiny. If this barrier were to open I would fall and die immediately—

'Hey, what's up?' Saint asks as I squeeze his arm tight. 'I thought you liked this ride.'

'I thought so too ... oh no!' We start to descend and my stomach feels like it's in my throat. I squeeze my eyes shut. 'This was a mistake. I want to get off.'

'It's a bit late for that,' Saint says.

For a moment we're at the bottom of the wheel and I can breathe again, everything feels normal, but then we start to rise once more. I do not want to go round again!

'You need a distraction,' Saint says. 'Look at me, Eva.'

I slowly open my eyes and Saint places his hand on my cheek and softly moves my head so my eyes are locked on him.

'Just focus on me, okay?'

I look into his eyes. He has perfectly symmetrical bushy eyebrows and nice shaped lips. Really nice.

'Okay,' I whisper, and Saint's eyes begin to explore my face. His hand is still on my cheek and the other is on top of my hand that's resting on his arm.

My heart is racing but I don't think it's from the ride any more. His mane of hair frames his face and I have a sudden urge to run my fingers through his curls.

135

'You have nice hair,' I say.

Saint smiles. 'Thanks. You do too. Feeling better?'

I nod, hoping he doesn't let go and he doesn't.

Our chests are rising and falling in perfect sync and I don't know if it's because we're stuck on this ride eighty feet high in the air and the only way I can get through it is to stare at him, but this pull to get closer to him is getting stronger and stronger. I want to know what it would be like to touch Saint's lips with my own and explore each other.

Or do you just want to win the dare? Oyin's voice says in my head, making me jerk back.

Saint's hand falls from my face and he frowns. 'What's wrong?'

'Sorry I . . .'

His hand that sits on mine has the dragon tattoo. The artwork is intricate and the creature stares up at me, and now all I can see is Saint's face when he mentioned New York. Does he miss her? Is he still in love with her? I like being this close to him, but do I even like him? Or am I just trying to win the money?

The thoughts are racing through my mind so fast that I move my hand off Saint and face forward, trying to ignore the way my stomach turns as we descend.

'Eva?' Saint asks.

'Sorry, I just need a minute,' I say.

He nods and faces forward and we sit in an awkward silence. There was a moment there and I ruined it and I have no idea how I feel about it.

*

Saint insists on walking me home once we get off the Ferris wheel, which I'm grateful for. I feel slightly off balance, and I'm convinced I'm not walking in a straight line. Okay, so clearly when it comes to Ferris wheels and me, we are not a vibe. Saint's walking close to me but there's a weirdness in the air. I think I did want to kiss him and I think maybe he wanted to kiss me too. What is happening? The only boy I've ever wanted to kiss was Jayden and now all I can think about is his cousin. I was only meant to get a date from Saint, but when we were alone in the sky I felt safe and comfortable and it felt . . . right.

I glance at Saint, who has his hands in his pockets, face forward. He is handsome. Not my usual type. I like my guys broader, sportier, more rugged with main character energy and Saint is the complete opposite, but for some reason I'm drawn to it. To him.

'Feeling better?' he asks, glancing at me.

'Yeah, thank you. Who knew heights were a big deal for me?' I say. 'Maybe not the best ride.'

'Maybe not.' Saint smiles. 'I was looking forward to ramming you in the bumper cars.'

I scoff. 'Please, you wouldn't even catch me.'

'Oh yeah?' Saint raises an eyebrow.

'Yeah!'

We burst out laughing and now we're closer so our arms are brushing against each other when we walk, making sparks fly on my skin. I wonder if I'm having the same effect on him. I hope I am.

'If you got a tattoo, what would it be?' Saint asks.

'Oh, I dunno. I've never really thought about it. I guess just something pretty, like stars or hearts or something,' I say. 'What did the dragon symbolize?'

Saint glances at it. 'You ever watched *Game of Thrones*?'

I stop in my tracks. 'I love *Game of Thrones*,' I gasp. 'Wait! Is that Drogon?'

'Yes! Wow, most people don't clock it. My ex, we used to love watching *Thrones* and so I get Drogon and she got Rhaegal.'

'You said it was a "set",' I say, and Saint frowns. 'You're missing one – Viserion.'

Saint laughs. 'That's very true. You know your dragons!'

'Don't get it twisted, I'm a massive GOT fan. Why do you think I have a friend called Sansa?' I say, and Saint chuckles. 'Okay, I know what I would get if I got a tattoo. A White Walker.'

'You can't get a White Walker!' Saint says, outraged. 'They're evil.'

'No, Cersei and her incestuous self is evil. The White Walkers, the Night King are the core of the show,' I argue.

'The Starks are the core of the show, Eva!'

We go back and forth reliving the epic-ness of *Game of Thrones* and I'm having so much fun that I don't even realize we're nearly at my house. What I don't need is Dami making another scene if a boy comes to our front door, so we stop some feet away.

'I had fun tonight,' I say.

'Me too,' Saint replies. 'I can't actually remember the last time I had so much fun.' He rocks back and forth on his heels. 'So, you got any plans for tomorrow?'

'Well, I'm obviously going to binge watch all of GOT,' I say, and Saint laughs. 'I'm going to church with my grandma and then I'll come by the store to film some content.'

'Oh, sick! And Benji will have this week's pay for you as well,' he says.

I'd almost forgotten about the extra money coming in from this job.

'I guess I'll see you tomorrow then?' he adds.

'Tomorrow.'

And it feels like the most natural thing to stand on tiptoes and wrap my arms round his neck for a hug. Saint pulls me close, his strong arms round my waist, and my face disappears in his mane of hair. It smells good, of argan oil and coconut. His hands gently squeeze my sides and my heart races. For a moment we're still, connected with each other, and I don't want him to let go.

TWENTY

'Eva?'

Saint and I quickly push away from each other. Amara is on the pavement in front of us holding a Sainsbury's shopping bag in one hand and taking out her AirPods with the other. She's wearing a long floral dress with rings on her toes and gold anklets. She looks at me and then at Saint with a smirk on her face.

'Oh, hey.' I take another step away from Saint for good measure. 'I didn't know you were coming back tonight.'

Amara is looking at me expectantly and I frown at her, not sure what else she wants me to say.

'Hi, I'm Amara.' She holds out her hand to Saint, who shakes it. Oh right. I should have introduced them.

'Nice to meet you. I'm Saint.'

'Love that name!' Amara grins. 'Like Saint West.'

Saint frowns. 'Err . . . okay.' Saint is probably the last person who wants to keep up with the Kardashians so I doubt he even knows who she's referring to.

'So, what's going on here then?' she asks nosily.

'Nothing!' I say, too quickly, gently pushing Amara to the door. 'I'll see you tomorrow, Saint.'

But Amara twists her body so she's out of my grasp. 'You hungry, Saint? I'm making fish tacos.'

'Grandma already brought food!' I tell her. What is she doing? She can't even cook!

Amara shrugs. 'I thought we could mix it up.' She shakes her shopping bag. 'There's plenty here.'

'Err . . .' Now Saint is looking from me to Amara.

I'm swiping my hand across my neck and shaking my head to signal no, but Amara links arms with Saint and starts walking with him to the door.

'Come on, it will be fun,' she chirps. 'You can tell me all about how you met Eva. I want to know everything!'

'O-okay,' Saint stammers as he lets himself be dragged to the house. 'We met at Carnival.'

Amara gasps. 'You did? Didn't she look amazing?'

'*What are you doing?*' I mouth, and Saint shrugs in response.

'Come on, Eva!' Amara sings.

I throw my head back and let out a silent scream as I follow them. They're waiting for me by the door because Amara doesn't have a key and, for a second, I'm tempted to keep her locked outside.

'What have you two been up to today?' Amara asks once we're inside. The house smells of peppers and spinach from Grandma's cooking.

141

'We had work and then went to a funfair,' Saint explains. He looks round the hall with interest, taking in the family pictures. I guess it was too busy to take in much at my birthday party.

Amara's eyes light up. 'Like a date?'

'Amara!' I snap.

'Sorry,' she says, not sounding sorry at all. She holds up the Sainsbury's bag. 'It won't take long to make. Saint, make yourself at home.'

'Like you do,' I mutter under my breath.

Saint follows me into the living room where Yum-Yum is lying on the couch. Mum and Dad would go mad if they saw him there. He sits up when I flick the light on but then snuggles back down when he realizes it's just me. It's hot in here and I turn the fan on before sitting down next to Yum-Yum stroking his head.

'He's cute,' Saint says coming over to join me.

'He's not—' but I'm surprised when Yum-Yum purrs even louder when Saint pets him. I was going to say he's not the friendliest cat and is known to hiss at any new person when they come into the house. It took him ages to warm towards Amara.

'What's his name?' Saint asks as Yum-Yum rolls onto his back and begins to gently paw at Saint's hands.

'Yum-Yum. Wow, he really likes you!'

'Everyone likes me.' Saint grins and I scoff. 'You okay with me being here? Sorry your sister—'

'She's not my sister,' I explain, as Yum-Yum jumps off the

couch and leaves the room. 'She's my brother's girlfriend. She's been staying here while my parents are away. And it's fine that you're here. As long as you don't feel pressured to stay?' And I hope he'll say no.

Saint shakes his head and the butterflies in my stomach flutter. He sits close beside me even though the couch is massive.

'What are we going to do while we wait for these tacos?' His leg brushes against mine and my heart jumps. There's this electricity between us that's been building since the funfair and I'm tempted, so tempted, to just lean forward and kiss him.

I always thought I wanted my first kiss to take place somewhere romantic with a guy I'm crazy in love with, but there's just something about Saint. Something different. Something better. It's like I know he would value this kiss just as much as I would. All thoughts of the dare have gone out of my mind. We're alone in the room and Amara is busy in the kitchen. This seems like the perfect time. I slowly move forward. Saint's eyes widen as he realizes what I'm doing and I'm praying he doesn't push me away. But then he moves towards me. I can hear my breaths loud and quick in my ears and my heart is racing so fast ...

'Are you allergic – oh!' Amara covers her mouth with her hand.

I close my eyes and let out a deep breath. Saint immediately faces forward towards the blank TV. Amara and her stupid timing ... She is really pissing me off.

'Sorry, sorry! I just wanted to check if Saint had any allergies.'

'Nope. None,' Saint says.

'Okay, thanks,' she says quickly before mouthing '*Sorry*' at me as she leaves.

Saint smiles nervously at me. Do we try again? Or was that a sign? Maybe kissing Saint is a bad idea.

'Let's watch *Game of Thrones*,' Saint suggests, making the decision for me. 'Favourite episode?'

'That's an impossible question,' I say, hoping I don't look as hot and flustered as I feel. I grab the remote and switch the TV on. 'I have at least ten favourite episodes.' I scroll through options until I find the boxsets to download.

'Ten? Please! There's maybe five.'

'Five?' I protest. 'We'll have to binge watch them all.'

'We'll have time to watch one today, maybe two. We might have to finish watching it another day.'

Is he suggesting spending more one-on-one time with me? The thing with Saint is, if I was going by his tone alone, I wouldn't think he was flirting with me. But I'm beginning to realize that he's someone who flirts by teasing. Come to think of it, he's been teasing me a lot lately.

'I want to watch either Battle of the Bastards or The Red Wedding,' I say.

'You know the episode is not actually called The Red Wedding,' Saint says. 'Let's watch that one.'

Amara is playing music on her phone as she cooks and the smell of fried fish wafts into the living room and smells really good. I wonder if she was lying when she said she couldn't cook just so Dami wouldn't expect her to. Dami's forever asking for specific dishes and yet he never raises a finger to help, so I don't blame Amara if she did lie.

I stand up and turn off the light. I can feel Saint watching my every move, which makes me feel warm all over. Now we only have the glow of the TV. I sit back down close to him, tuck my legs under my butt and, without thinking, lean in to him, almost like we're snuggling, and Saint brushes his hair over his shoulder and moves his head to the side so it's resting on top of mine. And it feels like the most natural thing in the world.

Usually, I hate it when people talk through a film or TV show no matter how many times I've seen it, but it's fun seeing Saint so animated with his opinions on what should have happened. We're at the part where Robb Stark gets stabbed in the heart.

'This is all on Robb, man,' he says.

'No it's not! He was in love,' I argue.

'If he just married that Frey girl, no one would have died. Arya could have been reunited with her brother and mum – and then maybe the finale would have been better.'

I burst out laughing.

We bitch and moan and laugh throughout the rest of the episode and I'm disappointed when it ends. I'm already looking for another episode to watch when I remember that we still haven't eaten the fish tacos and they should be ready by now. Lord, if Amara has burned them after all this!

'One sec,' I say as I head to the kitchen.

Amara is on her phone, leaning against the counter. Next to her is a plate of delicious-looking fish tacos.

'Why didn't you call me?' I ask as I pull two glasses from the cupboard.

'You sounded like you were having fun and I didn't want to disturb you.'

I can feel her watching me as I fill up our glasses with ice-cold lemonade – the only thing Dami is good at making.

'Yes?' I ask without turning round.

'Are you and Saint together?'

'No, we're just friends.' I close the fridge door and she's looking at me with an eyebrow raised. 'What?'

'Friends, Eva? I'm not a dummy. He's cute and there's definitely a vibe between you both.'

'Do you think?' I can't help but ask.

Amara nods. 'He's much better than that Jayden. Dami told me he came round.'

I frown. 'Wait, do you know Jayden?'

'He works at Sainsbury's, right? I go there sometimes and he's always flirting with me and the customers, forever trying it on.' Amara shudders. 'You can do so much better.'

Jayden tried to move to Amara? How am I only finding out so much about Jayden's character today? Amara hands me plates and the tacos as well as a packet of gum. I look at her questioningly.

'For the fish breath. So you can both ... you know.' She winks at me and turns back to her phone.

TWENTY-ONE

I'm sitting in my seat with Grandma's bag on my lap as she heads to the back of the short queue waiting to talk to the pastor. The church service ran over by an hour but it's finished now. This isn't my family church, which is very organized and starts and ends on time, but I go with Grandma to her church once in a while. She's always complaining that she's the only one who doesn't have family that attends service. Basically, she guilt-trips me into visiting. Whenever I suggest she comes to mine, she screws up her face and says my pastor is too 'new age'. Grandma's church is made up mainly of Nigerians and Ghanaians, and I find the pastor and the congregation a little dramatic, but it can be quite fun.

I love the outfits. Everyone comes in their Sunday best, in their traditional attire, slyly competing with each other. I dress up more when I come to this church as Grandma doesn't think jeans are appropriate in the house of God. So today I'm wearing this blue maxi dress as it's the only thing I own that's not low cut and virtually touches the floor.

'Hey, Eva.' A pretty woman with waist-length braids waves at me and I wave back. That's Sadé, the young woman Grandma thinks would be a good wife for Dami, but after last night I feel a bit more protective of Amara.

Despite fish breath being an absolute turn-off, Amara left Saint and me to eat our tacos together in peace, and it was really nice hanging and chatting with him. He left when Dami texted that he was on his way home. I didn't need my brother ruining what had been a really fun day. Since last night, Saint and I have been texting back and forth and he suggested if I was free tonight we could continue our *Game of Thrones* marathon at his house, which I'm down for. Somehow, our discovery that we both love GOT has seeped into our text conversations and now we only seem to communicate through *Throne* GIFs. His church service finished ages ago, so I've already got multiple GIFSs from him. I chuckle as I look through them.

I'm just responding to Saint's latest message when the Bad Bitches WhatsApp group goes off.

Sansa
Empty house today and tomorrow. Sleepover? Maybe the last one before we go off to uni? 😔

I usually talk to my friends every day and we did say that we would spend as much time as possible with each other before we all leave for uni, but, truthfully, I was looking forward to hanging out with Saint again tonight. But I guess I'll have to

148

make do with just seeing him at work later. Sharisha, Oyin and Fatima quickly all give Sansa's message a thumbs up. I can't be the only one not going. I add my own thumbs up to the post.

I'm greeted at Harley's World of Comics by a life-size Super Mario that makes me stop in my tracks.

'It's good, right?' Benji says as he adjusts the black moustache on his face.

I look at him, my eyes travelling up and down from his blue dungarees and red long-sleeved top to his massive hat with the 'M' on it. Did I miss a memo that it was a fancy dress day?

'Why are you dressed like – oh.'

Saint walks out from behind the till dressed in a similar costume but he has a green-sleeved top instead. Is it weird that I'm still attracted to him despite him being dressed like Luigi? He grimaces as Benji grins.

'Get it? I'm Mario because I'm short and round, and he's Luigi because he's tall and slim.'

I press my lips together trying desperately not to laugh out loud, especially when Saint looks like he wants to die, but my shoulders start to shake and a giggle escapes my mouth.

'See! I told you this isn't what she wanted!' Saint protests. 'We should have cancelled it today.'

'What I wanted?' I echo, confused. 'Cancelled what?'

'Every first Sunday of the month it's Cosplay Sunday,' Saint explains. 'So we have to come in a costume. This was obviously Benji's turn to pick a character to dress up as, but if a customer comes in cosplay then they get twenty-five per cent off. I told him that for TikTok you probably wanted us in everyday clothes.'

'Wait, this is really a thing you two do?' I ask, and they both nod.

I've never seen cosplay in real life before. It's kind of ballsy that they're going to be dressed up like this at work all day, but I guess it's not so different from me dressing up at Carnival and parading down Notting Hill with feathers and sequins.

'This isn't what I envisioned,' I confess. 'But this could be your USP and I'm sure other cosplay lovers will be obsessed. How do people know to dress like this without you having a strong social media presence?'

Benji shrugs. 'Word of mouth I guess. I've been doing this for years.'

'This is tame for him,' Saint explains. 'Last month he came as IT – you know, the clown – despite it being thirty degrees and not Halloween.'

'There's no rule to say I can't be a scary clown in the summer,' Benji counters, and they go back and forth like an old married couple.

I go on TikTok and am surprised to see that cosplay is huge on here. Literally thousands of searches. There are costumes from nineties movies, superheroes, and a ridiculous number of girls in a sexy two-piece blue outfit which I discover is Kitana from *Mortal Kombat*. Hmmm, I wouldn't mind an outfit like that. I'm so busy flicking through account after account that I miss what Benji says to me.

'Sorry?' I ask, looking up.

'I said we got you a costume as well.' Benji grins.

Oh no. I definitely don't want to dress up.

'Is it cute?' I ask wearily.

'I think so,' Benji says at the same time as Saint replies, 'Absolutely not.'

'Am I Yoshi or something horrific?'

Saint laughs. 'You're going to hate it.' He walks off to get it.

'No you won't,' Benji protests. 'I think you're going to look great, and it will complete our look.'

When Saint returns, my jaw drops. Yep, this is going to be terrible.

The pink satin material is so big that it obscures Saint's view and he has to use two hands to hold it.

'Barbie?' I ask. That wouldn't be so awful I guess. I did love the movie.

'It's better!' Benji rubs his hands together. 'And she's blonde too.'

Saint holds it up properly. It's a light and dark pink mess of a dress with a frilly pink collar and a blue gem in the middle of the chest area. It's basically an ugly pink ball gown.

'Who is this meant to be?' I ask, touching the cheap material.

'Princess Peach,' Saint and Benji say in unison and when I don't respond Saint adds. 'You know, from *Super Mario*?'

I haven't played any *Super Mario* games since I was a kid. Of all the things to cosplay as, and to be fair some of those outfits I just saw online were very cool, Benji thought this was the best way to introduce the store to TikTok?

151

'Yeah, no, I'm not wearing that. No way.' I shake my head to emphasize the point.

Saint gives Benji a knowing look.

'But you'll be the only member of staff not dressed up,' Benji protests. 'People go all out on Cosplay Sunday and I don't want you to feel left out.'

Left out? I couldn't be more relieved if I tried.

'It's okay,' I say. 'Maybe next time.'

No one points out that this is just a temp job till Bournemouth so I won't even be working here next month, but Benji pouts anyway. A customer walks in dressed from head to toe like Ash from *Pokémon*, complete with the red-and-white cap over a black wig, a blue-and-white jacket, and a toy Pikachu stuck to her shoulder. Benji walks over to greet her.

'Wow, he wasn't joking,' I say, watching them admire each other's outfits.

'Last month we had a group of guys come in dressed as the *Teenage Mutant Ninja Turtles*.'

I gasp. 'You're lying.'

Saint shakes his head. 'Full on green body paint too. It's even madder at Comic-Con. Everyone goes full out so you don't feel weird that you're in a full costume all day. If anything, you'd feel silly not to be in one. You'll see every type of character there. You ever been?'

'No but it actually sounds cool,' I say truthfully. 'Is there one coming up?'

'Yeah, after the gamer event in Bournemouth. I'm thinking I might go as Goku Black. The costume is pretty easy. Just got to figure out what to do with all this hair.' Saint laughs but stops when he sees my confused face. 'Goku Black?'

I have no idea who that is.

Saint frowns. 'From *Dragon Ball Super*. Goku! I thought you were going to watch it?'

I hold my hands up. 'Wait, there's a *Dragon Ball Z* and *Super*? Who's got time for all that? What is the costume anyway?'

Saint crosses his arms over his chest. 'I'm not telling. You're going to have to watch it.'

I roll my eyes. 'Fine! I'll watch your stupid *Dragon* shit.'

Saint laughs. 'That's the spirit. Man, it's hot in here.' He takes off the hat and his hair's tied up into a top bun. He looks adorable.

'I'm kinda liking this look,' I tease.

Saint raises his eyebrows. 'Really? This is doing it for you?'

I laugh. 'I think so. Maybe you should grow a moustache?'

Saint glances down at the fake black moustache and wiggles his mouth so the moustache twitches from left to right, making me grin. 'You would walk down the street with me like this?'

I shrug as he moves closer. 'Maybe.'

'Maybe?' he asks.

He's standing right in front of me and even though he looks ridiculous, that pull is back, where all I want to do is kiss him. My phone buzzes and I gesture at Saint to give me a second. I glance down at Oyin's message in the Bad Bitches chat . . . and it's as if ice has suddenly been poured over me.

I turn my back to Saint in case he sees it.

I'd completely forgot about the dare and now she's reminded me. It's like there's this sinking feeling in my stomach.

'Eva?' Saint says.

I hastily lock my phone so the screen turns black then I turn back round. These feelings towards Saint ... they're real, but how can they be when I've come into this under false pretences? What if something happens between us and then he finds out that it was all for a dare? He would never believe me if I told him that what I feel for him is real. *I* wouldn't believe me if it was the other way round. I would probably hate me. The idea of Saint hating me makes my heart ache in a way I haven't felt before.

'Eva?' There's concern in his voice. He touches my arm.

'I'm fine,' I say brightly. 'Should we get started?'

'Right. Okay.' Saint walks towards Benji, then stops, turns round and looks at me. 'You sure you're okay?'

I nod. 'Positive.'

This isn't going to work. Either I have to stop these feelings I've got for Saint or I need to forfeit the dare. But honestly, I don't know which one to choose.

TWENTY-TWO

I can't believe Benji was right. I'll never ever say it out loud, but I do feel a bit left out. Every single customer that's walked through the doors has been dressed in cosplay, and . . . some of the outfits! Like, the effort people have gone to is something else. Plus the hair, the make-up – I definitely underestimated how serious they are. I haven't felt left out enough to put on that ugly Princess Peach dress, but I kind of wish I had something.

'I think I've got enough,' I say, stopping the recording. 'I'll make a TikTok account for Harley's World of Comics tonight and will post it.'

'Thanks, Eva,' Benji says. 'Oh, before I forget.' He reaches behind the till and hands me a brown envelope. 'You've been so great and we really appreciate you. Did you confirm if you're coming to Bournemouth for the day?'

'I'll be there. My brother will be fine with it.'

I peer inside the envelope and it's the thirty pounds I'm owed for this week's work. Throughout the day I've felt like I was being hit by waves of guilt every time I looked at Saint. Since that message from Oyin, I don't know how to act around him, and I know by the looks he's giving me that he's trying to work out why I've suddenly been off. But now, holding this money, it's like those waves of guilt have grown into a tsunami and I'm drowning.

'Thanks, Benji,' I say, putting the envelope in my bag. 'I'm gonna head off.'

'Eva, hold up.' Saint hurries over to me having just finished with a customer. 'Are you sure everything is okay?'

'Yep, all good,' I say, turning away from his face because lying to him like this is too hard.

'You got plans? I wanted to see if you would like to grab a bite to eat. There's this restaurant nearby called Tu. Thought it would be cool to go there – don't worry, I'll change first! And then maybe come back to mine? Watch some GOT?'

I know the restaurant. It's got this gorgeous greenery with fairy lights and flowers that hang from the ceiling with a massive cherry blossom tree in the centre that's featured as the backdrop in many Instagram pictures. It's romantic as hell and exactly how I can win the dare. Saint has done exactly what I wanted him to do for me to get this money to fix Dad's car. The problem is I didn't count on me developing feelings for him. This yearning to be around him is strong and all I want to do is say yes and have a romantic night with him, no strings attached.

'I have a girls' night tonight,' I hear myself say.

The girls would understand if I cancelled – hell, they'll be gassing me up to get my money, but I just can't do it. I need time to think about this.

'Oh, okay,' he says, but he can't hide his disappointment. 'Maybe next time?'

I smile in response because if I agree to a 'next time' then it will happen and I will have completed the dare. But do I want that? And what happens to me and Saint after this stupid dare is over?

'See you later, Saint,' I say, heading for the door.

'Bye. Have fun,' he calls.

Once I get round the corner from the store, I lean on the wall and close my eyes, trying to calm down my racing heart. God, what have I gotten myself into?

When I get to my house, I can tell Dami and Amara are in because the living room window is wide open and I can hear Jhené Aiko's soulful voice from the driveway – she's literally all Amara listens to. My stomach rumbles loudly. I haven't eaten since after church when Grandma brought me a saltfish patty from the West Indian restaurant around the corner.

'Eva?' Amara greets me in the hall. 'There you are. Your parents have rung like three times to talk to you.'

'Is everything all right?' I ask, concerned.

Amara nods. 'They just wanted to check in with you.'

'Oh, okay. I'll call them later.'

'How was your day?' She glances at the living room door before lowering her voice. 'Did you see Saint?'

157

'At work,' I say, and Amara holds her hand to her chest like I said he brought me roses or something.

We go into the living room where there's a plate of fried plantain and buttered hard dough bread. Not exactly a meal but I'm too hungry to care. I help myself and sink into the couch.

Dami eyeballs me. 'Who's Saint?'

How the hell did he hear that? I quickly glance at Amara and she subtly shakes her head. She didn't tell him about Saint coming over.

'My friend. He's the one who got me a job. Actually, next Wednesday I'm going to Bournemouth for the day. We're throwing a Retro Gaming event for work.'

Dami raises his eyebrows. 'You and Saint are going to Bournemouth?'

'*And* our manager. For *work*,' I add, seeing as Dami seems to be forgetting that part.

'Right. What about uni shopping? Mum gave me a checklist of things we need to get. You're moving to Nottingham the week after Mum and Dad get home, right?'

'Err . . .' I play with a loose strand of string on my dress.

I've tried to put off thinking about uni but I know I'm only two weeks away from going. I can't help thinking of Saint saying that he's taking a gap year. Maybe I could persuade Mum and Dad to let me do that. It would give me time to work out the best career for me. I could work, maybe travel . . . but I already know it won't happen. Mum and Dad will shut that idea down straight away.

' "Err"?' Dami prompts.

'Babe!' Amara snaps. 'She's had a long day. Stop hounding her.'

Dami and I both stare at her. It's not like Amara to have my back and tell Dami off.

'I wasn't hounding her! Was I hounding you?' Dami asks defensively. 'You know what, yeah? You just let me know what's up, innit, and then we can sort it. How about you call Mum and let her know the info?' He sits back in the couch with his mouth set.

'I'll do that now.' I stand up and smile gratefully at Amara. 'Sansa's having a sleepover tonight. Probably the last one me and my friends will have before uni.'

'Sounds fun.' Amara puts her arm round Dami; Dami crosses his arms in response. 'We'll get some alone time, babe,' she says soothingly.

Dami grunts. Just stubborn for no reason.

I go up to my room and call my parents. Mum answers on the second ring but the line is bad today and it keeps cracking up so all I can hear are her broken words.

'Mum . . .? Mum? Can you hear me?' I ask but there's no response.

In the end I shoot her a message that I'll try again tomorrow. Sansa's sleepover isn't starting for a few hours so I lie on my bed, grab my laptop and search gap year ideas. I'm amazed at the amount of information – volunteering, travel, part-time courses . . . I'm not sure exactly what I want to do, and I honestly don't know if I'm brave enough to travel by myself, but deep down I know going to study law in another city is not the right move for me.

But how do I tell my family that?

TWENTY-THREE

Sansa lives in a five-bedroomed modern house in Ilford. The type that has spotlights everywhere and long heaters that cover an entire wall. Sansa's mum owns a very successful chain of yoga studios. It's just Sansa, her mum and her little brother that live here but her mum and brother have gone to see her aunty for a few days, so we have the house to ourselves.

I was going to message Sharisha to ask if she wanted to meet up so we could come together, but then I decided to make the TikTok account for Harley's World of Comics. I followed a bunch of comic book people, edited and posted the video, and packed my overnight bag. Just as I was about to leave, Yum-Yum came in from the garden and decided to use his litter tray – something he always does just when I have things to do and places to be. Then Dami told me to clean it up before I left. So, by the time I was done at home, I was running late.

Sansa opens the door in denim shorts and a crop top. 'Eva!'

We hug tight like we haven't seen each other for months. 'Come in.'

I take my shoes off at the door and follow her down the spacious hallway to the living room. Fatima and Sharisha are already there, and I hug them both. There are two pizza boxes, a bowl of crisps and lots of drinks on the table.

'Where's Oyin?' I ask.

Fatima rolls her eyes. 'Logan asked her to hang out so she said she'll come later.'

'Really?' I take a seat next to Sharisha. It's not like Oyin to blow us off for him.

'But it's not even a date. It's literally a come-over-to-my-house situation,' Fatima continues.

'She shouldn't be dropping us for a guy,' Sharisha says. 'She needs to drop him.'

'Well, I guess she won't see Logan either when she goes to uni,' Sansa says, sitting down opposite me. Always the diplomatic one.

Sharisha laughs. 'Of course not! Logan and her aren't a forever situation. Ugh! She can do so much better than him. Do you think I would let a man move to me after he already tried it with my friend?'

I always find it awkward when they bring up the me-Logan-and-Oyin situation and I'm just glad that she's not here to listen.

'Enough about them.' Sansa claps her hands excitedly. 'I'm going on a date with Anthony!'

'Anthony who helped at my party?' I ask, and Sansa nods. 'That's great! I like him. Where are you planning to go?'

'To that funfair that's not far from Westfield.'

'Oh, I went there yesterday with Saint—'

My friends all look at me.

'You went on a date with Saint?' Sansa asks slowly. Then she gasps. 'Eva, you won the dare!'

I shake my head. 'It was more research for this gamer event that's happening at work. Definitely not romantic.'

'Oh. So he hasn't made a move yet?' Fatima asks.

'Well, he kinda has . . .' I begin.

Sharisha frowns. 'What? You didn't say anything.'

'It only happened earlier today.' I fill them in on Saint asking me out and yesterday at the funfair and him coming to my house.

Fatima shakes her head. 'I'm confused. He wanted to take you to Tu and you said no? I hope it wasn't just for this sleepover, because we would have understood.'

'No, it wasn't that.' I sigh and look up to the ceiling, knowing I just need to say it. 'I think I . . . I think I like Saint. Like, *really* like him.'

There's a moment of stunned silence. Fatima's eyes are bulging, Sharisha's mouth drops open, and Sansa puts her hands on either side of her head like it's going to explode.

'Damn.' Fatima finally says. 'I didn't see that plot twist.'

'What do I do?' I ask desperately. 'I can't tell Saint I like him because of this stupid dare and every time I'm around him I feel guilty and gross for what I'm doing.'

'And he's Jayden's cousin,' Sharisha adds.

'Exactly! And did I tell you that Jayden came by my house

to apologize for the party? I think he was also going to ask me out.'

'No way!' Fatima says.

'But then I found out that it was him who made that list in college. You know, that one that labelled all the girls.'

'Whoa, whoa, time out!' Sharisha holds up her hands. 'Jayden did *what*? Nah, this is getting really messy.'

'It is!' I cry.

'Okay, let's all just take a deep breath.' Sansa inhales and exhales before eyeballing us. 'Come on, everyone do it.'

We follow her lead and it does help.

'Eva, is there any way you can get enough money from your job to fix your dad's car without having to complete the dare?' Sansa asks and I shake my head. 'Well . . .' Sansa shrugs helplessly. 'If you don't want to keep lying to Saint, maybe you should tell your parents the truth and deal with the consequences.'

'The truth?' Fatima snaps. 'No, girl, you need to just win this dare, fix the car and crack on with your life. Besides, Oyin will just give you another dare that will probably be worse. You're moving to Nottingham anyway, so what can even happen with Saint – or Jayden for that matter?'

I haven't told them yet that I'm wondering about taking a gap year. I think that might be a bombshell too many for one night. And Fatima's not wrong. If I did go ahead with uni, what could happen with Saint? And then there's Jayden, who I haven't spoken to since he came by the house. How would he feel if I said I liked Saint?

Sharisha is staring into space and I know she has an opinion about this which for some reason she's not voicing.

'Okay, I'm going to warm up the food,' Sansa announces. 'Let's just chill and I'm sure we'll think of something that will help you, Eva.' She smiles kindly at me before she picks up a pizza box. 'Fatima, can you grab the others, please?'

Once they've left the living room, Sharisha looks at me and I can see the hurt on her face.

'Eva, you didn't tell me that you liked Saint.'

'I didn't . . . it just kind of happened.' I groan. 'We've spent a lot of time together and he's so lovely and . . .' My eyes start to well up and Sharisha puts her arm round me.

'It will be okay.' She holds me tight and I sink into her. 'We'll figure this out together. I did ask my dad about a mechanic but it's still around the same price that we saw online. Girl, you know if I had the money I would just give it to you.'

'I know you would.' I wipe my nose with the back of my hand. 'Maybe Sansa's right and I should just tell the truth.'

Sharisha pulls away from me so fast that I fall into her lap.

'Sharisha!' I yell.

'I love your parents, but even I'm a little bit scared of them,' she says. 'You will never live this down if you tell them about the smashed car that happened at the party at your house – the party that they had no idea about.'

She's not wrong. I've never felt so conflicted before and I honestly don't know what to do. I wish I could go back in time and just not agree to this stupid dare. But who would have thought that I would *like* Saint?

Fatima isn't the only one who never saw that plot twist coming.

The doorbell rings and Sharisha and I look at each other.

'Sansa! The door!' Sharisha calls.

'It should be Oyin. Can you let her in?' she shouts back.

'One sec, girl.' Sharisha uses my legs to hoist herself up. I wipe my eyes, checking my phone camera to make sure it doesn't look like I've been crying. My eyes are a bit red but nothing crazy.

I can hear voices in the hall and I frown. Sharisha walks back into the living room, her eyes wide, and mouths, '*What the hell?*'

Then behind her Oyin appears, but so do Logan, Miles and Jayden.

TWENTY-FOUR

'Eva!' Oyin squeals as she hurries over to me. She doesn't give me a chance to stand up. Instead, she throws herself at me and we end up falling on the floor, which makes the boys laugh. 'Oops, sorry!'

'It's okay,' I say. Oyin manages to untangle herself from me and gets to her feet, extending a hand to help me up.

'I didn't know they were coming,' I say quietly.

Oyin shrugs. 'They just tagged along. You think Sansa will mind?'

Even if she did, Sansa most likely wouldn't say it out loud.

'You see Jayden's here?' Oyin not so subtly nods her head towards the door where the boys are hovering awkwardly.

'Yep. I see him.'

Jayden waves shyly at me and I force a smile back. Great. This is the last thing I wanted to deal with. It doesn't help that he looks super cute in a white tee and jeans, but looking at him all I can think about is Saint.

'Hey, boys.' Sansa's voice is an octave higher than usual.

She doesn't hug them as she's carrying the pizza boxes. 'I didn't know you were coming over.'

'We were meeting up with Logan, who was dropping Oyin over here,' Jayden explains. 'And I wanted to holla at Eva.'

Everyone looks at me and my face goes warm. Sharisha puts her hand on my arm and gently squeezes.

'Let's eat first, there's enough for everyone,' Sansa says brightly, but she throws a sharp look at Oyin, who completely misses it because she's too busy pouring herself a drink.

Jayden's heading my way to sit on the other side of me but thankfully Fatima plonks herself down, so he has to sit elsewhere. I help myself to an American Hot pizza and for a moment all I can hear is the sound of everyone eating.

'So, what did I miss?' Oyin asks, looking at each of us with a smile on her face.

Sansa and Fatima glance at me, but Sharisha says, 'Nothing much. Waiting on you.'

It's hard to miss the sharp 'you' in Sharisha's tone, but Oyin either doesn't catch it or ignores it, because she says brightly, 'Logan and I were just hanging out.'

'Hanging out? Is that what you're calling it?' Miles says, elbowing Logan, and the boys laugh.

'Miles, grow up,' Sharisha snaps.

I do not want to think about Oyin and Logan doing it.

'I'm getting some water,' I announce to the room. Logan's sitting on the floor with his long legs stretched out so I have to step over him, his eyes following me.

The kitchen, like the rest of the house, is immaculate. I love

168

the white island in the middle of the room and there's always a full bowl of fresh colourful fruit that sits in the centre. I run the water at the sink, lean on the counter and take a deep breath. All I wanted was a night with my girls – most likely our last night together before uni starts – and the guys are ruining it.

Picking a clean glass from the side, I fill it up from the tap and down it, instantly feeling better.

'Hey.'

I spin round and Jayden is in the doorway.

'You okay?' he asks.

'Thirsty.' I hold up the glass and fill it up a second time.

'Can we talk?' he asks, walking further into the kitchen. Usually when I'm around Jayden, I feel flustered, but right now there's nothing. Actually, more than anything I just want to be left alone.

'About what?' I ask, leaning on the counter, keeping a bit of distance.

'Sorry that I came by your house the other day,' he says. 'I hope I didn't cause any shit with your brother?'

I shake my head. 'Dami was just being protective. Sorry that he spoke to you like that. I've been meaning to text you, but I've been caught up with work.'

'You work with Saint, right?'

A stab of guilt punctures my chest hearing him say Saint's name.

'I didn't know you were into comics,' he adds.

'I'm probably more into it now because of him,' I admit.

'But I'm helping more with the social media side of stuff. It's fun.'

'That's cool. Saint was telling me about the Retro Gaming event. I might come down.' Jayden grins. 'See you in action.'

I'd normally have a flirty response ready to throw back but this time I stay silent instead. There's noise coming from the living room and I'm sure Sansa is making them play a board game. Her family are board game enthusiasts.

Jayden frowns. 'Are we okay? You seem a bit off.'

'I know you made the list, Jayden.'

Jayden has one of those faces which can't hide what he's thinking. I watch in silence as his face goes through several stages: confusion to realization to worried. He sits down on a breakfast stool. 'List? What list?'

'Are you really playing dumb?' I question.

'What do you want me to say?' he argues. 'It was just a stupid thing I did ages ago. Why are you even bringing it up?'

Is he for real? He has no idea how that stupid list affected me and so many other people.

'Besides, I called you "the pretty one", so what's the big deal?' he continues.

'The "big deal" is I don't want to be judged only on my looks. And I don't want to be labelled by anyone – and definitely not by a guy,' I reply, and Jayden just sighs. And that really pisses me off. 'Neither did any of the girls in college,' I continue. 'Who do you think you are, deciding what people should be known as? Did we label you? What name would we give? "The basic one"?'

'Really, Eva?' Jayden scoffs. 'If I'm so basic, why you always trying to move to me?'

'I've never moved to you! You're always complimenting me, hollering at me. Maybe you're getting me confused with the other girls you're dealing with.'

Jayden laughs and says matter-of-factly: 'Ah, so you're jealous. The list isn't that deep so I don't get what you're so mad about.'

Lord, what did I see in the boy? He has no understanding of what I'm saying at all. He can't even see how his actions and words are so awful. At least I feel some sort of shame, some guilt for this dare, but Jayden doesn't seem to think that there was anything wrong in the slightest with his behaviour towards me or any of the girls in college.

'Can you just leave me alone for a minute?' I say.

Jayden rolls his eyes. 'Eva, man, why you acting so emotional?'

'"*Emotional*"?' I yell.

'What is going on?' Sansa walks into the kitchen and stares at me and Jayden. 'We can hear you shouting.'

'It's nothing,' Jayden says as I cross my arms.

Sansa gives me a pointed, questioning look, and I shake my head. I'm so over whatever the hell this was with him.

'We've just started Truth or Dare so come on,' Sansa says.

Jayden and I look at each other before I follow Sansa out of the kitchen with Jayden trailing on my heels.

Everyone looks up when we walk in and we join the seated circle, but I sit next to Sharisha away from Jayden.

'You good?' Sharisha whispers to me.

'Tell you later,' I respond.

'Okay, let's continue,' Sansa declares. 'Who just won?'

'I did,' Miles says. 'And I pick Jayden. Truth or dare?'

Jayden shrugs. 'Dare.'

'Kiss the girl that you fancy the most.'

Sharisha moans loudly. 'Are you tone deaf, Miles? Didn't you hear them arguing?'

'What? They can kiss and make up,' Miles argues.

Jayden looks over at me and raises his eyebrows, as if asking me whether we should, and I scoff. He has another thing coming if he thinks I want *him* to be my first kiss.

'All right then, let's make it truth,' Jayden says, his mouth set in a hard line.

'Hmmm, truth ...' Miles frowns as he tries to think of something.

'Oh, I've got something,' Logan pipes up, and I don't miss the glance he throws at me, which for some reason instantly makes me feel on edge. 'It's just a yes or no answer.'

'Okay,' Jayden says.

Logan grins. 'Do you know about Eva's dare?'

My stomach churns like I'm about to be sick.

'Dare?' Jayden questions. 'How did she get one? We were in the kitchen.'

'Logan!' Oyin snaps, at the same time as Sansa says, 'Fuck,' before accidentally-on-purpose knocking over the drink by her feet. A dark stain of Coke appears on her carpet. 'Shit! Jayden, can you get me some warm water and white vinegar, please?

From the bathroom. Two floors up. And Miles, grab me some cloths from the kitchen, please. There's some in the cupboard.'

If Jayden and Miles think it's weird that Sansa has asked *them* for help, they don't show it. They immediately get up to get the stuff.

Once they're gone, Sansa rounds on Logan, furious in a way I've never seen her before. 'What the *hell* are you doing?'

'What?' Logan laughs. He goes to pour himself a drink and Oyin snatches it from his hand and places it on the table. Logan looks at Oyin and says, 'Hey! If you didn't want me to say anything then why did you tell me?'

'Oyin?' I say in disbelief and Oyin freezes. *No. There's no way.* My heart drops. Oyin told him about the dare. How could she do that to me? Why would she risk having Jayden find out about this?

'Girl, you better speak!' Sharisha snaps at Oyin.

But Oyin doesn't say anything. Instead, she's looking anywhere but at us. I've known Oyin since we were eleven years old and we've always been close. Our secrets stay between us. And our dares have definitely always stayed within our circle, so what possessed her to tell Logan, of all people?

Miles comes back into the living room with multiple cloths and Jayden bounds down the steps with a bucket of water and white vinegar spray.

'Is this all – what's up?' Jayden asks, looking around the room, clearly feeling the tension.

'Nothing, man.' Logan chuckles.

'Can you all just get out?' Sansa yells, in a way that's so unlike Sansa. She's looking directly at Logan. 'I didn't even invite you here – you or your friends, and all you're doing is pissing me off.'

'But . . . I just . . . the cloth . . .' Miles trails off.

Logan kisses his teeth. 'Let's bounce. I need to go home.' He looks at Oyin. 'You coming?'

I stare at Oyin, who actually looks like she's thinking about it. What has got into her? How has this guy got her in such a chokehold? This is not like her at all.

'I'll walk you out,' Oyin says in a small voice and hurries past us.

'Is she for real?' Fatima mumbles.

Jayden glances at me but doesn't say anything. He leaves the bucket on the floor and heads towards the door. The door slams, and only then does the tension in my body ease.

TWENTY-FIVE

I collapse onto the sofa with my hand on my chest, willing my heart to calm down. I really thought Logan was going to tell Jayden about the dare. What would Jayden have done? What if Logan tells him anyway?

'What just happened?' Fatima asks, looking around the room. 'How did that escalate so quickly?'

'Why is Oyin telling anyone about the dare?' Sharisha asks. 'Especially Jayden's best friend. Is that their pillow talk or something?' Despite the upset, that makes me chuckle.

Sansa ties up her blonde hair into a top bun. 'I shouldn't have yelled like that, but, honestly, Logan was acting like such a dick.'

'Nah, I'm proud of you, girl,' Sharisha says, hugging her. 'You cussed that boy out.'

'Thank you, Sansa,' I say.

Sansa hurries over to me, puts an arm round my shoulder. 'Are you okay, Eva? What was all that with Jayden in the kitchen?'

'We spoke about the list and he just didn't get it.' I rub my eyes, suddenly feeling exhausted. 'Can you imagine how mad he would be if he knew about Saint? And that I like him? I just . . . I just can't do this any more.'

'You want to stop the dare?' Sansa asks softly.

I nod and instantly this weight that I didn't realize I had seems to lift from my shoulders. This whole thing has felt like it's been spiralling out of control and I need to get a grip on it before it blows up in my face. The last thing I want to do is hurt Saint, so even if Logan decides to drop the bomb – and I wouldn't put it past him – then at least I'd know I wasn't part of it any more.

'But the car, Eva. How are you going to fix it?' Fatima asks. 'Babe, I really think you should accept Saint's date, sort the car and then put all of this behind you.'

'But she *likes* Saint,' Sharisha reminds Fatima. 'I don't think she can just "put it behind her" that easily.'

I'm racking my brain trying to figure out how I can have Saint *and* sort out the car, but I'm coming up empty. All I know is I can't keep doing this dare.

The doorbell rings and none of us move.

'I'm tempted to leave her out there,' Sansa says before she reluctantly hoists herself up and goes to answer it.

Sharisha is already positioned next to me, her hands on her hips, ready for anything. I really don't want to fall out with Oyin. All I want is to understand why she did what she did, but when Oyin's backed into a corner she can get super defensive.

Sansa and Oyin appear a moment later and Oyin locks eyes with me.

'Logan said he won't say anything.'

I wait, thinking there's more she's going to say, but she doesn't add anything.

'*Wowww* ...' Sharisha drags the word out. 'You're not even going to apologize?'

'I didn't mean to tell him,' Oyin replies. 'It just ...' She shrugs.

'But you did!' Sharisha snaps. 'You told Logan. We don't tell anyone about the dares, you know that.'

'Like I said, it was an accident.' Oyin's jaw hardens. 'I didn't think he would bring it up like that in front of everyone.'

'Didn't you?' I ask. 'What did you think he'd do with that information? You didn't think, even for a second, that he might want to tell Jayden? His best friend? He may still do it.'

Oyin sighs like we're exhausting her. 'He said he won't, so he won't.'

'Oh, come on, Oyin. We all know Logan doesn't always tell the truth,' Fatima points out, and Oyin flashes her a sharp look.

'What do you mean by that?' Oyin counters in a hard tone.

'The whole thing with Eva,' Fatima says. 'He was on her like mad, asked her out – what, just a few days into college – but then tried to play it down when he moved to you. He still looks at Eva like she's the sun or something. It's like he's obsessed.'

177

I so wish she never took it there. Oyin juts out her chin and glares at Fatima.

'Logan doesn't like Eva, he likes me! And can I remind everyone that Eva decided to throw a party behind her parents' back and she accepted the dare, which wasn't forced on her. She knew the risks of accepting a dare involving Jayden's cousin.'

'*She*'s right here!' I yell. 'You knew I was in a difficult position, especially when I had no job to fix my dad's car. You could have borrowed or loaned me the money if you'd really wanted to help. As I saw it, the only way I could get the money was to take the dare.'

'You're all ganging up on me and how exactly is any of this my fault?' Oyin asks, looking at each of us, and I almost laugh because this girl must be joking.

'You. Told. Logan.' Sharisha claps after each word, saying exactly what I was thinking. 'That is one hundred per cent your fault, Oyin.'

'*And* you brought them to my house without asking me first,' Sansa says. 'That wasn't cool, and you knew I would find it really awkward to tell them to leave.'

'You know what? Everyone is clearly Team Eva here and no one even wants to hear me out,' Oyin shouts. She picks up her tote bag.

Sharisha rolls her eyes. 'Where are you going?'

'Home! You lot are cussing me, cussing my man and I'm not here for it.'

'Please save the "my man, my man, my man" energy,'

Sharisha says, and Fatima bursts out laughing. 'Logan is not your man and you're not his girl. He's a friends-with-benefits at best.'

The hurt flashes in Oyin's eyes. I don't want her to feel ganged up on, I don't even want her to leave, but I do want her to apologize for telling Logan.

'Fuck off, Sharisha,' she snaps, heading for the door.

'What did you say?' Sharisha shouts, lungeing for her, but Sansa and I pull her back. Sharisha is not the one to get into a fight with because she would win. Easily.

For the second time tonight the door slams shut and the echo seems to vibrate through the house.

'Bitch.' Sharisha shrugs me and Sansa off and storms to the kitchen.

Sansa takes a deep breath, her cheeks flushed. 'I just need a minute,' and she goes upstairs. We look up to the ceiling as we hear her footsteps overhead.

'I'll go talk to her,' Fatima mutters and I nod.

I already know Sharisha wants space so I stay on the couch wishing the day could rewind. I wish I'd said no to this sleepover. I'm not sure what to do with myself so I go on TikTok to see how my video for Harley's World of Comics is doing – and I gasp when I see over six thousand views and five hundred new followers. Damn! This community is strong. I take a screenshot and send it to Saint followed by a series of fire emojis and smiley faces with sunglasses on. Saint types back straight away.

> Superstar! Benji will actually cry lol

> Thanks! We need to post more and your followers will go up so quick x

I hover on the keys wanting to talk more but also not sure if I should, especially with what happened today. Then I see Saint typing:

> What you up to?

I smile, glad he too wants to continue talking.

> At Sansa's for a sleepover ...

Do I mention that Jayden was here today? No. Maybe not a good idea.

> Not going great so just sitting on the couch lol. You?

> Nothing. Wish we were together doing nothing.

And the butterflies are fully whizzing away in my stomach. I wish we were together too. This last night with my girls is a hot mess and I'm not sure how it's going to get any better, but at least right now I have Saint and talking to him is already making me feel calmer. I don't care about the dare any more. I don't want to force anything between us. I can just be me and honest from now on. So I respond without overthinking it:

I wish that too x

TWENTY-SIX

By the time Saint and I finish our conversation, none of my friends have come back to the living room. So in my new spirit of being honest I do something I told Saint I was going to do – I watch *Dragon Ball Z*. It's actually easy to find as there are episodes on YouTube and they are short, under fifteen minutes each. There's even an episode giving a summary of that Frieza character that Saint was wearing on his T-shirt at Carnival. I'm surprised that I actually like it! It's nice to put the names to the characters that Saint mentioned and the storyline is surprisingly really good. Before I know it, I find myself clicking on the next episode.

It's only when Sharisha slumps down next to me, looks at my phone and asks, 'Why are you watching DBZ?' that I stop. I've already watched four episodes.

'Oh, Saint asked me to watch it and I said I would. I'm trying this new thing where I actually do what I say I'm going to do.'

'Oh yeah, honesty is back in fashion,' Sharisha teases, but her eyes tell a different story.

'You okay, babe?' I ask.

She sighs. 'I wasn't cool to Oyin. I shouldn't have said that about Logan, even though it's true.'

'The whole thing was a lot,' I say. 'We do need to chat with her, but I think everyone needs to cool down first. Sansa and Fatima haven't come down yet and I feel bad that all this shit kicked off in Sansa's house. All the girl wanted was a sleepover.'

'Ugh, I know!' Sharisha glances at my phone where it's frozen on a female character with blue hair.

'That's Bulma,' I explain, and Sharisha's mouth twitches. 'Yes, I've become that person.'

'Tell me now if you're going to start doing cosplay so I can end our friendship!'

I laugh out loud. 'Cosplay isn't too bad.'

Sharisha's eyes look like they're going to pop out of her head. 'What has Saint done to you?'

I grin. 'All this comic book and anime stuff is actually kind of cool. I'm looking forward to the gamer event. I just wish I had a games console or something that I could practise on.'

Sharisha shakes her head. 'You lost me when you called all of that cool. Come on, let's go check on the girls.' She holds out her hand and I take it.

We find Sansa and Fatima sitting on the floor against Sansa's bed in her large bedroom. They've changed into their pyjamas and have on matching face masks with cucumbers on their eyes.

'Err, what's going on here?' Sharisha asks.

'She said this would make her relax,' Fatima says, her mouth barely moving.

'Where did you get the cucumbers from?' I ask. I don't remember her getting them from the kitchen.

'My mini fridge.' Sansa points at the small pink mini fridge in the corner. Of course she has one in her bedroom. 'Help yourself. There are masks in the bathroom.'

Unlike us, Sansa has an en suite. Her mum decorated it for her so it's all modern with gold accents. There's a basket on the counter filled with different face masks, and face wipes on the side. Sharisha and I grab one each to wipe off our make-up.

'That feels nice.' The sheet mask instantly cools my face.

'Mmm, this smells good.' Sharisha massages her mask on her cheeks. 'I already feel calmer.'

We head back into the bedroom and I grab some cucumber slices and hand two to Sharisha. She puts on her Spotify and 'Dancehall Queen' by Beenie Man blares thorough her speakers.

'Sharisha!' we all yell.

'Sorry, sorry – wrong playlist.'

A second later, Aaliyah's gorgeous tone fills the room. I join the girls and rest my back against Sansa's bed, close my eyes and place the cucumbers on top of my eyelids so everything is blacked out.

The next morning the mood is much more positive and we joke around as we eat our homemade pancakes, which Sharisha's made and served with maple syrup and lots of strawberries and blueberries. After the face masks last night, we watched a movie, and although Oyin was still on our minds and we failed to come up with a solution that would make everything right, it did end up being a nice sleepover.

'You working today, Eva?' Fatima asks.

'No, they're packing stuff up today for the gamer event so I'm there tomorrow. Saint said he will send me the info for Bournemouth tonight. You guys should come!'

They glance at each other and I laugh. It was worth a shot.

'What do you like about Saint?' Sansa asks, leaning forward on her elbows. 'Is he different to Jayden?'

'He is. I feel like Saint is just himself and is comfortable about it. He doesn't care about being cool or what people might think of him, he just does him and I like that. Also, he's really easy to talk to. We actually were speaking about a gap year.'

'A gap year?' Sharisha frowns.

'Saint's taking one. Until he said it, I never thought about it but I'm kinda feeling the idea. I don't think moving to Nottingham right now is the best thing for me.'

'Oh, wow,' Fatima says, surprised. 'When did you start feeling like this? I thought you were excited to get away from your parents.'

'I was. I mean, I am.' I shake my head. 'You know how my parents pressured me into studying law?' The girls nod. 'I thought moving far away would be fun and putting some distance between me and my parents would help me become more independent. But the closer it gets to freshers' week and starting uni, the more I'm panicking about leaving.'

'I feel the same,' Sansa confesses. I can't hide my surprise. Sansa has always wanted to study philosophy and has been nothing but excited about going to the University of Manchester, but I guess that's how I seemed to them as well. 'I'll be away from my mum, my brother, you guys,' she explains, 'and it's just really daunting.'

'It's *so* daunting!' Sharisha agrees. 'I'll be in Guildford at Surrey, Fatima in Reading, Oyin in Bristol. Why didn't we pick the same uni, or at least unis that are close to each other?'

'Because we're stupid,' Fatima says, and we laugh. 'Seriously though, I think we're all feeling the same, like it's really scary, man. Even though Oyin is on some next nonsense right now, you girls are my best friends and I really hope we stay close, despite the distance.'

My eyes start to feel hot and before I know it I've burst out crying. I don't know whether it's because I'll miss my friends or that I've finally admitted out loud how I feel about uni. Maybe it's the fight with Oyin, or finding the money to fix Dad's car, the stupid dare, or Jayden – or everything mixed in together. Sharisha, Sansa and Fatima quickly wrap their arms round me, telling me it's going to be okay.

'Sorry, guys.' I wipe my eyes with my T-shirt and sniff. 'I don't know what's wrong with me.'

'Don't apologize, babe,' Sansa says. 'You had to get that out. Crying is good for the soul.'

'You got me going now,' says Sharisha, dabbing at her eyes. 'Trying to ruin my lashes and shit.'

I laugh through my tears. Even though I opened up, I still don't know what the right route is for me going forward, but I do know that as long as I can keep my friends close I can get through anything.

TWENTY-SEVEN

I get back home late in the afternoon desperate for a nap. I don't know why but I can't get a decent night's sleep unless it's in my own bed, and now, with this thirty-degree heat, I'm finding it hard to stay awake.

'Hey, Yum-Yum.' My cat is sprawled out on the hard floor by the door in the hallway and I tickle his ears before he lazily swats me away. 'I know,' I say. 'I just want to sleep too.'

My hand just reaches the banister when Dami calls me from the living room.

'What's up?' I ask.

Dami is standing beside two boxes filled to the brim with comic books and a familiar grey boxy console by his feet.

'I was thinking about the gamer thing you're doing for work,' he begins. 'Sorry that I wasn't more supportive about you getting a job. I know how hard you've tried, so I figured you should probably know more about what you're walking into,' he says.

This is probably the nicest thing my brother has ever done for me.

'Dami!' I squeal, wrapping my arms round him, and he pats my back gently in response. 'How did you even get all this?'

'It was in the dumping room,' he explains. 'Right at the back. I didn't even remember that Raheem gave me the SNES and all the games when he outgrew it. I figured we can play some of the games and read the comics so at least you have some knowledge at the gamer event.'

'I've done my own research already!' I respond. 'I even watched *Dragon Ball Z* last night.'

Dami raises his eyebrows. 'Really? Who's worse, Cell or Majin Buu?'

'Majin who?' I respond and Dami laughs. 'I only watched four episodes from the Frieza Saga.'

Even Dami can't hide how impressed he is. 'Look at you!'

I flick my hair. 'I know! Come on, let's play.' All my tiredness is immediately pushed aside by my excitement. The games are spread out on the living room table – *The Legend of Zelda*, *Final Fantasy VI*, *Mortal Kombat*. I smile and think of Saint when I see *Street Fighter* and *Mario Kart* next to each other.

It takes Dami a minute to set up the SNES and he makes me blow on the cartridges for ages to clean out the dust.

'Do you remember any Chun-Li fighting moves?' I ask Dami.

'Of course! That's important shit to remember. Pop in the game.'

At first I'm doubtful that Dami would remember anything, but he picks Chun-Li, so I pick Ken, and he completely destroys me doing all of Chun-Li's classic fighting moves.

'The champ is back!' Dami shouts as I'm KO'd again.

'Ugh! I forgot how annoying you are when you win things. Right, teach me.'

It takes me a while to lock down the sequences, but it'll be worth it to see Saint's face. It's important to me that he should know that I've tried to understand his world a bit more . . . and I want to beat him. Dami may be an obnoxious winner, but he's a good teacher and this explains why I used to be so good at video games when I was younger.

We play until the sun sets, forgetting to eat lunch, but this has been the best day with my brother and I've missed hanging out.

'We haven't spent time like this for a minute,' Dami says, reading my mind, his eyes on the screen.

'I know. It's been so much fun. Thanks again for all this.'

Dami pauses *Mario Kart* as our racers are on Rainbow Road ready to start the race. 'I'm proud of you, you know,' he says and laughs when my eyes widen. 'Nah, seriously, Eva. Going to uni, moving away, getting a job. It's big moves.'

I shuffle uncomfortably in my seat. 'Do you ever regret it? Dropping out of uni?'

Dami shakes his head. 'It was the right move for me. Uni itself just wasn't what I thought it would be and it didn't make sense to stay there just because Mum and Dad wanted to hang a picture of me graduating in the living room.'

I remember the day when Dami said he'd dropped out. Mum and Dad were beyond livid. I don't think I've ever seen them so angry. They told Dami that he would be a failure, that he was an embarrassment to the family, but Dami stuck to his guns and refused to budge. I wanted to defend him, but I didn't want to get shouted at. But now those same words that my parents rained down on Dami might be coming towards me and I don't know if I can handle it as well as Dami did.

'I'm sorry I never backed you with Mum and Dad,' I say.

One corner of Dami's mouth lifts up. 'It wasn't your job to, Eva. Even though I'm still figuring out my life and what works best for me, at the end of the day I'm happy. Admin isn't my dream job, but the people are cool and I've got Amara.' At that a goofy grin spreads over his face.

'Wow! She's got you hooked,' I tease.

'Shut up, man.' Dami laughs.

'Do you think you two are a forever thing?' I ask curiously.

For ages I thought Amara was just another one of Dami's unserious relationships, even though she's been around longer than the others. But lately, being around Amara has made me see why Dami likes her. And I like her being around.

Dami shrugs. 'I think so. She's a good one, despite what Grandma thinks! You like her, right?' I nod. 'Well, that's all I care about.'

'Awww, are we having a mushy sibling moment, Dami?'

He kisses his teeth. 'The problem with you, yeah, is one compliment gets you excited.'

I laugh. 'I live for a compliment!' And Dami rolls his eyes

in response. 'Seriously though,' I say, 'now that I'm older, I get the whole uni thing a lot more now. And you're right: if it's not for you then it just isn't.'

Dami stares at me. 'You okay, Eva? Something you want to tell me?'

I want to tell him how I feel about uni and how afraid I am about dealing with Mum and Dad, but confessing to a member of my family, even though it's Dami, isn't something I'm ready for just yet.

Dami frowns. 'It's not Dad's car, is it?'

I can tell by his face that he thinks that's what's on my mind and already I can feel the frustration radiating out of him. I know I need to tell him that I don't have enough money to fix it so we're going to have to claim it on Dad's insurance, which is another thing Dad will be mad at me about. But a selfish part of me is enjoying the time I'm spending with Dami and I don't want to ruin it.

'Nope, nothing.' I force a smile on my face. 'One more game and then onto the comics, yeah?'

Dami nods and un-pauses the game, and I try to focus and ignore all the things I still need to sort out.

TWENTY-EIGHT

Harley's World of Comics is absolutely manic today. I should have asked more questions when Saint asked me if I minded coming early to help get everything ready for the gamer event, but all I thought about was that I could spend time with him. Something should have clicked in my head when he said to wear clothes I don't mind sweating in. I didn't expect it to be this chaotic. Despite them working all day yesterday there is still so much left to do.

The people who can't make it to Bournemouth and don't have access to a computer at home will be able to come into the store to play. Benji's girlfriend, a woman called Dove, will supervise. All of us work together to dismantle some of the shelves to create more space, plus pack up the comics and graphic novels that we're going to sell once we're in Bournemouth. There's a group of guys setting up the hired screens, the various consoles and headsets. When I'm not helping to move things, I'm filming for TikTok.

It's boiling in here and Dove is currently on the phone trying to hire some big fans. Saint has taken off his work T-shirt so he's only in a white vest top. He has a muscled slim build and for a moment I forget that I'm filming for work and I'm focused on him and the muscles visible in his back.

'Eva?' Benji calls. I drop my phone and it hits the floor hard.

'Shit,' I hiss. I bend down to pick it up, check it carefully and sigh with relief that the screen isn't cracked. Saint gives me an amused smile and I hope it's because I was having a clumsy moment and not because he knows I was checking him out.

'You okay for the six a.m. pick up?' Benji asks.

I hold my groan. I'm *so* not looking forward to it. We're setting off really early for Bournemouth to be there in time to help set up. Thankfully, Benji has a team down there who have already started, so hopefully there shouldn't be loads for us to do. I'm not an early bird and I'm notoriously useless in the mornings without a cup of coffee inside me first.

'Me, you and Saint. Road trip!' Benji sings.

I lock eyes with Saint and I can't help but smile. Two and a bit hours together in the car. Kind of makes the early wake-up call easier to handle.

'Can't wait,' I say.

We work solidly for a couple more hours, sweating in the heat, until Benji and Dove say they're going to buy us lunch and slushies from somewhere nearby. The guys setting up have gone and all the computers are lined up in a row. There are some new posters for the gamer event that we need to place around the store but, other than that, it looks sick. I can already picture it full of gamers tomorrow and it feels good to be part of making that happen.

I sit on the floor resting my back against the till stand, fanning myself with one hand even though it doesn't seem to be making any difference.

'I'm starving,' Saint groans as he joins me on the floor, our arms touching, hands grazing against each other, and I want to hold his but I'm nervous to make the first move. We sit like this for a few minutes, our hands dancing close. until Saint gently moves his fingers so they slip in between my own and I don't dare move in case he changes his mind. His thumb traces along my hand like he's drawing a pattern but I'm not sure what. He repeats it over and over again and I copy the pattern with my other hand on the wooden floor. A love heart.

'What are you hungry for?' I ask and Saint looks at me. His eyes trace my eyes, my nose, my lips, where he pauses for a moment.

'I don't think I should say,' he whispers as he moves closer to me.

My heart hasn't stopped racing since his hand touched mine, but now it's gone up a notch and it's practically sprinting.

'Maybe you should show me,' I say. I'm desperate for him to kiss me.

We're practically in each other's faces, so close that I can smell his minty breath. I close my eyes as his lips trace my jawline and a shiver runs through my body.

'So beautiful,' he whispers in my ear before he places a soft kiss on my neck.

It takes everything in me not to jump on him right here. Every part of my body is alive and anticipating the next touch from Saint.

'Not here,' Saint says, placing a kiss on my shoulder.

'Why?' I moan like a child, and Saint laughs, his dimples appearing.

'I don't want our first kiss to be here, at work.'

I smile. 'So, there will be a kiss?'

'There will most definitely be a kiss,' he says confidently, and I love it. 'But I want it to be memorable, romantic—' Saint shrugs. 'Blame the poet in me.'

'I love that.' I run my finger down the side of his perfect face because I just want to touch him in any way possible. 'Do you know what would make it even more romantic? A spoken word piece curated for me.'

'What makes you think I haven't already written one?'

Is he for real? I pull away from him to see if he's joking and I can tell from his expression that he isn't. *Saint wrote about me?*

'Can you recite it?' I ask.

Saint shakes his head and my shoulders sink.

'Not that I don't want to,' he explains. 'I don't know it off by heart yet.'

I smile. 'If I come to yours, will you read it to me?'

Saint raises his eyebrows. 'When?'

'After work?' I ask, praying he'll say yes.

Saint pauses for a moment. 'Okay.'

'Yay.' I cheer and clap my hands and Saint laughs. 'Maybe

tomorrow after the gamer event is finished we'll have time to go to the beach.'

'At sunset,' Saint adds. 'I'll try and make it happen. That would be a good date.'

Date. Before, that word would have made me excited in a different way. I would have won the dare and got the money to fix Dad's car. And even though I don't have the money, Oyin can dare me something else, I really don't care. Because right now all I feel is excitement about my first *real* date with Saint.

'I can't wait,' I say. Saint holds my hand again and I look down at his light hand holding my dark one.

The door opens and Benji and Dove arrive back with bags of some takeaway food and slushies, but Saint doesn't let go of my hand and I don't pull away either.

'Oh, this heat!' Benji moans loudly. 'Saint, come and grab this.'

'Benji!' Dove hisses and gestures not so subtly at us holding hands.

Benji notices and mouths an 'O' shape before he smiles at us. 'It's like Naruto and Hinata.'

'Oh my days, we're *not* like them,' Saint argues. 'First off, I'm not an orphan!'

'You know what I mean,' Benji replies.

I'm grinning at this exchange, not because I agree with Benji but because, thanks to Dami, I actually know what they're talking about!

'Don't worry, we'll be downstairs.' Benji throws an

exaggerated wink at Saint, who chuckles and shakes his head. Dove rolls her eyes.

'Take your time,' Dove says to us.

I lean into Saint, resting my head on his shoulder, and he rests his head on top of mine, his curls tickling my forehead and I lose track of how long we stay like that.

TWENTY-NINE

I'm excited but nervous as we walk to Saint's house. I've never been to a boy's house before unless it was a house party. And I've definitely not been alone with a boy in a house before ... well, except for Jayden in my room. I shake my head. *Do not think about Jayden.*

Saint lives in a two-storey terraced house in West Ham and, when he opens the door, I can hear a woman's voice singing along to something on the radio.

'My mum,' Saint explains, stepping aside for me to walk in first.

'Your mum?' I hiss, pulling up my vest top so the neckline sits higher. 'Will she be okay with me being here?'

'Of course!' Saint says. He locks the door. 'I'll introduce you.'

'Okay,' I reply, even though my heart is racing and my mind is already scrolling through the various killer looks I've seen Grandma give the girls Dami has brought home. God, please let his mum like me.

I follow Saint past the family pictures: a picture of him with his mum and dad; pictures of his twin brothers; pictures of him standing between his twin brothers. We walk into the kitchen. His mum has her back to us. She's wearing fitted jeans and a colourful Aztec patterned top, and she's stirring some type of batter in a bowl.

'Hey, Mum,' Saint calls and his mum immediately looks round at him, her face breaking into a wide smile.

Saint is literally her twin, with the same eyes, nose and mouth. Her skin is a darker shade of brown and flawless.

'Hey, darling,' his mum says in a strong London accent. She catches my eye and gives me the warmest smile, making my heart calm down. 'And who's your lovely friend?'

'This is Eva.' Saint grins at me. 'She's been helping out at the comic store and is coming to Bournemouth tomorrow.'

'Hello, Aunty.' I bend my knees to greet her in the traditional Nigerian fashion, but Saint's mum dusts her hands down on her jeans and opens up her arms. Before I know it she's enveloped me in a tight hug.

'It's nice to meet you, Eva.' She pulls away and studies my face. 'Wow, you are gorgeous.'

'Thank you,' I say, my cheeks warm. 'I love your top.'

She looks down at it. 'Thanks. It was a birthday present from my boys.'

'I picked it out,' Saint insists.

His mum chuckles. 'And his brothers insist that they did. What are you two up to?' She doesn't say it with the suspicious tone that my family would use if I'd brought

Saint home with me to my house. His mum genuinely seems interested.

'I was going to show her my latest spoken word piece and maybe we'll watch some *Game of Thrones*,' Saint replies.

'Your spoken word?' Saint's mum raises her eyebrows at me. 'He must like you, Eva.'

'Mum!' Saint groans, and his mum laughs, making me grin. 'Come on, Eva.' He grabs my hand in front of his mum and she doesn't tell him off for it.

Wow, she really is laid back. My mum would never.

Even though his house is smaller than mine, there seems to be so much more space. No clutter anywhere. We go upstairs and Saint opens the door to his room. I'm expecting to see comics everywhere and figurines, but it's pretty tame. A perfectly made big bed, a wardrobe, a chest of drawers, and a desk that's piled with notebooks in different colours. There's a wall with posters of different anime characters and a few pictures that I go and look more closely at. They're mostly of Saint with people I don't know. There are girls in a few of them and I wonder if any are his ex.

'Where are your comic books?' I ask.

'In the room next door. We've been transforming my brother Israel's room into a library.'

I've never met anyone who has a home library before. Not even Sansa in her massive house has one.

'Can I see the library?' I ask.

'Err . . . sure.' Saint picks up a black notebook from the top of the pile on his desk. 'Follow me.'

When he opens the next door on the landing and leads me inside, I gasp. The room is lined all the way round, floor to ceiling, with white bookcases. Half of them are empty, but half are full of paperbacks and comic books. The paperbacks are colour-coordinated, forming a pretty rainbow, while the comic books face outwards and are arranged by series. There are boxes filled to the brim with more books and comics waiting to be stacked, so the library is very much a work in progress.

'This is so cool,' I say, and Saint grins. 'Must have taken you ages.'

'Yeah, it's a lot, but when it's finished it's gonna be sick.' He walks to the other side of the room and grabs two massive grey beanbag chairs. 'Feel free to sit.'

Trying to sit cute in a beanbag when I'm wearing a short skirt and desperate not to flash my knickers is a myth, but I try my best. Saint flops down beside. He's still holding the black notebook and he suddenly looks nervous.

'Can you turn round?' he asks.

I frown. 'What?'

'I just . . . I'd feel more comfortable if you weren't looking at me when I read it out,' he explains.

How can he read out his words to a packed room of strangers but can't say it just to me? But I don't want to push in case he changes his mind. I twist myself away from him until I'm facing the window. Behind me, I hear Saint take a deep breath and clear his throat.

'*Kiss me under the lights of a thousand stars. Kiss me where*

202

my heart beats a melody that sings your name over and over again.'

I catch my breath as he speaks the words that I know are about me.

'Kiss me in the dark and leave traces of light on my skin.'

I can't help but turn my head slightly. Saint's eyes are closed. His hand is on a page in his open notebook where he's written the lines of his spoken word piece and the title is underlined. *Eva.*

'Kiss me above the clouds and take me to paradise.'

My stomach swoops like I'm right there, flying with him. I can't stop staring at his lips, wanting more than anything to kiss him exactly how he's describing it.

'I can feel you watching me,' Saint says, and he opens his eyes.

'What? No!' I quickly turn back round, biting my lip. Shit. He wasn't meant to see me.

Saint kneels beside me and lets out a low chuckle. 'You couldn't help yourself, could you?'

'No,' I admit, and Saint smiles. 'That was really beautiful.'

Saint glances at my lips and my heart skips. 'I have the best muse.'

'You do?' I ask breathlessly, leaning forward.

'Yeah,' he whispers.

I close my eyes inhaling him, wanting him—

'Saint! Eva! Food's ready!' His mum, calling from the stairs.

Saint groans and places his head on my shoulders. I could cry. We just needed one minute. One minute!

'Saint?' his mum yells again.

Saint turns away from me and yells at the door. 'Coming!' We look steadily at each other. 'I'm sorry,' he says gently.

'It's okay.' I stroke the side of his face with my finger and Saint catches my hand and entwines it with his own. 'We still have tomorrow at the beach.'

'Can't wait.' He stands up first, then helps me to my feet, and because I can't get enough of him I wrap my arms round his neck and he holds me tight round my waist so we're entwined with each other.

I wish we could stay like this forever. But we only get a minute because we both know Nigerian mothers are very impatient.

THIRTY

My alarm goes off at five a.m. and for a moment I'm just confused. Why am I getting up this early? Then I remember: Bournemouth. My eyelids are so heavy I can barely keep them open. Yum-Yum is sprawled out at the end of my bed in a deep sleep. I reach over and turn off my phone alarm and see a message from Saint.

> Hope you're up! Mum packed us some snacks. See you at six xx

I reply back with a love heart and sit up in bed, rubbing my eyes and yawning. My mind skips back to yesterday and how fun it was having dinner with Saint and his mum and dad, who came home half an hour after we started eating. The food was so good! Akara, beef suya and fried rice. I loved the way they all bounced off each other, laughing and joking, filling me in on their shared memories, and I couldn't help but feel envious. I wish I had that easy relationship with my parents.

I can totally understand now why Saint is so comfortable just being himself. From the few hours I was with them, I saw how much his parents really listen to what he's saying, always trying to understand where he's coming from. That explains why Saint can take a gap year and work on comic books and just do *him*.

Mum called me last night as I was going to sleep and I deliberately didn't answer as I didn't want my good mood to be ruined. I was worried she would ask me about uni, seeing as I didn't give Dami any clear answers the other evening.

I'll deal with it once this event is over, I tell myself.

I shoot a text to Grandma reminding her that I'll be out for the day and Dami will be at work, so she doesn't need to come by today.

The house is quiet and I get ready as quick as possible, not wanting to disturb anybody. I'll be running around a lot in Bournemouth, so I put on a pair of denim shorts and a fitted red top that shows an inch of skin. I team these with my new birthday trainers and, lastly, my sunglasses resting on top of my head. My charger is in my bag so I can get all the content needed. I leave a Post-it note on the fridge reminding Dami that I'll be in Bournemouth and I add Saint's number, for just in case he can't get hold of me for any reason.

Saint gives me a missed call to signal that they're outside. For some reason I expected Benji to be driving a van – until I remember we only have two boxes to take with us to Bournemouth. It's a bright day and already warm. Benji and Saint wave at me through the window of the shiny black Ford.

'Morning!' I say as I open the door and get in next to Saint at the back. The windows are down and the air conditioning is on, so it's nice and cool.

'Hey, Eva.' Benji points at my dad's car, still sitting there under its cover. 'New car?'

'I wish. Need to get a smashed window fixed,' I reply.

'Oh, really? Dove's brother is a mechanic, if that helps? I can call him, get a discount.'

'Are you serious? That would be amazing! Thank you, Benji!

'Sure. No problem. I'll shoot him a message once we get to the beach. Right, any requests?'

'I'm easy,' Saint says. He's wearing black shorts and a black T-shirt with a slogan on it – TALK ANIME TO ME.

'Me too,' I say.

Benji puts on the radio and starts humming along to the song. He signals and we drive off.

I turn to Saint. 'How many people are you expecting today?' I ask.

'A few hundred.'

'What?' I'm truly amazed. I imagined maybe forty people max. 'You serious?'

'Yeah. It's gonna be busy. Then there's the people joining online as well, don't forget. Oh, and Jayden said he might pop by.'

Jayden? I haven't spoken to him since the argument at the sleepover. Does he know about the dare? Is he going to say something to Saint? And does this mean Logan's coming too?

I shake my head. No, if Jayden knew about the dare he would be blowing up my phone.

'I thought you said Jayden didn't come to your events?'

'Yeah, he usually doesn't.' Saint shrugs. 'He messaged me last night about it. I did offer him a lift in the car with us instead of getting the train, but the six a.m. wake-up call was a no.' Saint laughs.

I look out of the window, silently stressing and staring blankly at the empty motorway. Is Jayden really coming? Should I message him to ask? The only person who might know Jayden's plans is Oyin, but if she knew he was coming wouldn't she give me a heads up? But then again, after the sleepover, maybe she wouldn't. I haven't spoken to her either since then. I'm sure that if Jayden knows something it's because of Logan, and that's on her.

I open the Bad Bitches chat. There's been nothing new on it since Sansa invited us for the sleepover. My fingers hover over the keys as I ponder whether I should say something or not. Oyin did say Logan wouldn't say anything and she seemed pretty certain about that.

I clear my throat. 'Is Jayden coming alone?' I ask.

Saint shrugs again. 'Who knows! He might not come at all.'

And I hope that's true.

I try to put Jayden out of my mind and focus on Saint, but it's difficult and more than once Saint has to repeat what he's just said as I'm distracted. Thankfully, he appears to think it's just tiredness and I don't correct him. In the end, the journey doesn't seem to take as long as I thought it would. We get through the delicious snacks Saint's mum packed for us on the way.

When the sea comes into view I can't help getting excited. The last time I went to the beach was on a family holiday to Spain when I was twelve.

'Did you bring your swimsuit, Eva?' Benji asks.

'Oh no, I didn't even think.' I had no idea we would even have time to go in the sea.

'He's playing,' Saint says. 'There's usually no time to do that. Hopefully, we can make an exception today.' Saint gives Benji a knowing look; Benji gives him a thumbs up back. Saint glances at me. 'Sunset date, remember?'

Like I'd ever forget. I'm glad it's at the forefront of Saint's mind.

'Can't wait,' I say, all thoughts of Jayden forgotten.

We pull up outside a leisure centre a few minutes from the beach. A huge sign outside reads HARLEY'S WORLD OF COMICS RETRO GAMING DAY. There's a nice cool breeze here, possibly because we're so close to the sea. The seagulls fly above us and I breathe in the sea air. It's quiet and peaceful and I wish we could stay out here a while longer.

Saint and Benji take a box each out of the boot and I follow them towards the main entrance.

'Are we taking over the whole building?' I ask, gazing up at the massive centre in wonder.

Saint laughs. 'No, just the sports hall – but that's pretty big.'

The sports hall is the closest room to the door and I can already hear voices from inside. The double doors are open and I gasp when I glimpse inside. There's a very big stand with the Harley's World of Comics logo as well as the gamer posters that have been blown up and stuck all round the walls. There are rows and rows of screens of different sizes with all types of consoles, including SNES and PlayStations, with signs above them saying what year they were made ranging from 1976 to the 2000s. There are two-player games all the way up to sixteen-player games, and a VR station. A pop-up shop area where we'll sell comics. Sponsored stands are being set up and I can see containers filled with toys, artwork, board games and T-shirts – and at least twenty helpers running back and forth to get everything ready in time.

'This is amazing,' I say. 'You do this every year?'

'Yep.' Benji looks on. 'Our fourth year now and it only gets bigger and better. Of all the things I've done, this is honestly the one I feel proudest about.' He rubs his hands together. 'Right, Saint, can you and Eva set up the comic book stand? And then explain to Eva what she needs to do? I just need to touch base with the team here.'

'No prob. Come on, Eva,' Saint says.

Benji hands me the box he was carrying, which I end up dragging across the floor as it's too heavy for me to lift properly. There are a few sealed boxes already by the comic book stand.

'Let's take them all out, lay them on the floor, and then we can decide where they should go,' Saint suggests.

'Wait, let me set up my phone. I can do a time lapse.'

I prop it up on the table and Saint opens the sealed boxes

while I unpack the ones that we brought with us. There are hundreds of comics, some I recognize and most I don't. I group all the ones that are from the same series together, creating piles across the floor. It's tiring work but there's also something quite therapeutic about it.

Saint's phone rings and I glance at it. My heart stops when I see it's Jayden.

'Hey,' Saint says, holding the phone between his ear and shoulder so it doesn't disrupt his flow. 'Yeah, we're here . . . ah okay . . . Eva?' I look up and Saint glances at me. 'Yeah, she's here . . . okay, cool . . . bye.'

I can't tell anything from Saint's expression.

'Was that Jayden?' I ask, playing innocent.

'Oh, yeah. He wanted to know if we'd arrived and if you were here.' I can tell by Saint's tone that he's puzzled, confused even, then he confirms it by asking, 'Are you and Jayden close?'

'Err . . . I mean, we're okay. Why?'

'No, nothing. I just clocked that he's asked about you a few times.' Saint shrugs. 'Okay, let's see where we're at.'

Grateful for the change of topic I stand next to him, admiring the piles and piles of stock. Saint's eyes are taking everything in and he starts pointing at the stands, telling me where things should go, and we start to put everything together. By the time we're done, hours have gone by. I'm starving, but with all the comic books displayed in order, it really does look like a shop.

Saint checks his phone again and I'm praying it's not

Jayden. 'We're going to open soon. Let's grab some food from the green room.'

He holds out his hand – the first time today he's tried to hold mine – and I sigh, relieved that we're okay. So I take his outstretched hand, and curl my fingers round his.

THIRTY-ONE

I can't even hear myself think. There's music playing from the speakers, chatter and yells from the gamers and staff, as well as the noise from the various games. Saint alternates between manning the comic book stand and checking in on the gamers. I do multiple loops recording footage, going on live, taking pictures, and I'm genuinely loving it. I'm hoping that there's time to play some of the games with Saint because I really want to show off how hard I've been practising.

My phone battery flashes fifteen per cent so I head to the green room where I left my bag and phone charger. Inside, there's a long table with a spread of sandwiches, crisps, biscuits and lots of juice and water, as well as several couches and chairs. Apart from me, the room is empty. I help myself to a chicken sandwich as my phone charges. We've kept some stock back here as well, including some graphic novels, so I pick one up and start to read.

'I need to remember this,' Saint's deep voice says, and I

look up as he takes a picture. 'Reading a graphic novel. Never thought I would see the day.'

'Hey! I better not have been mid-chew!'

'Nah, you look cute. One more.' He pulls the phone in front of him to take a selfie and I do the peace sign in the background before he collapses next to me on the couch. 'Just sent them to you. Having fun?'

I nod. 'Just charging my phone. When are we playing a game?'

'You mean, when am I kicking your ass?' Saint asks.

'Err, mine? I recall destroying you. Badly, might I add.'

'You're pretty cocky for what was clearly a fluke.'

'A fluke!' I spring to my feet. 'Come on, let's play something right now.'

'You sure? You're not going to sulk when you lose, right?' Saint teases.

'Keep that same energy, Saint,' I say, and he laughs.

We head out into the hall and I remember that *Street Fighter II Turbo: Hyper Fighting* was placed near the middle so I head there. There's a little bit of a wait before we jump on the consoles and I study the buttons, remembering the moves Dami taught me. The fighters appear on the screen and I get first pick so I choose Chun-Li.

'So obvious,' Saint says.

'Shut up, Saint!'

He cackles and hovers on Ryu.

'And you call *me* obvious?' I say.

'Hmmm, okay.' Saint moves his curser over Chun-Li. I'm

about to question what he's doing when he selects her and now it's Chun-Li verses Chun-Li. Mine is in a blue costume and his in grey.

'What the hell?' If he knows all the same power moves as me, how am I meant to win?

'Still obvious?' Saint asks, and I use my hip to nudge him.

Round one flashes and we're fighting in China, Chun-Li's home. The background is of a street market with a butcher's and chickens in cages. I glance at Saint and he's laser-focused on the game. If I remember what Dami taught me, I should be okay.

Fight!

Saint doesn't waste any time trying to kick my Chun-Li in the legs, so I jump and stamp on his Chun-Li's head making her fall to the floor. A quarter of his life has gone.

'Fuck's sake,' Saint mumbles, and I grin.

He punches at me and I block it. He keeps coming at me and I keep hitting block. He jumps at me and I get a kick in so his Chun-Li falls again. I still have my full life and his is now down halfway. His Chun-Li pops up from the floor and does a Spinning Bird Kick, but miraculously I do a Sweeper with my Chun-Li so she doesn't get hit by the power move.

'Oh, come on!' Saint yells.

I bite my lip, staying super focused, and press the combo buttons. My Chun Li's leg rises up and moves up and down so fast that her foot becomes a blue fire flame – the *Hyakuretsukyaku*. She's hitting Saint's Chun-Li, who falls in slow motion to the floor.

'Yes!' I yell. KO.

Saint groans.

Round two and three aren't any better for him. He blocks a lot more than the first round, but I wait it out and attack when he has a moment of not defending himself. At one point his Chun-Li is so dizzy that she has yellow stars rotating round her head. He gets a few kicks in, but I grab his Chun-Li by her top and dash her to the floor, finishing with a Spinning Bird Kick, and he's knocked out.

'Nope, we're going again,' Saint says.

He grabs my hand and leads me down the row to *Street Fighter V*, which I've never played before. I'm hoping the combos are similar. This time Saint picks Ryu and I go for Chun-Li again, hoping she won't let me down.

The graphics are a million times better here, way more life-like and the bodies somewhat exaggerated. Chun-Li has gone from a petite figure to looking like she's had a BBL.

'Chun-Li's got some thighs on her!' I say, and Saint laughs.

The game begins and we're on a bustling side street and I'm taken aback by the extra graphics, like when I hit Ryu these flames appear. The combo moves I know from *Street Fighter II* aren't working the same in this version so I'm just pressing anything, hoping if I'm consistent something magical will happen. I manage a *Hyakuretsukyaku* and it looks way more aggressive with these graphics, so I keep doing it and then the graphics slow down. The angle of the video changes so Chun-Li's Lightning Kicks are now from Ryu's point of view and I can see him being knocked around.

'Okay, this is sick!' I say.

'You should see *Street Fighter VI*. The graphics are so good!'

For a moment I think I'm totally going to win, but Saint does a series of combo moves and on every round he completely destroys me. Once he hits me with the *Hadoken*, Ryu's fireball, it's a KO.

'Ugh! That's so annoying.' I cross my arms over my chest.

'I can see you practised though. It was impressive,' he says kindly.

I huff in response. My practising didn't seem to help with the updated version.

Saint puts an arm round me. 'Are you sulking?' he asks.

Yes.

'No,' I say.

He kisses my cheek, sending a shiver through my body. 'Let's go play something else.'

By the time I start heading back towards the green room to get my phone, we've played *Mario Kart* and *Donkey Kong*. Saint actually jerked my controller mid-game so my Princess Peach hit a wall just so he could overtake me in the race.

The energy in the hall is so infectious that I can see why people get excited about gaming. I kind of wish I was here as a guest and was able to try everything. My hand is on the door of the green room when I hear a loud cheer to my left and I glance over. Someone must have won—

I freeze as I see two familiar figures in front of the *Pokémon* stand.

Jayden and Logan.

THIRTY-TWO

'*Shit!*'

I hurry into the green room and shut the door behind me, resting my back against it, breathing hard. Why are they here? Is it to support Saint or actually to out me? I grab my almost-charged phone to write in the Bad Bitches group chat that the boys are here, but because my hands are shaking so much I keep misspelling the words. I yell, jabbing at my phone, trying to get the message across.

My friends respond instantly, with multiple variations of *What the hell?*

> Do you think Logan will say anything to Saint?

I wait. A message pops up.

> **Oyin**
> I promise he won't, Eva. Don't worry.

To be honest, it doesn't reassure me, but I'm glad she's talking. I'm hoping no one challenges her and thankfully nobody does. My phone buzzes again in my hand.

> **Fatima**
> But you pulled out of the dare anyway, so if he says anything at least you can say you're not doing it.

> **Oyin**
> Wait! What? When did you pull out???

I put my phone in my pocket. If the girls don't fill Oyin in, then I'll do it later. Maybe I won't even bump into the boys. There are so many people and I'm walking around filming. I should be able to spot them first so I can avoid them.

Seeing as I can't hide in the green room forever, I head back into the hall, and Jayden and Logan are gone. Relief floods through me and I continue filming. The Retro Gaming event finishes at seven but at half six Saint texts me to come and meet him at the comic book stand.

I head over, still keeping an eye out, but there's been no more sign of Jayden and Logan. Thankfully, they're not at the stand either. Maybe they've already left, seeing as we're almost finished.

Benji is on the stand helping the line of customers. Saint waves when he sees me and says something to Benji, who nods, and Saint hands him a bunch of keys. Then he steps out from behind the counter holding a carrier bag.

'We've got to be back before eight, so we have a bit of time,' Saint says.

I frown. 'Time for what?'

'Our date! Did you forget?'

'No, of course not. I just thought because it's so busy ...'

'They can handle it.' Saint holds out his arm. I giggle as I link arms with him and we head out of the hall.

The air is much cooler now and there are people hanging around with carrier bags that I recognize from our event. Saint hasn't mentioned Jayden or Logan. Maybe he didn't see them or, if he did, they didn't say anything worth repeating. I hope so. Saint heads to the boot of the car and pulls out a cute wicker basket with a tartan blanket. He then empties the carrier bag into the hamper and I see Nigerian meat pies, strawberries, a pot of cream and bottles of drink.

'Saint!!!' I squeal. 'You made us a picnic?'

That's the nicest thing any guy has ever done for me.

'Thank God for the fridge in the green room! Mum made the pies. I figured we can sit on the grass by the beach before we walk along the sand.'

'Saint, this is ...' I don't even know how to articulate how amazing and sweet this is. 'Thank you.'

We walk towards the beach and we manage to find a patch of grass with trees that shade us from the last bit of sun. Saint lays out the blanket and we sit. He hands me a meat pie that's cold but tastes so delicious.

'Your mum made these?' I ask. They're better than my grandma's and Grandma's are top-tier.

Saint nods. 'Good, right?'

'So good.' We sit in silence as we eat and I could happily eat a second pie because they are so moreish.

'You have some ...' Saint leans over and brushes some golden flakes of pastry caught in my braids.

'Thanks.' Typical. I brush my braids back over my shoulders to reduce the risk of any more embarrassing moments.

'Okay, out of ten, what would you give the event today?' he asks.

'Ten,' I say without hesitation and Saint raises his eyebrows. 'No, I'm serious. It was so good and the vibe was amazing. I feel like I would actually come back here as a visitor.'

'Really? Maybe you should come to Comic-Con on Sunday in Olympia. That's a whole cosplay thing though.'

'Maybe I will,' I say. 'If it's as fun as today.'

'Well, that is high praise from someone who came into the shop pretending to get something for her brother.'

I gasp. 'How did you know?'

Saint laughs. 'You never followed through with actually getting anything. So, what made you come in the first place?'

'Err ...' I look out to the sea to give myself time to think. There's no way I can be honest and mention the dare. 'I dunno. Guess I was just intrigued by you.'

Saint tilts his head to one side. 'Why?'

I shrug. 'You're different to the guys I know.'

I expect Saint to push it more, but he doesn't. Instead, he nods and pulls out the strawberries and cream.

'Tell me something about you that I don't know yet,' Saint says.

'Hmmm ... I guess ... I mean ...' Why am I nervous to say it? It's not like Saint will take the piss or anything. 'I've never been kissed.'

Saint lowers the strawberry that was heading to his mouth and stares at me wide-eyed. 'What?'

I smile nervously. 'It's true.'

'So you mean, if me and you kissed today—'

'You would be my first,' I confirm.

'Wow,' Saint says softly. 'I wasn't expecting you to say that. Can I ask why you've waited?'

I shrug. 'Just wanted it to be special.'

I watch him carefully, hoping he doesn't pull a face or anything, but instead Saint smiles.

'I hear that. Kissing is intimate. You don't want to be doing that with everyone,' he says.

And I'm filled with relief by his response. 'That's exactly how I feel! I've never met anyone that agrees with me on that.' He really is something. 'Okay, your turn.'

Saint bites into a strawberry as he thinks. 'I got into a relationship with my best friend but we broke up when her family moved to New York and I was happy about it.'

'Happy?' I frown. 'Why?'

Saint sighs. 'She'd mapped out our entire life together and I realized we didn't want the same things. To be honest, I miss her friendship more than anything else. We broke up a year ago and she was my first serious relationship. She actually

222

got me into spoken word.' Saint smiles sadly. 'How did you manage not kissing with your exes?'

'Never had a boyfriend.'

Saint's mouth drops open. 'How have *you* never had a man?'

I look at the grass and play with a strand by my feet. 'Haven't found the right one ... yet.'

The seagulls squawk above us as they circle over the beach.

'You are full of surprises, Eva. For the record, I'm glad you pulled up at Harley's World of Comics,' Saint says, biting into another strawberry.

I can't hold back the grin that spreads over my face. 'Yeah? Why is that?'

'For one, you are beautiful,' he says matter-of-factly, making my cheeks grow warm. 'And judging by the guys that kept looking at you at your party, you seem like the kind of girl that could get any guy she wants, yet you came to seek me out. I'm glad you did.'

He holds out the cream and I take a strawberry and dip it in. When I bite into it, the flavours dance on my tongue and it's refreshing and sweet. Maybe the dare wasn't such a terrible thing. Without it I wouldn't have got to know Saint on this level and realized what a sweetheart he is. Maybe we can grow into something beautiful.

'I'm happy I met you too, S—'

I'm distracted by the buzzing of a wasp flying near my head! I scream and jump up, knocking my drink over. The wasp hovers over the strawberries and Saint waves it off, laughing uncontrollably at me.

'It's not funny!' I hate wasps. Great. Everyone is looking at us now.

'It's gone. Relax,' Saint says, but I keep looking around me every few seconds. 'You know wasps are also at the beach, right?'

'Oh, hell no! I'm not trying to get stung.'

He laughs. 'I'll protect you. Let's finish this and we can walk around for a bit.'

The conversation between us is so easy. By the time we've finished the picnic and thrown the rubbish away, I feel like Saint and I are even closer. We walk down to the beach hand in hand, the sky now a beautiful mix of purple, pink and yellow. Saint holds me steady as I take off my socks and trainers, and he takes his off too. The sand is warm under our toes and the sea breeze gives us goose pimples on our skin. I want to remember this moment forever.

'Let's take a picture,' I say.

We put our stuff down and Saint stands behind me, putting his arms round my waist, and my heart begins to race. I angle the camera so it can capture only us against the stunning background. We look like the cutest couple ever.

'Love it,' I say and, as I turn back to him, Saint's hands are still round me.

I catch my breath as he gazes at me, and this gorgeous backdrop is nothing compared to Saint. I stand on tiptoes and wrap my arms round his neck. His hair brushes against my skin, my breathing is fast with anticipation. His eyes search mine, wanting to know if it's okay. If I think of a perfect moment for a first kiss, this is it. I tilt my head slightly to the side and lean forward ...

When our lips finally touch, warm and soft and perfect, sparks tingle my skin and I feel like I'm floating. Our lips move in unison as we start to grow familiar with each other's touch. His tongue meets mine and I pull him even closer, his body clinging to mine. I lose track of how long we kiss, it feels like hours. When we pull apart, my lips are already puckering up wanting more.

The perfect first kiss.

We grin at each other and Saint pulls me into a tight hug, his face nestled against my neck, and over his shoulder I see an outraged Jayden.

THIRTY-THREE

'Oh no!' I hiss and gently push Saint off me.

He frowns and follows my gaze. His frown gets even deeper when he's notices how pissed Jayden is.

'Hey, I thought you left,' Saint says.

Jayden clenches his fists. 'Are you for real? *You* and *her*?'

This can't be happening. How did Jayden even know that we were down here on the beach? Did he follow us? Was he spying on our date?

Saint steps away from me and looks from me to Jayden. 'Yeah,' he says slowly. 'What's the problem?'

Jayden laughs harshly, no humour in his voice. 'Eva, how are you here kissing my cousin, when me and you are together?'

Saint's eyes flash dangerously at me. 'What? You're with Jayden?'

'Well … no, we were never together.' Which is true, although not the whole truth. 'We liked each other before, but nothing ever happened.'

'So this is why you started acting all off with me?' Jayden asks, charging towards me.

Saint steps in front, blocking him.

'What you doing, man?' Jayden yells, fury in his eyes.

'Don't step to her like that, J,' Saint says, and Jayden moves closer, so they're face to face.

'Guys, please!' I beg, looking around for assistance, but the beach seems to be deserted now.

'Me and her had a blow out just the other day. She was still on me,' Jayden argues.

'She's never mentioned you, cuz,' Saint says.

Jayden's nostrils flare. 'You calling me a liar?'

Saint glares at him. 'Yeah.'

Before I know it, Jayden pushes Saint hard and he stumbles back into me, knocking me to the sand.

'Eva!' Saint cries.

'It's okay,' I say quickly. 'Jayden, can you stop?'

'Are you for real?' he shouts, and I flinch. 'Acting like some hoe. Coming between me and—'

But whatever else Jayden was going to say is interrupted by Saint, who punches him so hard across the face that Jayden goes flying.

'Stop!' I scream, as Jayden lands on his bum, hitting the sand with a hard thud.

Someone is running at us, and I quickly try and get to my feet.

'Call her that again and see what happens!' Saint yells. Jayden sits holding his jaw.

I stand in between them with my arms out. 'Stop. Fighting. Please!'

Jayden scrambles to his feet and they glare at each other. I have no idea what to do and how to make this stop.

'Jayden!'

Logan runs towards us and pulls Jayden back by his arm. 'Allow it, man. Those two – it's not even real.'

I freeze.

'What?' Jayden snaps. 'What you saying, man?'

'It's a dare. She's doing this to get money to fix her dad's car. Eva don't even like Saint like that.'

And suddenly it's like everything is moving in slow motion. Jayden and Saint both look at Logan, confused; Logan is pointing at me; but all I can hear is a buzzing in my ears, a buzzing that won't stop, that's getting louder and louder. My chest feels tight, everything looks fuzzy, like I'm about to pass out.

Jayden's eyes widen as he looks back at me, but it's Saint's expression that hits me the hardest. Saint's head drops to his chest and he squeezes his eyes shut like the words are too painful to hear. Watching him makes every bit of my heart break into a million pieces.

'Is that true, Eva?' he asks, so softly, his face a mixture of hurt and shock and disbelief all in one.

'I ... no ... well, yes – But I ended it ... because I like you *so* much. I swear, Saint, this – all of this, you and me – it's all real.' Tears course down my face before I can stop them. 'Please, Saint. I'm telling the truth.'

Logan scoffs. 'Nah. She's a hustler, man, and she ain't worth you two fighting like this.'

'Shut up, Logan!' I scream, and Logan scoffs again in response.

'This was a dare?' Jayden shakes his head. 'Are you for real?'

'I'm sorry.'

Saint can't look at me. I reach for his hand and he opens his eyes, steps away from me with a look of pure disgust on his face. He doesn't have to say anything for me to know that this is all over and he wants nothing more to do with me. I want to tell him how much he means to me and I never meant for this to happen, but I can barely see through my tears.

Without another word Saint storms off, not looking back. Jayden looks me up and down and kisses his teeth. Then he turns on his heel and follows Saint up the beach.

Logan smirks at me. 'He was always going to find out,' he says. Then he just shrugs, like he hasn't just thrown a bomb, and walks off.

I'm crying so hard that I'm struggling to breathe. I lean over, with my hands on my thighs, and snot drips from my nose, my tears stinging my eyes. I've ruined everything.

I sit on the sand, my knees pressed to my chest, hugging myself, looking out to sea. My throat feels raw, my eyes hurt and I'm exhausted. I know I need to head back but my body doesn't move. Saint's face keeps playing over and over again in my head. I ruined the one good thing I had going. Right now I hate myself more than he does. My phone keeps buzzing in

229

my pocket, but I don't take it out. Logan's smirk. He'd been waiting to say his pathetic little speech, and he enjoyed seeing everything go up in flames. I fucking hate him. Oyin promised me he wouldn't say anything.

'Eva?' I look up and Benji waves his phone at me. 'Where's your phone? I've been calling you.'

'Sorry.' My voice comes out croaky and I cough to clear it. 'Where's Saint?'

'He's in the car.' Benji waits a beat. 'Did something happen? He looked really upset.'

He didn't tell on me. Even now, he's being the bigger person.

'I think I should get the train,' I say, standing up and dusting the sand off me.

'Don't be silly.' Benji picks up the picnic basket and hands me my trainers. 'Let's head back.'

I'm nervous about facing him again. Together, Benji and I walk back in silence. I can feel him glancing at me, but he doesn't ask me anything else.

Saint is sitting in the front passenger seat of the car and I wish he would look at me, but he doesn't. Benji puts the stuff in the boot and I get into the back by myself.

'Today was good,' Benji says cheerfully, but his smile wavers when neither I nor Saint respond. 'Oh, Eva, this is for you.' He hands me a brown envelope. 'Your money for the week and the contact for Dove's brother, for your dad's car.'

Saint scoffs and gazes out of the window. I wish Benji had given this to me in private. Now it's just reminded Saint of what's happened. I got with him for the money.

Benji looks at him and then at me.

'Thank you,' I say quietly.

'Any music requests?' Benji asks but he's met with stony silence. 'Last chance, or it's comic book podcasts for the next few hours.' He chuckles to himself, but it quickly trails off when we don't react.

Benji puts on the podcast, starts the car, and we make the long journey back home.

THIRTY-FOUR

It's dark travelling back to London and Saint and I don't say a word the whole time. I will myself to sleep so I can wake up once we're back, but I don't manage to. I should edit the videos and post them on TikTok, but I can't bring myself to look at them, so I spend the journey staring out of the window, sick to my stomach that I put Saint through this.

We pull up outside my house and I'm relieved to be home.

Benji turns to me. 'Thanks again for today, Eva.'

'Thanks, Benji. I'll post everything on TikTok tomorrow, if that's okay.'

'No problem. Have a good evening.'

I hesitate, not sure if I should say anything to Saint. He's looking down at his phone not paying attention to me.

'Goodnight,' I say and climb out of the car. I watch them drive off. Is that the last time I'll see Saint? My job was linked to the gamer event, and that's now over. The idea of not spending any more time with him makes me start crying all over again.

232

I wipe my eyes, trying to pull myself together and look reasonable as I go into the house. Dami and Amara's laughter carries from the living room into the hallway. I take a deep breath and peep round the door.

'Hey,' I say.

'Eva!' Amara pauses the TV.

'How did it go?' Dami asks.

I sniff. 'Yeah, it was good. I'm going to rest.'

Dami frowns. 'You okay? Are you ill?'

'No,' I say, but it comes out high-pitched and I burst out crying. Again.

Amara hurries over to me, enveloping me in a tight hug. Dami uncurls himself from the couch and hovers behind her.

'Did something happen? Did someone hurt you?' he asks.

I shake my head.

'It's okay,' Amara says, rubbing my back. 'We'll have a chat later?'

I wipe my nose with the back of my hand and nod.

Dami comes over and places his rough hand on my forehead. 'You're not warm. What's going on?'

'Babe, leave it,' Amara says firmly. 'Eva needs to sleep. Can't you see she's exhausted?'

Dami looks like he wants to say more, but he eventually nods. Amara squeezes my arm and I've never been more thankful to her. I head upstairs and shut my door, sitting on the floor with my head in my hands. Yum-Yum rubs his face against my leg and purrs, before settling himself beside me, his ginger fur tickling my skin.

Dami and Amara's voices travel up the stairs and I hear my name. I don't want anyone to bother me, so I take off my clothes, put on a T-shirt and get into bed, where my tears leak into the pillow.

I don't leave my bed for three days.

My door opens and closes multiple times as Dami and Amara come in to check on me. I know I'm worrying them as I can hear snatches of their conversations from downstairs.

'She hasn't eaten or taken a shower,' Dami says. 'I'm gonna have to call Grandma.'

'Just give her time,' Amara says.

'Three days, Amara!' Dami shouts. 'Something is really wrong.'

I sit up in bed, hating that they're arguing over me. I'm sticky, sweaty, smelly and hungry, but it's like I've got no energy to do anything. Shit. I forgot to post the footage from the gamer event. What I don't need is another person being mad at me. I step over my sandy beach clothes abandoned on the floor and take my phone out of my bag.

Multiple missed calls from my friends: the Bad Bitches chat has forty unread messages. Nothing from Saint, but there's a text from Jayden and I hesitate whether to open it. I can see part of it and as soon as I read *I should have known you were a bitch* I press delete.

I take a deep breath and open the videos. It's like taking a bullet. Turns out Saint is somehow in all of them and clearly, subconsciously, I wanted to watch him. I miss his slow, lazy walk and the way he teases me. I miss him so much. All I want to do is call him, but I can't forget that look he gave me at the beach. I'm scared I'll make him dislike me even more if I bother him.

It's hard to edit the videos when he's in so many shots, but I think about Benji, who hasn't even pressured me yet about posting and I don't want to take advantage. I post all the content and then, because I obviously like to torture myself, I look at the pictures Saint and I took of us together in the green room and at the beach. We were so happy. And I fucked it all up. My phone flashes low battery and, as I cross the room to charge it, I catch myself in the mirror. My braids are in a knotty mess and I have days-old tear-stained mascara marks on my cheeks. I not only feel dirty, I look it too.

There's a gentle knock at my door.

'Eva?' Amara calls.

'Come in,' I say, and if she's alarmed at the sight of me, she doesn't react. She's carrying a bowl of rice and stew with plantain.

'Dami's gone to work. You've got to eat, babe,' she says.

I step aside and she hands me the bowl before she opens all my windows, letting the fresh air in. Then she gathers up all my dirty clothes and puts them in my wash basket. The rice and stew is flavoursome and delicious, the plantain sweet, and my stomach rumbles as I eat.

'Better?' Amara asks, and I nod. 'There's more downstairs if you're still hungry.'

She waits patiently as I eat and once I'm done she takes the bowl from me and puts it on the desk. She sits down beside me on the bed.

'I smell,' I warn her.

'Not too bad,' she teases. 'Are you feeling better?'

I shake my head. 'I've really messed up, Amara.' I thought I had used up all my tears, but they start to race down my face again and I aggressively wipe them away.

Amara holds my hand. 'Whatever you tell me, Eva, it will stay between us, okay?' She doesn't break eye contact and I know I can trust her. She still hasn't told Dami that Saint came round.

'Okay.' I take a deep breath and tell her everything, starting with Jayden, then the car window breaking, the dare . . . I tell her about Saint, about Oyin and Logan, and the beach. The only thing I keep back from her is my uni plan because that might just be too much for one outburst.

Amara doesn't interrupt me.

'Wow,' she says once I'm done. 'Have you spoken to Saint at all since?'

'No. And he hasn't reached out either. Not that I can blame him.'

'Your friends? Have you told them?'

I shake my head. 'They've been messaging. I don't know if they know what happened though.'

'Right. And this Logan guy, do you think maybe he's been wanting to sabotage you since you turned him down?'

I frown. Surely not. That would be ridiculous for Logan to

hold onto a no that happened at the beginning of college. But then, I have caught him staring at me. And that smirk on the beach after he told Saint and Jayden the truth ...

'I don't know ...'

'Hmmm. Either way he sounds like a dickhead. First things first, we have to sort out this car. Your parents are back on Wednesday, right? How much money do you have?'

'I think sixty pounds. Hold on –' I get off the bed and grab the brown envelope that Benji gave me and count it out, surprised to find he's paid me more than I was expecting – 'and with this and my birthday money it's more around a hundred and twenty.' I hand all the money over together with the business card with Dove's brother's contact. 'Apparently, he'll give me a discount. I searched online and the repair should cost around four hundred.'

'Cool. I'll call them. And I'll top up this money and I'll sort out the car.'

'No, Amara, I can't ask you to do that.'

'You didn't ask!' Amara says. 'I'll sort it out, okay?'

'I'll pay you back. I promise.'

Amara waves her hand as if to say *It's all good*. 'What you need to do is take a shower, talk to your friends and think of a way to apologize to Saint.' She stands up. 'Look, Eva, I won't lie, you have done some dumb things this summer.'

Okay, I deserve that, but it still hurts.

'But I look at you like a little sister and I've got your back, okay?'

'You do?' I ask, surprised.

'Of course!' Amara narrows her eyes. 'You don't look at me like a big sis?'

To be honest, no. It took me a while to warm to Amara and I sometimes felt she got really sensitive whenever Dami and I teased each other or reminisced about something and she would be left out. But I've felt comfortable opening up to her recently, more so than I have with Dami. Also, her mothering me the last few days has been nice, especially because she doesn't breathe down my neck like my own mother does.

'There's no denying that you meant well,' Amara continues. 'And anyone with a brain can see how sorry you are. Now you need to show Saint that. I could see how much he likes you. You just need to get him to listen.'

'How, though?' I ask.

'I don't know. You know him better than me. Just think about it.'

'Okay. Thank you, Amara. I really do appreciate you.'

She beams at me, and I can tell how much my words mean to her. Maybe she's right. Maybe I just need to get Saint to know how sorry I am. Somehow.

'Oh.' Amara pauses at the door. 'Your grandma is on her way to check on you. Dami called her in a panic. I'll probably be in Dami's room when she comes.'

Grandma has made it very clear that she doesn't think Amara is a good fit for Dami, but if Grandma could only see the Amara I know, she would definitely change her mind.

'I'll put in a good word for you, I promise,' I say, and Amara smiles.

Once she's gone, I scan the messages from my girls and it's clear they know some of it. Oyin had an argument with Logan and wants to meet me. Everyone is asking if I'm okay and wants to know what's going on with Saint, so I type:

> Sorry for going AWOL. Can you lot come round tonight pls? I need your help.

THIRTY-FIVE

Grandma grabs me in a big hug when she sees me and pats my back. She's always heavy-handed so it kind of hurts, but I don't say anything. I'm feeling more human now that I've showered, brushed my teeth, fixed my hair and changed my clothes. My sweaty bed sheets are in the wash. All my friends responded and are going to come by this evening, but Oyin messaged me separately and asked to meet earlier – just us two. I've agreed, but in truth I'm nervous about it.

'How are you, sugar?' Grandma asks, searching my face. 'Dami said you were sick.'

'No, Grandma, I just … got myself into a situation, but Amara helped me with it.'

'Amara?' Grandma says, narrowing her eyes suspiciously.

'Yes, Amara.' I gesture to a kitchen chair and Grandma sits down, with a big sigh as she stretches out her legs. I sit opposite her.

'I brought you some pepper soup because I thought you couldn't leave your bed. What happened?'

I hesitate, not sure how much to tell her.

'Is it about the blanket on your father's broken car?'

'Grandma!' I exclaim. 'You knew the window was broken?'

'Of course I did! You think I believed that you had covered it because of the sun?' Grandma laughs loudly, showing off the gap in her teeth. 'When are you going to fix it?'

'Soon – Amara is sorting it.'

'Eh?' Grandma pauses, then nods her head approvingly. 'She just needs to learn to cook, that girl, and she might be okay.'

I laugh. 'She can cook,' I say, remembering the fish tacos Amara made for me and Saint. That pang of hurt flashes across my chest when I think of him. 'And she's good for Dami. I really like her. She's kind of like the big sister I never had.'

Grandma shrugs. 'If you like her, then she is okay.'

I hope this means she'll stop pushing the church girl on Dami, but I won't hold my breath.

'And? Something else is bothering you.' Grandma points her finger at me. 'I can tell.'

I cannot go into the whole Saint situation with Grandma. The last thing I need is her telling my parents I have a boyfriend or something stupid.

'It's about uni. I don't . . . I'm not sure about it.'

'Ah! You don't want to be a lawyer?' Grandma exclaims, throwing her hands in the air. 'What will you do? You want to be poor? On the streets?'

'Grandma, please! I'm not sure yet,' I say honestly. 'And moving to Nottingham, I don't think it's the right thing for me to do – not right now anyway.'

Grandma is quiet, which is unusual for her, and the longer she doesn't speak the more nervous I get. I can't tell from her expression if she's mad or disappointed, and I would hate if she was either.

'Eva,' Grandma begins, 'do you know that I sat right here with Dami when he told me he wanted to drop out of university?'

'Really?' I can't hide my surprise. I had no idea that Dami spoke to Grandma.

'And I'll tell you what I told him. I'm not happy about it, but it is your life. Pray, ask God for guidance and do what you think is best.'

I wait for her to add a 'but' which doesn't come. Is Grandma really saying she supports me not going to university?

'Now, your parents will have something different to say.' Grandma laughs and my heart sinks. 'But I forced your father to go to university even though he said he wasn't sure.'

'Dad didn't want to go?'

Grandma shakes her head. 'I was very stern with him and said he must go, he wouldn't be successful without it. That was the mentality then, but things are different now. It's okay to take time to think. But . . .'

There it is, I think, *the 'but' I was expecting.*

'But you cannot be home just sleeping and doing silly things. You need a plan. You have to work, maybe go to another country. This is not the time for you to go to the disco.'

I laugh. 'It's called a club, Grandma.'

She has a point though. If I take a gap year, what do I want to achieve? How am I going to fill my time? I haven't even checked yet how to defer my place at uni. There's still a lot I need to think about, but just talking about it with Grandma has made me feel a whole lot better.

'Thanks, Grandma.' I kiss her cheek and she pats my arm. 'What are your plans today?'

'I was going to make some pounded yam, meat stew and egusi stew for your dinner.'

'Mmmm, yes please.' I'm about to leave the kitchen when an idea hits me. 'Amara's upstairs and she said she would like to learn how to cook the traditional dishes.'

'She is upstairs?' Grandma raises her eyebrows so high they disappear into her wig. 'The English girl wants to cook my food?'

'Grandma!'

'And you don't think *you* should learn?'

I sigh. 'How about you teach both of us, then? It would be nice.'

Grandma shrugs. 'Okay.'

'I'll call her.' I take the stairs two at a time and knock on Dami's door. Amara is on the carpeted floor sorting out her make-up.

'Hey,' she says. 'Everything okay?'

'Grandma wants to teach us how to make some traditional food. You in?'

Amara points at herself. 'She wants me?'

I grin. 'Yes!'

'Oh shit.' She stands up and looks down at her short, low-cut dress. 'Okay. Let me change and I'll be right down. What should I wear? I don't want to offend her.'

I already know Grandma will look Amara up and down with a critical eye, trying to find any reason to suggest that she's not good enough for her only grandson.

'I'll help you look,' I offer.

Cooking with Grandma and Amara is more fun than I thought. Amara plays Fela Kuti, who was my grandad's favourite artist, and the joy that appears on Grandma's face is priceless. She seems pleased with Amara, who is legit working up a sweat as she stirs and stirs the pounded yam, although I'm criticized for not stirring hard enough and Grandma prods my skinny arm. When Amara finally stops to take a breath, Grandma inspects the pot and I hold my breath in anticipation. Grandma takes a bit of the pounded yam and tastes it.

'This is good.' She smiles at Amara. 'Well done.'

'Thank you, Aunty,' Amara says, and when Grandma turns away from her, Amara punches the air.

Now it's my turn.

'Eva. Ah ah!' Grandma scolds. 'What is this? It's meant to get thicker and smoother.'

'My arm hurts,' I moan, and Grandma rolls her eyes. She nudges me out of the way with her hip, adding more yam powder and water, and I watch happily from the sidelines.

THIRTY-SIX

The pounded yam and stew is as delicious and filling as ever. Amara did a great job and I can tell Grandma is impressed with her. When we sit down to eat I know Grandma slyly thinks Amara will pick up a knife and fork, but she eats with her hands like the rest of us. I knew Grandma just had to give her a chance, and it's clear to everyone how much Amara cares about our family and I'm glad Grandma can finally see that.

Once Dami gets home and Amara fills him in on the updates about Dad's car, Dami insists that Amara is definitely not going to use her money. He offers to put some of his savings towards paying for the rest of it, provided I pay him back every last penny. We're taking the car in on Monday to get it fixed. Words can't even express how thankful I am that Dami and Amara have sorted it. At least that's one less thing in my life that isn't shit.

In the evening, Amara and Dami go out for dinner and Grandma has already left for bible study, so I tidy up the living room, only stopping when the doorbell rings.

Oyin looks as nervous as I feel when I see her on the doorstep in a black maxi dress. I haven't been outside for several days and the soft breeze and heat feel nice on my skin.

'Hey,' I say stepping to the side, not ready just yet to greet her with a hug.

'Hi, Eva.' Oyin walks into the hallway, not attempting to hug either. 'How are you?'

I lead her to the living room and sit on the couch. 'Could be better. You?'

She sits down opposite me and sighs. 'I ended things with Logan.'

'What?' I definitely was not expecting that. 'You serious?'

Oyin nods. 'I swear, Eva, I didn't mean to tell him about the dare. It just happened and I regretted it as soon as it came out. He promised me he wouldn't say anything and I trusted him.'

'Did you know he was going to Bournemouth?'

'I didn't, not until you wrote it in the group chat. But I didn't want you lot to know that I hadn't known he was going.' Oyin fiddles with the straps on her bag, avoiding my eyes. 'I called him, but he didn't pick up. I texted him to keep it quiet.'

'Did he respond?' I ask.

'No. I kept messaging him and he wasn't responding. Even with that, I didn't think he would say it.'

'But he tried to say it already at Sansa's house,' I argue.

'Yeah, but he was drinking alcohol earlier that day so he was tipsy – not like that's an excuse,' she adds quickly when I open my mouth to protest. 'I'm just really sorry, Eva. Logan is a dick, but I was the idiot for trusting him.'

'Thanks for apologizing. Why didn't you want us to know that you had no clue he was coming to the Retro Gaming event?'

'Because of Sharisha and Fatima. I didn't want to give them more to say. After the blowout at the sleepover, I started thinking maybe he doesn't really want me. Maybe I was always just second best to you.' Oyin's voice catches at the end and I hurry over to sit next to her.

'Don't cry, Oyin.'

'It's just hay fever,' she lies as her eyes water. I put my arm round her. 'I know he asked you out before and yes, that kinda bothered me, but when Logan was with me, he seemed all about me. But to be honest, it was always in the back of my mind. Like, if you wanted him, would he go?'

'Oyin.' I rub her arm. 'You are so gorgeous, and any guy is lucky to have you. Trust me, I don't fancy Logan.' I don't even like him as a person, but I don't say that out loud.

'But I don't feel that in here.' She presses on her chest. 'I was even jealous of you that the boys labelled you "the pretty one". And you were so upset about it. I kept thinking I would love to have that. Every guy I like never likes me back or it takes them ages to see me as anything attractive and it's ... exhausting.'

I had no idea that Oyin felt like this. To me, Oyin is always confident and self-assured. I know we all have our insecurities, but I didn't think she thought guys weren't attracted to her.

'Well, I'm here to remind you that you're a queen and only deserve the best,' I say. 'You seemed different with Logan, not entirely yourself. Trust me, babe, you're going to get so much

247

better than him and it will be with someone that you can trust and depend on because that's what you deserve.'

Her bottom lip wobbles dangerously. 'Thank you, Eva,' she says as she reaches out to me, and this time we do hug. It feels good to have my friend back.

I don't know how long we stay like that, but when the doorbell rings, I apologetically pull away.

'Does it look like I've been crying?' Oyin asks, wiping her eyes.

'No, you look great. And don't feel like you have to tell the others what you told me if you don't feel ready. I won't say a word.'

Oyin looks relieved and smiles. 'Thanks, girl.'

Sharisha, Fatima and Sansa are on the doorstep with a shopping bag that they hand to me.

'What is this?' I peer inside and laugh. There's Ben & Jerry's Cookie Dough, three different types of gossip magazines, and a ridiculous amount of face masks and bubble bath. 'Thank you, girls!'

'I'm so sorry, Eva,' Sansa says, hugging me tight. 'I know how much you liked him.'

I shrug in response, not knowing what to say. They follow me to the living room and the atmosphere tenses when they see Oyin. Sharisha sits on the other end of the room, far away from her. Knowing that there's one way to put everyone in a better mood, I grab five spoons from the kitchen, hand them out and open the ice cream.

'Dig in!' I announce.

'We got that for you,' Fatima protests.

'And I want to share it with you all. Look, I know things were left in a shit place at Sansa's and we all said some harsh things.' Sharisha crosses her arms over her chest in response. 'But thank you all for showing up for me.' I sigh. 'So, shall I tell you what happened with Saint?'

My friends glance at each other.

'I mean, if you're okay to?' Sharisha asks softly, and the others murmur in agreement.

I nod. For some reason it's harder telling my friends than it was telling Amara. Maybe because Amara was more detached from the whole thing, whereas this whole situation started at Carnival, so all of us here are involved.

'So now Jayden wants to make a move!' Sansa tuts. 'What's he been doing for the past two years?'

'Exactly!' Sharisha replies. 'And that fucking Logan—'

'Is an arsehole and I'm done with him,' Oyin announces, and the girls look at her in surprise.

'Seriously?' Fatima asks and Oyin nods.

'And, Eva,' Oyin says, 'I'm sorry that I didn't just offer you the money for the car. At the time I did think the dare would be a bit of fun, but this whole thing just went completely left. I'm so glad that the car is being sorted without your parents knowing.'

'Thanks, Oyin, but you were right: I didn't have to accept the dare,' I say.

That's the hardest thing about all of this. I wasn't forced into it, I *chose* to manipulate Saint. And now I've hurt him in a way that I don't know is forgivable.

'I had no idea that you fell for him,' Oyin says. She squeezes my hand. 'Have you spoken to him?'

I shake my head. 'I miss him so much and I wish I could just tell him how sorry I am. Everything that I feel about him is real and I've never felt like this about a guy. But what am I meant to do? I can't just go to the comic book shop and bother him at work. I've really messed this up.'

Oyin's looking steadily at me, a slight frown on her face. 'So, you still owe me a dare, right?'

Sansa's spoon clatters to the floor. 'You're not serious?'

Sharisha kisses her teeth. 'This girl, man, I swear . . .'

Fatima's shaking her head in disappointment.

'You owe me a dare,' Oyin repeats, still looking straight at me.

Has she just forgotten our heart-to-heart that literally happened moments ago? Why the hell is she bringing this up? I'm so ready to cuss her out, when she says, 'I dare you to fight for Saint and get him back.'

There's a stunned silence. Sharisha jerks her head back in surprise and Sansa gasps.

'You know what,' Fatima starts and we all stare at her, but she's only got eyes for Oyin. 'That's the best dare so far.'

Oyin smiles. 'I think so too.'

'B-but . . . how?' I've been racking my brain trying to think how I can talk to Saint but I haven't got any answers.

'Has he not got another spoken word event coming up? Maybe you can go to that?' Oyin suggests. 'Ooh, maybe you can perform something to him?'

That makes us laugh and whatever tension is in the room is now calmer. Oyin's got a point. It *would* be easier to approach Saint at an event. At least that way there'd be less chance of it becoming a scene. Then I remember—

'He's going Comic-Con tomorrow!' I practically shout in excitement. 'Oh shit, where is it again?' I tap my thigh as I try to remember. 'Olympia.'

'Perfect! You can go and talk to him.' Sansa grins.

Fatima frowns. 'Err, have you ever seen Comic-Con? There's thousands of people there. You'll never find him.'

And all the hope I had shrivels up.

'Way to kill the mood, Fatima.' Sharisha rolls her eyes. 'Is he going in cosplay? That can help narrow it down.'

'Yes! He's going to be Goku Black but I don't know what that character looks like.'

'Already on it.' A few seconds later, Oyin shows us a picture of Goku, an anime character with black spiky hair, in a long-sleeved black top with a type of grey vest over it and a red sash round the waist, and what looks like black hareem pants. 'I don't think he would be able to put on a wig with all the hair he's got,' she adds.

There will probably be hundreds of people in this same outfit, but I have to try and find Saint.

'I'm gonna go,' I declare.

'I'll come with you,' Sharisha says.

'And me,' Sansa echoes.

'Me too,' Fatima says.

'I'm buying us tickets,' Oyin says, and she smiles sheepishly. 'The least I can do.'

My heart swells with love for my friends and how they've all come through for me.

'What are we going to wear though?' Sansa says. 'Don't we need to dress up too?'

We fall quiet thinking but I come up blank. A meow comes from out in the hall.

'Sorry, guys, let me just check on Yum-Yum.'

My cat is staring at me with his big green eyes and, when I get closer, he shoots up the stairs. This usually means he wants or needs something, so I follow him up to my bedroom and he goes straight to my dresser, where my birthday cards are still set out. One of his toys, the little ball with the bell inside it, is stuck underneath. I crouch down, pull it out and throw it to the other side of the room, where Yum-Yum runs after it. As I stand up, the card Saint made me catches my eye – and suddenly the idea comes to me and I know exactly what we should wear. Saint will definitely pay attention to me when he sees me at Comic-Con.

THIRTY-SEVEN

Five girls walking down the street in full carnival costume literally stops the traffic. The line for Comic-Con goes all the way down the outside of the building, and maybe it's because we're not dressed as comic book characters and our costumes are so bright and our feathers are massive and colourful . . . but everyone is looking at us. I scan the line trying to see if Saint is there, but no luck.

'Why did this feel so normal in Carnival and now all I want to do is cover up?' Fatima says, hugging herself.

I can't lie, I do feel pretty exposed, but it's not like any of us had time to get a whole new costume.

'Thanks again, girls,' I say. 'As soon as we find Saint we can go.'

'Do you know what we didn't think about?' Sharisha says. 'What if Saint isn't here? What if he changed his mind?'

We all look at each other with the same alarmed expressions It didn't even cross my mind! I could cry at the idea that I'm so close to talking to him.

'Wait – I'll call his shop,' Sansa suggests. 'I can ask for Saint.'

'Good idea,' I say. I give Sansa the store number and she dials it.

'Hello? Yes, I'm wondering if I can speak to one of your workers ... yes, that's right – Saint ... Oh, really? ... Of course ... no problem. Thank you!' She hangs up and grins. 'He's here.'

'Phew!' I place my hand on my heart and it's racing. I've never wanted anything more than getting back on good terms with Saint. Now I'm praying that by the time we finally make it inside, he won't already have left through the exit on the other side of the venue.

'What's the plan when we see him?' Oyin asks. 'Are we blocking him?'

'Blocking him?' Sharisha exclaims, and Oyin gives her a look. They still haven't spoken about what happened at Sansa's party, but I'm grateful that they're at least trying with each other in order to help me.

'I can't force him to talk to me,' I say.

'Oh yes we can,' Fatima says. 'We did *not* do all of this for him to just air you.'

I bite my lip. What if Saint does storm past me? Yells at me in front of everyone? If he gives me that disgusted look that he did on the beach, I legit will have a breakdown. I take a deep breath. *Stop it, Eva, think positive thoughts*, I say to myself.

We eventually get to the front of the line and Oyin shows our tickets to security. We have to walk through a long corridor where there are some people in normal clothes and I wish I'd thought to check. I just assumed everyone had to come in cosplay. Once we get inside the venue, I gasp. It's like the gamer day on steroids. There are three floors and massive exhibitions of everything from comic books to TV shows to merch, and there are lots of hallways off the main space suggesting that there are even more rooms. It's also completely rammed.

'Damn!' Fatima whistles. 'This is crazy.'

A couple of kids run past us dressed as Black Panther.

'Can I have one please?' Sansa asks a girl in a black Comic-Con T-shirt, who hands her a programme and a map. 'Okay, let's see . . . Hmmm, there's a lot going on.'

That's an understatement. There is too much going on. There are celebrity signings from actors and authors, panel talks and every room is jam packed with different things to do. How the hell am I meant to find Saint in all of this?

'Do you have any idea what he would come here to do?' Sansa asks.

I try to think, but I can't recall him saying anything significant. He could easily be at the graphic novel stand or Marvel HQ. There's a whole section dedicated to anime, and he is going as Goku Black . . . unless he changed his mind.

'I have no idea,' I confess. Where do we even start?

'Let me see this.' Oyin takes the map off Sansa and scans it. 'Right, we're here, in this hall.' She points at the map. 'It's busy but I reckon that, if we're just looking, we can do this whole room in maybe fifteen minutes. We'll need to split up though, so some of us can do the pathway on the left, someone else the centre and then someone does the right. Once we get to the end of the hall, come back down the same way, just in case we missed him. Let's meet back here and then we'll try another room.'

I'm so grateful that someone's taken charge of this because I'm at a loss. I'm desperate to find Saint in this chaos and my head hasn't stopped swivelling.

'And if you see Saint, put an "S" in the group chat and stall him,' Oyin adds.

'Stall him how?' Sansa asks nervously.

Oyin shrugs. 'Just say it's your first time here. Ask for tips but do not mention that Eva is here.' Oyin glances at me. 'Is that okay?'

I nod. I don't want Saint to run a mile knowing that I'm looking for him.

Because Oyin hasn't really cleared the air with anyone but me, I decide to partner up with her and take the middle lane, Sharisha goes by herself to the right, and Sansa and Fatima go together to the left.

'Excuse me, excuse me,' I say, trying to get past without my feathers getting destroyed.

'I had no idea this was a whole thing,' Oyin says. 'It's like another world, isn't it?'

'I'm kinda used to it because of working at Harley's World of Comics and the gamer event . . . wait!' I stop mid-walk and Oying bumps into me, but I barely notice because I swear that I just saw Saint. I keep staring, praying that he'll look at me, but when the guy eventually turns round, it's not him.

256

'We'll find him,' Oyin says reassuringly and I nod, even though I don't fully believe it.

We get to the end of the aisle and meet the others, who've had no luck either, so we head back through the hall – but still no sign of Saint.

'I think we should split up and check the rooms off to the side.' Oyin opens up the map again. 'Let's go with the areas that we think Saint will be interested in. Give us the top five, Eva.'

'Right, okay . . . err . . . comic books, anime, *Dragon Ball Z*, the gaming section and . . . oh, *Game of Thrones*.'

Sharisha frowns. 'Are you sure you two had things to talk about?'

I playfully nudge her. 'You know I love *Thrones* and I got into the other stuff. Saint made it all seem so . . . I dunno . . . fun.'

'She *really* likes him,' Fatima says, dragging out the 'really', which makes us all laugh. 'Okay, girl, let's get your man. I'll take comic books.'

'Anime,' Sharisha says.

'I guess I'll do *Dragon Ball Z*,' Oyin says.

'Gaming section,' Sansa says.

Which leaves me with *Game of Thrones*. There are a few actors here from the show so maybe he went to get something signed. We all take a picture on our phones of the programme and the map.

'Keep an eye on the group chat,' I remind them and they nod. 'See you in a bit.'

I have to head up to the second floor which is where the signings are. There's a group of people in the Ghostface mask from the *Scream* movies and when they see me staring, they wave their fake knives at me. I wave back politely.

When I get to the right place for the signings, I can see from the door that the actors are seated all the way up at the front of the hall and the long lines of fans stretch out across the room. I'm trying to see which actors they are when one of the stewards approaches me.

'Have you got a ticket?'

'Yeah.' Oh, shoot, Oyin has my ticket on her phone. 'My friend has it. Do I need to show you my ticket even though I'm inside?'

'No, you need a separate ticket for the signings.' She pats the stand next to her that says PLEASE HAVE YOUR TICKET READY. 'Who are you coming to see?'

'Oh ... err.' I glance at the programme on my phone and say the first name I see.

The girl nods. 'And maybe call your friend so they can show me the ticket?' Someone is waving for her attention. 'Hold on, I'll be right back,' she says before she goes to assist a group of people and I take that chance to slip into the room.

THIRTY-EIGHT

My costume is way too colourful to stand at the back and not get caught so I wander down the lines trying to see if I can spot Saint. I don't recognize the six actors. Maybe because they're not in their costumes. There are security people surrounding them and more stewards at the front of the queues checking tickets again.

I put on my friendliest smile as I wander around the room, hoping that no one will question what I'm doing. A woman who was taking pictures of the actors is marched out by a security guard gripping her arm and she's shouting, 'I couldn't afford a ticket!' Damn. Okay, that's what I need to avoid.

I scan up and down the lines but there's no sign of Saint. My phone beeps and I quickly look at it hoping there's been a sighting but it's just my mum telling us her plane time home. I have to wait several minutes for the steward at the door to be distracted again before I can get out of the room safely. The group chat is quiet and I can't help but feel deflated. Why did I think this was going to work? For all I know Saint could have already left – or maybe he hasn't even arrived yet.

'Sorry, excuse me?' A man and woman approach me with a camera. She has an Australian accent. 'Your costume is amazing. Can we take a picture?'

'Oh yeah, sure,' and I force a smile on my face and pose.

As they snap away, over their shoulder I see a mixed-raced guy in a black and grey top with a red sash round his waist. His thick hair is out and he's peering from left to right as he looks at the map in his hand. It's like my heart leaps out of my chest into my throat.

'Sorry, I need to . . .'

I don't even finish my sentence as I hurry towards Saint.

He hasn't seen me yet and he's still some distance in front of me. He's heading for the stairs that go up to the next floor and I'm pushing past people, trying not to lose him. I follow him up the stairs, my heart racing, palms sweating, praying that he'll give me a chance to speak. He heads into a room on the right but there are people in front of me also going in so I have to wait for a moment. At last I head inside – and bump right into Saint, who's just on his way back out of the room.

'I'm sorry – Eva?' Saint's eyes widen. 'What in the—'

'Hi, Saint!' I say brightly. 'What are you doing here?'

I was not meant to say that! The room he's in is actually a pop-up bookshop, heavy on the comic books.

'Well . . . err . . .' Saint is looking around, obviously thinking why wouldn't he be here. This is very much his domain. 'I wanted to buy something, but then remembered there was a stall downstairs that I want to check out first.' He waits a beat. 'And you?'

'Oh, I ... I wanted to get something for my brother,' I say without thinking.

An amused smile spreads across Saint's face. 'Your brother? Feel like we've had this chat before?'

I forgot that this is what I said to him the first time I came into Harley's World of Comics. *Smooth, Eva.*

'And you came dressed in your carnival outfit.' He looks me up and down, making me feel hot all over. 'I always liked this outfit.'

'Really?'

Saint shrugs, like he didn't just compliment me. So I look at him up and down, taking my time. He shakes his head but he's smiling.

'Made this outfit yourself?' I ask.

'No, I bought it. I have the wig too, but all the hair wasn't working.'

'You look good,' I say. He looks incredibly cute.

'Thanks,' he says. 'So do you.'

For a moment we're just staring at each other and it feels so easy and natural to be around him, to flirt with him, like nothing had even happened, but then memories of the beach flash in my mind and I wince.

'Saint, I actually came here to apologize to you. I'm so sorry for everything that happened.' He crosses his arms over his chest and doesn't respond. 'When Oyin dared me to do it,

261

it started from this stupid game of dares we'd been doing for months—'

'Was dancing on me at Carnival one of them?' he asks.

I hesitate, not wanting to add more salt to the wound. But lying hasn't done anything good for me, so I nod. I can't tell from his expression what he's thinking, but he gestures at me to carry on.

'So when my dad's car got damaged, Oyin dared me to get you to ask me out on a romantic date and if I passed the dare she would give me the money to fix the car. That was it. I could tell you weren't into me, but I had no other way of getting the money to fix it so I figured I would try.' I take a deep breath. 'But then we got closer and I saw who you are – smart, funny, kind, sweet … and being around you felt like the best thing ever. I started to fall for you.'

Saint uncrosses his arms.

'Most of our tastes are pretty different, but you invited me into your world and I didn't want to leave. I ended the dare before we went to Bournemouth because I knew by then that the way I felt about you was genuine and way stronger than just wanting to win the money for the stupid car.'

Saint frowns. 'Is that why you said no when I asked you out on a date?'

I nod.

'Oh. I thought maybe I read the signs wrong.'

'No, you really didn't.' I take a step forward and Saint doesn't move. 'I like you so much, Saint, and I know I need to earn your trust back. I'll do whatever it takes.'

'Oh, Eva.' Saint sighs and my heart drops. 'It's not like I don't believe you, because I do. I know you wouldn't come here dressed up if you weren't being earnest, but ... well, Jayden said you two were together.'

'We were never together,' I protest. 'Yes, me and Jayden liked each other but nothing has ever happened between us. Ever.'

'He said he was your first kiss,' Saint says uncertainly.

'No, he wasn't!'

I swear I'm going to kill Jayden.

'He said he came to your house not long ago,' Saint continues.

'He did, and my brother told him to go away. Jayden didn't come inside – and I've never kissed a guy before you. You're the only guy that's been invited to my house.'

'Really?' Saint slowly smiles and the butterflies that I thought were dormant are back. 'So, I was for real your first kiss?'

I nod again and, as soon as Saint grins, his cute dimples appear. I reach forward and take his hand and he lets me. My skin zaps with his touch.

'Do you think we can start again?' I ask.

Saint's thumb gently runs across my hand and my body comes alive. I know that I'll do anything to make us work. If he just gives me a chance.

'I don't know, Eva,' he says gently, and I have to bite down on my lip hard to stop myself from protesting. 'I really like you, and thank you for explaining and apologizing and for

263

coming here.' He takes a step back from me, dropping my hand. 'But this is a lot. I just need time to think.'

'Okay,' I say, even though I'm desperate to know how much time he needs. What are the chances of us trying again? I just want some hope that I haven't fucked everything up completely. I want to ask, but I'm so scared that he might say something I don't want to hear.

'I'm gonna head downstairs, but it was good seeing you, Eva,' he says, already walking off.

'You too,' I say, and he raises his hand in goodbye. I watch him go until I lose him in the crowd, and then the tears fall down my face.

I don't know how long I stand propped up outside the pop-up bookshop. A part of me was hoping that Saint would come back, but he doesn't. My phone has rung twice but I ignored it both times when I saw it wasn't Saint, but when Sharisha texts that she's worried I ring her back.

'Eva! We've been looking for you. Where are you?' she asks. I can barely hear with the noise from the bookshop.

'Third floor,' I say. 'I'll meet you by the stairs.'

'Okay, we're coming,' Sharisha says. 'Did you see Saint? We've looked everywhere and had no luck.'

'Yeah, I saw him.' My voice breaks at the end and I quickly press my lips together and look around, hoping that no one heard me. Everyone is too busy shopping to pay any attention to me.

'Oh, babe, are you okay? Hold on ... girls, it's this way ... sorry, we're almost there. So many damn people.'

I sniff and wipe under my eyes, praying I can control myself enough that I don't have a full breakdown in front of all these strangers. Even though I know my friends are coming, I hold the phone tight to my ear like it's a lifeline keeping me afloat.

'Do you see her?' Sharisha's voice calls and she's looking from left to right because I'm still in the corner, so I step out and her eyes widen. My friends hurry over to me at the same time as I burst into loud, noisy tears.

'Oh, Eva ... What happened?' Sansa asks as Sharisha grabs me into a tight hug. Everyone is staring at us and we must look a sight with our carnival costumes and me bawling my eyes out.

Sharisha pulls away, gripping my arms and looking me in the eyes. 'Should we get out of here?' she suggests, and I nod.

Oyin pays for a taxi to take us back to my house. On the way I tell them everything that happened in my chat with Saint.

'So now I don't know where we are. It's just ...' I shrug pathetically. I went there to get answers and I've left even more deflated and unsure of what to do.

'You can't wait around for a guy, Eva,' Fatima says gently. 'I know you like Saint, but who knows how long he needs? Plus, you're going to uni soon anyway.'

'I'm not,' I mumble, but they hear me.

'You're *not* going to uni?' Fatima asks.

I shake my head. 'I'm taking a gap year.'

Oyin gasps and I remember she had left Sansa's when I first mentioned this to the girls. 'What did your parents say?'

'I haven't told them yet. But I spoke to my grandma and she's supportive.'

'We've got your back, okay?' Sharisha grabs my hand. 'It's all going to work out. And you and Saint will figure it out.'

'But maybe I didn't fight for him enough,' I protest. There must be more I could have done to show him how much he means to me. Maybe I should have kept ringing him, pleaded with him to forgive me, instead of wallowing in my bed for days like some victim.

'Babe, you went to Comic-Con in your carnival outfit,' Oyin says. 'Trust me, that speaks volumes and I think Saint heard you. Just give him space, yeah?'

'Yeah, maybe you're right,' I say.

I gaze out of the taxi window at the traffic before closing my eyes and offering up a silent prayer: *Please, God, let me and Saint be okay again.*

THIRTY-NINE

'Looks as good as new,' the mechanic says, handing Dami the car keys. 'New window, fixed up any marks, and we hoovered up any remaining pieces of glass inside the car. Might want to get it washed though.'

'Thanks, man.' Dami shakes his hand. 'Lifesaver.'

Amara squeezes my shoulders and I smile gratefully.

'Eva, I swear if you do this again—' Dami begins.

'I won't. Promise.' I hold out my pinky and he eyes me suspiciously before clasping it with his own.

'At least it's sorted now,' Amara says. 'Let's go get the car washed and then tomorrow we need to go food shopping and stock up and clean the house properly so your parents aren't coming home to a shithole.'

'You mean *Eva* will be cleaning the house,' Dami adds.

'I'll do whatever,' I say, and Dami and Amara stare at me because I never offer to clean up.

'What's up with you?' Dami frowns.

I shrug. 'Just trying to take some responsibility.'

He grunts in response. 'Let me finish paying up.'

My phone buzzes and like always I hurry to open it, hoping that it's Saint, but it never is. I know Comic-Con was only yesterday and he clearly needs more time to think, but it doesn't stop my heart jumping every time my phone goes off. There's a photo in the message and when I click it there's a screenshot of a possible job opportunity at Wonderland bookshop.

> **Sharisha**
> I think you should go for it x

How funny. A few weeks ago I would never have thought about working there, but now I can see myself fitting in. I send her a thumbs up and remind myself to apply and not overthink it.

'All right, cool, let's go,' Dami says, leading us to the car that the mechanic has parked outside the shop. Dad will never know this happened and I couldn't be more grateful to my brother and Amara.

'Can I drive, babe?' she asks as Dami unlocks the car.

'No,' Dami and I say at the same time.

Amara pouts. 'Why not?'

'My dad will go mad that I drove it. I'm not on his insurance and, knowing him, he's most probably memorized the mileage.' Dami shakes his head. 'He won't even let me pick them up from the airport. I love you, but no.'

Once the car starts, Fela plays from the speakers and Dami

stops Amara's hand as she goes to change the radio. 'Amara. He'll know someone's been in here.'

Amara tuts and rolls her eyes. I love that she thinks that Dami's exaggerating.

Once we get home, we're all exhausted but the car is washed and shiny and pretty in the driveway. Mum and Dad will be home in two days and we're going food shopping early tomorrow morning so we have time to clean the house.

I look more into the job vacancy at Wonderland bookshop. They want someone who can be in charge of the graphic novel section and run events specifically for that audience. It's funny, because with the amount of knowledge I've picked up from Saint and Harley's World of Comics I do think I could actually do this and feel confident about myself in the role. I mean, there's still so much more to learn but I think I have a good chance of getting the job.

I turn on my laptop and fill out the application, not giving myself time to talk myself out of it, and once I check it over for spelling, I hit send. There may be someone else more experienced who could get it over me, but it's the first step in starting my gap year, really exploring the things that I enjoy, and I'm excited about it.

Despite Dami's grumbling, he helps Amara and me to clean up the house from top to bottom. When I sort through the stuff in my wash basket I find the cushion that was ruined by a drink at my birthday party. I completely forgot to wash it and the stain

269

is now too set in to save it, so I throw it in the bin. Hopefully Mum won't notice one missing cushion.

Dami orders us a takeaway as no one can be bothered to cook anything and Grandma's food is finished.

'I've got to go soon,' Amara announces as she finishes her noodles.

'Go?' I frown then I remember that my parents don't even know that Amara has been staying here and of course she can't be here when they get back. It'll be weird with her gone and I'm surprised that it makes me feel sad. 'Do you have to?'

'Unfortunately.' Amara grins at me. 'You gonna miss me or something?'

'Maybe a little, yeah.' I shrug and Amara leans over and kisses my cheek.

'I'll miss you loads. I feel like we've bonded this summer,' she says.

'Me too.' It's funny that I never really opened up to Amara at all before this summer and yet now I kind of see her like a big sister. It feels good to have someone that I can talk to who I know won't judge me or snake me to my parents.

Dami frowns. 'Bonding over what?'

'Nothing,' Amara and I say at the same time.

I wake up to the bright sun streaming through my curtains, bathing my bedroom in yellow. Dami and I stayed up chatting after he took Amara home, and I told him about taking a gap year. He was surprised but supportive and showed me how to defer my place. I know I should have waited and spoken to my parents, but it feels so much like the right thing to do. Obviously I want Mum and Dad to support me, but even if they don't and I have to suffer their annoyance like Dami did, I'll just have to take it. Ultimately, this is the right thing for me to do.

I reach over to my phone and it's nine a.m. Wait, my alarm didn't go off! They'll be home by now. I scramble out of bed, slip on my slippers and head down the stairs.

'Mum!' I call.

'Eva!' Mum's voice carries from the kitchen and when I enter she turns away from the freshly boiled kettle and holds out her arms. I'm the perfect mix of my mum and dad but I've got my eyes and full lips from her. Her skin is darker now from the sun and, when she left she had her black wig on, but now she has these small, neat, long braids.

I grab her in a tight hug and it feels like it's been forever since I last saw her. She's a bit shorter than me so her head rests on my shoulder.

'My darling! How are you? How was your birthday?' she asks. She pulls away from me, smiling, but there's a slight crease in her forehead. 'Ah, you look different.'

'Do I?'

'You look mature.' Mum taps my nose gently, making me chuckle.

'Thanks, Mum. My birthday was good. Where's Dad?' I ask looking around the otherwise empty kitchen.

'He is upstairs unpacking. You know how funny he gets about stuff everywhere.' Mum pulls a face. She's the queen

271

of leaving her unopened suitcase in the hallway for weeks on end. 'Dami went to get me some painkillers from the shop. I have a headache from the flight.'

'Oh, sorry—'

'No, no –' Mum shakes her head – 'I want to hear about your summer. And university!' Mum clasps her hands excitedly and my heart sinks. 'Did Dami help you get your stuff? We need to figure out the best time to leave to avoid the traffic. Have you done—'

'Mum, I need to talk to you,' I cut in.

'Oh.' Mum holds a hand to her chest. 'Is it serious? Should your dad be here? Are you sick?'

'What? No!' Always *so* dramatic. 'It's about university.'

'Okay,' Mum says slowly. She sits down and I sit opposite her.

I take a deep breath. 'I've been thinking a lot about it these past few weeks and I don't think law is the right degree for me.'

'Ah, ah! What do you mean?' Mum demands sharply. 'If you don't study law then what are you going to do?'

'Well ...' I gulp and my throat is dry. 'I was thinking of taking a gap year just to help me decide.'

'A *gap year*?' Mum is on her feet. 'You want to be like your brother? With no ambition?'

'Mum, please—'

'You think we're here in this country for you to do nothing all day instead of going to university?'

'I'm not going to do nothing all day. I want to get a job.'

Mum scoffs. 'A job for minimum wage when you can be

a lawyer, have a successful career and earn good money. No. Eva, you are not taking a gap year so get that silly idea out of your head.'

'Mum!' She's not even hearing me out.

'What is all this shouting?' Dad walks into the kitchen. He's so tall that his head almost touches the top of the door frame. He pushes his glasses back as he looks between me and Mum. I must look as annoyed as her.

Mum points at me. 'Your daughter doesn't want to go to university. She wants to take a gap year.' She says 'gap year' like it's a dirty word or something. 'We leave Eva with Dami and look how she's thinking!'

Hold up. How did this become Dami's fault?

'Eva, is this true?' Dad's voice is gentle, which surprises me. He's usually there with Mum, yelling for no reason. Mum starts to pace the kitchen like she's gearing up for a battle.

'I want a gap year because I don't want to move to Nottingham and I'm not sure if law is the right degree for me. This has nothing to do with Dami at all. I only told him last night, so he had no idea. This is how *I* feel and what *I* think is right for me.'

Mum kisses her teeth. 'What's "right" for you? You don't know what's right for you. Please, Eva, I have a headache.'

'So I can't talk to you then?' I snap. 'You can't just dismiss my feelings because you don't want to hear what I'm saying.'

'Look how your daughter is speaking!' Mum says to Dad. Whenever she gets annoyed it's suddenly 'your daughter' or 'your son'.

Dad says something in Yoruba which I don't understand and Mum responds, but her words come out sharper. Dad sighs, rubbing his forehead, and Mum storms out of the kitchen.

'Mum!' I call after her, but I hear her footsteps on the stairs. I raise my eyes to the ceiling, breathing heavily. On one hand I'm pissed that she didn't even let me explain anything, but I'm also hurt that she just assumes I've not thought about it and this is just a whim.

'Are you sure this is what you want?' Dad asks, sitting down opposite me.

'It is,' I say. 'I'm not saying I don't want to go to uni ever, but I need a bit more time. Law was never something I was passionate about. I just wanted to make you both proud.'

'You know, your grandma already told me,' Dad said.

No wonder he didn't come in all guns blazing!

'So, you know I too wanted a gap year but was forced to go to university. I did resent her for it for years,' Dad says.

'Really?' Dad's never mentioned this to us. 'Then why were you so hard on Dami when he quit?'

'Because he didn't have a plan. You know how Dami was before, going round with those silly boys on the street. I was afraid without structure he would fall back into the same patterns, but Dami has done well and got himself together and I'm proud of him.'

I so wish Dami was here to hear this. Mum and Dad haven't told him that they're proud of him since he dropped out of uni.

'So, Eva, do you have a plan?' Dad asks.

274

'Kind of. The idea of moving to Nottingham, never having had a proper job and not knowing how to be responsible for myself, and then being far away from everyone and everything I know . . . well, all of that was scary. But I worked a few hours this summer and it was fun. It was good to learn something new. So I want to get a job, maybe travel, take up some new hobbies.'

Till now, I've usually spent all my spare time with my friends, hanging out, and maybe going on a few dates, and repeat that cycle again and again. But this summer I've tried new things and I enjoyed it. Plus, I was good at it.

'When I do go to uni, I want to know who I am and what I want to be. Not just go for the sake of it, drop out and still have to pay off the debt,' I finish.

Dad listens quietly. He sighs and I brace myself to be told, maybe in a nicer tone, that I am going to uni whether I like it or not.

'I understand,' Dad says, and I freeze. 'Let's make a plan and set some goals for what you want to achieve. But I'll need you to stick to it, Eva. Then maybe you can go to university next year.'

'Really?' I ask, already getting to my feet and running round the table to Dad to fling my arms round his neck. 'Thank you, Daddy.'

'It's okay.' He pats my arm. 'I'll talk to your mum. It might take a while for her, so be patient, okay?'

'I will.' I can't believe that Dad is going to support me on this.

It's scary not knowing how this year will go and not having the structure of education, but I'm determined to make it work. And with Dad's support – and hopefully Mum's too – I know it will be easier.

FORTY

Six weeks later

'Your son is going to love *Chainsaw Man*.' I put the graphic novel in a bag. 'Let me know if you need any more recommendations.'

'This is great. Thank you.' The woman smiles at me. 'I didn't have a clue what to look for.'

'No worries. Thanks for shopping at Wonderland. Have a good day.'

'You too.' She waves as she walks to the door.

I mentally give myself a high five, the way I always do when I manage to make a sale. I've been at Wonderland bookshop for the past five weeks. My interview with Mrs Anderson, the owner, was really good but I still wasn't sure if I would get the job, especially when she said that she would ask Harley's World of Comics for a reference. I still don't know if it was Benji or Saint who gave the reference, but whatever they said helped because I got the job!

It's always busy and noisy here but I love it. The only time

I had a pinch-me moment was when I met Trey Anderson and Ariel Spencer for the first time. They only work part-time, between his singing gigs and her art exhibitions, but they are the cutest, nicest couple. Now I'm not fazed by them being around, but it took me a minute. Sometimes I catch them flirting or gazing at each other across the bookshop and Saint always pops into my head.

Saint. I haven't seen or spoken to him since Comic-Con. He still only posts comic books. The last video of him is the spoken word event that I filmed and from time to time I rewatch it, and it transports me back. I wish I had a copy of the spoken word poem he wrote for me. Harley's World of Comics' socials have gone quiet so I assume they haven't had anyone take over since my job ended, which is a shame. It has a really good following now.

'Eva.' Trey appears from the basement holding a cardboard box in his hands.

Getting used to Trey's beauty definitely took me a moment. Tall, lean body, handsome, beautiful dark skin . . . Ariel is one lucky girl.

'Some stock came in this morning. Do you think you can find room for it?'

'No problem.' I take the box from him and walk it over to the graphic novel section, which is where I'm usually based. There are a few kids lounging on the beanbags reading and I smile at them as I place the box on the floor and rummage through, trying to see what's come in.

A gust of wind blows through the shop as the door opens.

I pick up a range of graphic novels in my arms, scanning the shelves to see where they would be best placed.

'I'm looking for a recommendation,' a familiar deep voice says behind me, and I pause, the graphic novels in my hand.

'What exactly are you looking for?' I ask, trying to keep my voice calm as I turn round.

'A present for my brother.' Saint grins, his dimples on display. He's wearing an oversized Naruto graffiti hoodie with dark combat trousers. His long curly hair frames his face.

'Is that right?' I question, smiling back at him.

'Hey, Eva,' he says.

'Hi, Saint.'

I'm unsure for a moment whether it's appropriate to hug, but he makes the decision for me and pulls me into a tight embrace. Oh, I've missed this. Missed him. His hair tickles my face and I gently swipe it away. I know we've been hugging for too long when the kids on the beanbags start to giggle.

'How are you?' I ask, pulling away, shooting my eyes to the kids, and Saint's eyes widen as he realizes we had an audience.

'I'm good. I've got a spoken word event tonight.'

'Oh, that's cool. What else you been up to?'

'I've decided next year I want to go to Japan, get involved with the anime community there.'

'To stay?' I ask, my voice having gone up an octave, which I hope he didn't notice.

'No, just for a month or so.' Saint looks around Wonderland. 'You like it here?'

'I do. Very busy and lots of crazy Trey and Ariel fans daily,

279

but everyone is nice.' I narrow my eyes. 'Did you give me the reference?'

'Yeah,' Saint says easily, and my heart leaps. 'I said they would be stupid not to hire you – but in a respectful manner, because Mrs Anderson would cuss me all the way out.'

I laugh. 'Well, thank you. I really appreciate it. It's the first tick against my gap year goals.'

'No way! So you took a gap year?' Saint asks and I nod. 'Wow, that's great, Eva. I'm really proud of you for doing that.'

'Thanks. It's been cool so far. Missing my friends loads though, but we talk all the time. Kinda living my uni life through them at the moment.' *And I miss you*, I want to add but I'm scared to push it. 'How's Benji and the store?'

'Benji's Benji,' Saint says, and we laugh. 'But it's good. Our social media's shit though so don't be surprised when we ask you to come and help us again.'

'Anytime,' I say.

Saint rubs the back of his neck. 'So ... are you around tonight?'

'Yeah,' I say too quickly, which makes Saint smile.

'You want to come to the spoken word event? Same spot as before. And maybe we can grab food after or something?'

Saint's tone sounds casual but his eyes betray him as I catch the second when he looks nervous. I bite my lip, forcing myself not to break out into a cheesy smile. This – *this* right here – is what I've been waiting for, *for weeks*. The number of times I've glanced up when the shop door rings, hoping it's him who's come in. The ideas I've come up with to have an event

around comic books, just so I have an excuse to call him . . .
And now here he is, so gorgeous and lovely, standing there in
front of me, giving me a second chance.

And I'm not messing this up again.

'I would love that, Saint.'

ACKNOWLEDGEMENTS

And then there were three! Thank you God for once again helping me to write another book. I have never felt more stressed than writing *The Love Dare*. There were so many things going on personally and then I had no idea what to write. The idea of not writing a Christmas book actually stressed me out! Which is weird when you think about it. What I did know was I wanted a book that reminded me of the fun bits of the nineties and I wanted to focus on the bet trope without the whole taking off your glasses and now you're suddenly hot.

I'm a kid of the nineties and watched on repeat *10 Things I Hate About You*, *She's All That* and *Never Been Kissed* – the perfect romcoms. I'm also a girl whose older brother forced her to grow up on comic books, video games and *Dragon Ball Z*... and who doesn't love *Game of Thrones*? So take this book as a love letter to that decade – ignoring GOT!

Saint is that guy who is just comfortable in his skin and not a try-hard. He owns his gifts and always strives to be true to himself. I think if my characters all hung out for the day then Saint, Quincy from *Only for the Holidays* and Santi, Ariel and Annika from *Love in Winter Wonderland* would be the best group of friends. Hmmm ... maybe that's a spin-off book?

Eva is that girl who seems to have it all but is in fact lost, which I think so many of us can relate to. I wanted her to fall for the guy that was from a different world and, instead of trying to change him, she gets locked into his world and appreciates how special he is. In doing so it opens up her expectations and choices. Like in Eva's family, my parents wanted me to be a lawyer but when I realized (at twelve years old) that being an author was in fact a job, I was sold. I also didn't want to go to uni and I wanted a gap year. But unlike Eva, I didn't take one, went to uni and ended up quitting like Dami. It's so important that we are confident in the choices that we make rather than just going with the flow.

I know Grandma is going to be a favourite and she's based on my great-aunty Sadé, who is my grandma's little sister and is basically like a grandma to me and my siblings. I didn't really get to know my grandmothers as they died when I was little, but my mum and dad always told me the best stories about their grandparents and great-grandparents, who they grew up with.

Someone asked me how I write love stories. I never thought I had a dramatic love life until I wrote these books with lots of my own experiences in them – good and bad – and I'm like, damn!

I wrote this one in two months and thought, *This is such*

a hot mess – so a massive thank you to my editor Carla for working your magic. I always think of you as one of the editing queens of romances so I appreciate that I got to work with you! Thank you to my previous editor Amina for helping me with the storyline and encouraging me to write a summer romance starting at Carnival. This was really fitting as I've visited Carnival so many times; even in primary school we used to have our own and come in costumes for the day! Like Eva I used to play the steel pans and the first styles of dance I learned were dancehall and soca. So it was fun to highlight a culture that I grew up around.

Thank you to my agent Gemma for always being the support I need.

Thank you to Zarah for taking me to a retro gaming exhibition so we could play all the old school games and I could do my research. Thank you to Anneliese for once again reading the book before I sent it in. Not sure how you always see the gem in the book before I do! Thank you to Arhvee for brainstorming ideas with me. You had some good ones! Once you started talking about copyright I backed out lol but I appreciate you helping me to start thinking of ideas again. Thank you to Helen for always being there and giving me the space to write.

Thank you to everyone at Simon & Schuster for once again helping me create a beautiful book. THE COVER! GORGEOUS!

Massive love to my family. Every time I write I throw bits of me in there, but also you guys. Your love, prayers and support are unmatched. Mum, are you happy I put your home town Suparé in the book? Every time I think of Suparé I can hear Dad saying, 'No one knows where that is. But they know Abeokuta.' Ha! And thank you to Gboli for forcing me to watch *Dragon Ball Z* every day after school when I was ready to have my *Sister Sister* marathon. It's actually inspired so many of my ideas.

Thank you to everyone who has read my books all over the world. The reviews, the TikToks, the pictures, showing up to my events ... you have made this Hackney girl so happy and I love and appreciate you all so much. Now to think of more stories!

ABIOLA BELLO

is a Nigerian-British, prize-winning, bestselling children's and YA author who was born and raised in London. She is an advocate for diversity in books for young people. She's the author of the award-winning fantasy series Emily Knight and was nominated for the CILIP's Carnegie Award, won London's BIG Read 2019, and was a finalist for the People's Book Prize Best Children's Book. Abiola contributed to *The Very Merry Murder Club*, a collection of mysteries from thirteen exciting and diverse children's writers which published in October 2021 and was selected as Waterstones Children's Book of the Month. Her debut YA, *Love in Winter Wonderland*, published in November 2022 and was an Amazon's Editor's Choice and was featured in The Guardian's Children's and Teens Best New Novels. *Only For The Holidays* published in October 2023 and was The Bookseller One To Watch, one of Waterstones Best Paperbacks of 2023 and was featured in The Guardian's Children's and Teens Best New Novels. Abiola won The Black British Business Awards 2023 for Arts and Media and The London Book Fair Trailblazer Awards 2018. She is the co-founder of Hashtag Press, Hashtag BLAK, The Diverse Book Awards and ink!

@ABelloWrites

HAVE YOU READ?

WILL TREY AND ARIEL FIND THEIR HAPPILY EVER AFTER?

LOVE in Winter WONDERLAND

ABIOLA BELLO

ONE

Trey's playlist: 'Let It Snow' by Boyz II Men

Seventeen days till Christmas

I'm about two seconds away from committing murder.

'But I thought it was two for one? I saw the deal in the bookshop window down the road,' the white woman with blonde highlights says.

She means Books! Books! Books! It's on the tip of my tongue to point out that we're clearly a different bookshop, but instead I flash my best smile – all white teeth. Next to her, her daughter's eyes flicker with interest.

'Don't get me wrong, I love a bargain as much as the next person, but we're independent.' I say 'independent' *real* slow. 'So you're helping the community when you buy from Wonderland. Plus, we're a Black-owned, family-run bookshop.'

Now the woman looks uncomfortable, catching eyes with her daughter, who huffs and says, 'Mum, it's fine. Just pay.'

The women looks like she's struggling to decide what to do. I bet now she thinks that if she doesn't support the bookshop I'll think she's racist. Truth is, I just think she's cheap.

'Look, I'll even throw in a couple of bookmarks.' I grab two from behind the counter and hand them to her. One says *Indie Bookshops Rule!* and the other says *Black Lives Matter*. We're such a subtle family.

The woman's eyes widen when she reads them. Then she reaches into her purse, pulling out her bank card, and I have to stop myself from punching the air in celebration. With this sale, we've reached our daily target, and Mum agreed that, if we did, I can leave early for Bebe's Christmas party. Bebe Richards is one of the girls in my friendship group at college, and one thing about her is she knows how to throw down. I have no idea why she's having a Christmas party on a Wednesday, over two weeks before Christmas Day, but I don't care. Anything that's not the bookshop or coursework sounds good to me.

'Thanks for shopping at Wonderland,' I say as I hand the woman her books with a grin. 'Merry Christmas.'

'And you.' She smiles back, but it looks forced. Her daughter, on the other hand, gives me a wink before they walk off. I smile and shake my head.

'Flirting with the customers again?' Dad walks up to the till and opens it, staring at the money and scratching the back of his head.

'We're on target. Slam dunk!' I shoot up my arms and flick my wrists, pretending to dunk like Kobe.

'Wasn't it busier this time last year?' Dad looks around the bookshop and I follow his gaze.

He's right. It's kind of quiet, but I'm sure it will pick up once it gets closer to Christmas. Dad's been paranoid ever since Books! Books! Books! opened. He thinks they've stolen all of our customers and tells me so after every shift. But we've been doing okay, and I think part of that is down to my epic playlist: 'The Best Christmas Songs by Black Artists' – '8 Days of Christmas' by Destiny's Child, 'This Christmas' by Chris Brown . . . and is it even Christmas without Mariah?

'Relax, Dad.' I put an arm round him. We're pretty much the same height now at six foot one, and with my wide-set eyes, broad nose, strong jawline and lean physique I'm my dad thirty-odd years ago.

Dad huffs in response.

'I'm leaving soon, but I can do a quick tidy and chat to some customers first,' I say.

Dad shuts the till and points in front of him. 'If those kids aren't buying, tell them to scat. How many times do I have to remind you, Trey? We're not a library. One day the bookshop will be yours and you can't have customers loitering around.'

I don't want the bookshop, I want to say, but – like always – I swallow it down. Wonderland was created by my great-grandad and is my family's legacy. It's the first and only Black-owned, independent bookshop on Stoke Newington High Street. Dad grew up here, and all he wanted to do when he was a kid was take over and be the boss. I want to be a singer, selling out arenas, but there are two problems. The first is my parents assume that Wonderland is my future, and I don't want to disappoint them. I pray all the time that my little brother Reon will be up for the task of running the bookshop. The second problem is I have a fear of singing in front of large crowds. I even get nervous when it's a small one. But if I close my eyes, or have a couple of drinks for Dutch courage, I can sing no problem. Part of my New Year's resolution is going to be to enter singing competitions, because I want to overcome my fear and really see where singing could take me, even though I know how hard it is to break into the music industry.

The loitering kids are gone now, but they've carelessly left a few books on the floor – no wonder Dad wanted them out. I return the books to the shelves and check in with a few customers to make sure they're okay before circling the rest of the shop.

I start quietly singing along to 'Let It Snow', which is playing through the speakers.

'Ooh, sing it, DeVante,' Boogs calls over at me as he walks into the shop.

I laugh. 'Wrong group, genius.'

'Is it?' Boogs frowns. 'Isn't this Jodeci?'

'Boyz II Men.' We dap, and I hug the petite girl in the colourful patchwork coat next to him. 'Hey, Santi.'

Santi flicks her long braided twists over her shoulder and raises her eyebrows. 'DeVante?'

'How would you know?' Boogs says. 'All you listen to is Coldplay.'

Boogs and Santi go back and forth and I shake my head. Boogs, real name Dre Deton, is my best friend. He moved to Stoke Newington just over a year ago. There was a rumour going round he used to be part of a gang in his old ends. The rumour was true, but we hit it off straight away. He's all light-skinned, light eyes, breaking girls' hearts with his pretty-boy face and fire dance moves (hence the nickname Boogs, short for Boogie), but that was until he met Santi Bailey. Technically, I got them together, because I'm dating Santi's twin sister, Blair. Identical twins with non-identical personalities – Santi dresses like she was a hippy in a past life, and she's always asking me for book recommendations, whereas Blair is a walking ad for Pretty Little Thing, and I can count on one hand the number of times we've spoken about books. On paper, I'm better suited to Santi, but somehow Blair and I work. I guess opposites really do attract.

ONE

Quincy

8th December

I've been in the supermarket for no more than five minutes when I hear, 'Oh, Quincy.'

I turn to see Mrs Huntington, a sixty-something white woman in a fur jacket who is decked out in pearls. Under the jacket she has a powder-blue shirt and matching skirt. She owns the Huntington's, a range of luxury cabins that she lets out here in the little market town of White Oak.

'Hello, Mrs Huntington. How are you?' I ask.

I'm surprised when she rests a gloved hand on my arm. Her face falls, and for a second I think she's going to tell me Mr Huntington has died – he's been ill for years. 'I heard about you and Kali, dear.'

And there it is. It's been a couple of months since we broke up, but word spreads fast, especially in somewhere as small as White Oak.

'What happened?' she presses, taking a step closer and wafting her floral perfume in my face. 'You were together for years, weren't you? I always thought you were such a gorgeous couple.'

I shrug like it's no big deal, but I can feel that familiar lump forming in my throat whenever I think of Kali. Despite everything, I miss her. How am I meant to move on when people keep bringing her up? Everyone wants to know why we broke up, but if I told them what went down, her reputation as a sweet and innocent girl would be ruined. God knows I've thought about spilling the truth, though. I bet if I told Mrs Huntington what happened, she'd die from shock right here in the supermarket.

'It just wasn't meant to be,' I reply then gesture at the full shopping basket in my hand. 'Cameron's in the car, so I better go and pay for this.'

'Oh, of course, dear. Don't keep your brother waiting. I'm sure you'll find another lovely lady to take to the Winter Ball,' Then her voice goes up an octave: 'I'm so pleased your family are hosting it this year.'

I force a smile, because even though I like Mrs Huntington, I know from her voice that she's lying.

The Winter Ball is a massive deal. It's held annually on December 23rd in the Renaissance Ballroom of the Tudor manor house that I used to think was a castle. Centuries ago, it was owned by a super-wealthy family who left it to the town back in the 1800s. The Winter Ball has been a tradition ever since.

My family are one of the few Black families here, and no Black family has *ever* hosted the Winter Ball before, despite my parents bidding every year to do it. This year the committee agreed.

'Yeah, we're very excited,' I say cheerfully. I start to walk away and her gloved hand falls from my puffer jacket. 'Say hi to Mr Huntington for me.' As soon as my back is turned, I roll my eyes.

Once I've paid, I carry the bags to the black 4×4 parked on the side of the road. The windows are down even though it's freezing, and Kendrick Lamar is blaring out of them. I'm convinced it's going to snow, but Mum says I shouldn't put that out in the world, because when it snows here, it *snows* – the roads close and everyone is housebound. All that time and money spent on the Winter Ball for nothing.

My older brother Cameron, or Cam as we call him, is bopping his head to the music. His long locs are swinging back and forth. Inside the boot are his DJ decks and business cards printed with the words KING CAM under a logo of a crown with headphones over it.

I go to his window and yell over the music, 'Cam, your decks are in the boot. Should I put the shopping in the back seat?'

'Nah, me and Stacey had sex on that blanket, and I still need to wash it.'

What the hell? I glance into the back of the car, and there's a grey fleece blanket bunched up on the seats. Stacey and Cam went to school together. I had no idea they were hooking up.

'I'll wash it when we get back,' he adds.

'That's nasty, man,' I say, and Cam laughs in response. I head back to the boot, rearranging it so I can fit the shopping in.

'Got everything?' he shouts when I get in the car.

The bass feels like it's in my bones. I lower the volume. 'The whole street can hear you,' I snap, and Cam grins.

Cam's twenty-one, three years older than me, and we couldn't be more different if we tried. He's loud; I'm more reserved. He has girls blowing up his phone all day and night; I've always been in a committed relationship. He has light brown locs down to his waist; mine are darker and only reach my shoulders. But we do resemble each other physically, both being over six foot with a slender build, rich brown skin and dark eyes. He's the local DJ and, when he pulls up anywhere, everyone knows it's him. Mum and Dad used to get constant complaints, but now that he's the go-to person for parties the whole town seems to put up with it.

Cam presses the gas, and the car pulls off fast. I put my hands out in front of me, catching the dashboard before I smack into it. He couldn't even wait for me to put on my seat belt. That's another thing: my brother drives like a maniac.

'Dickhead,' I say, pulling the belt over me.